THE FIFI CODE

EROS CRESCENT TRILOGY VOLUME ONE

RICHARD LEE

*Dedicated to a world in need of
love and imagination.*

Imagine a retired writer, living in a bush hut in a forest beside a river in rural Australia. He gets lonely sometimes. Drawing on the memories of an active life in long gone days in a big city, he sets out to write a simple fantasy, populated with events and people that he remembers and others that he invents. Welcome to *The Fifi Code*.

— THE AUTHOR

CONTENTS

PREFACE

THE FIFI CODE is a novel about love. It provides a window on women loving women both within and outside of an existing heterosexual relationship and when a man's love might just not be enough.

Meet the delightful Rosa Bennett's network of women friends and lovers, young and old, all of whom she is happy to share, both with her husband, and with her other lovers.

Discover too, the secrets of the special trigger word *Fifi* and the erotic instructions that accompany it that Rosa devised to prompt her very fit and virile husband Bertie in their lovemaking.

This story is a gentle and erotic fantasy rampage. It is a titillating story of sensual love and lust – often featured in unique and unexpected settings – and innocently enjoyed by all.

1

MORNING GLORY

LIVING AT THE BENNETTS' house in Eros Crescent was wonderful. Rosa and Albert Bennett were so friendly and loving, and the house, set in a beautiful garden, was filled with their stuff, accumulated over a long and happy life together.

I wasn't actually sleeping in the house; rather I had my own delightful granny-flat, built for Bertie's mother, who only lived in it for a year before she passed away. It had views of the garden and was very private. Rosa had suggested to my stepmother Helen, a long-time family friend of theirs who had taken me with her when she went to visit them, that I should move into the flat.

Rosa and Albert had married very early. Rosa had been only seventeen and Bertie almost twenty. The two of them were so handsome and they looked so innocent. I loved looking through their wedding photos and leafing through the family's early albums

Coming home to this house and the graceful air of comfort and nostalgia that I felt as I entered the hallway each afternoon was a relief from my hectic hours at university. The work demands of my third year of Psychology were extensive, so each night I would retire to the solitude of the book-lined study to prepare work for the next day, but not before I had cleared the dining room table and washed and dried the dishes.

Rosa said I didn't have to do that as she so enjoyed having me there, and she would have had to do all those things for the two of them anyway. I laughed and told her that I needed the exercise and that housekeeping skills might be useful if I ever found a husband, to which she would give an almost wicked chuckle, and answer mysteriously:

"It's other skills that will make the marriage, dear Alice. But you are right, being useful in domestic ways is a good thing."

It was not difficult to become besotted with Rosa. She radiated love and good-will, and I realised that she would likely become a role model for me as I grew to know her better.

Things suddenly changed. One day I received a text from Helen to say that Rosa had taken a turn and was in hospital and telling me to ring for details.

Helen and my stepdad collected Bertie and we met in the reception area of the hospital at around 4 o'clock, all of us feeling miserable at the possibility that this was something serious. Imagine our surprise when we entered Rosa's room and discovered her sharing a joke with two young nurses.

"Here they are," she called out. "I'd better look as though I'm sick or something I suppose, or they will think I'm tricking them."

The nurses left and Rosa put her hand out towards Bertie and said, "Nothing to worry about, Bertie my love. You've got me for a long time yet."

We all collected around the bed, smiling with relief.

"Oh Rosa, we're so pleased you are OK. Will you go home today?" said my mother.

"Afraid not, Helen. The bad news is that they want to keep me here for a while to monitor things."

Rosa looked at Bertie and smiled wistfully at him.

"It's been a long time since we were in separate beds Bertie. Hopefully it won't be for long my darling, otherwise I will insist they give me a room with a double bed."

Bertie laughed, and leant over and kissed her lovingly for what seemed like a long moment.

The house seemed so very quiet and still without Rosa. Even though she wasn't in any way noisy, one always felt that she was close by.

When she had been at home, I would meet her in the mornings in the kitchen or dining room. I would make myself a bowl of cereal and fruit and a coffee, and she would be in her dressing gown and elegant Chinese patterned slippers. She always appeared radiant at that time and I found myself wondering just how she managed it.

Now things were different. Rosa was no longer there.

With Rosa gone, I had an instinctive feeling that I should take responsibility for Bertie. Though he was intelligent, strong and a very self-sufficient seventy-year-old, he had in recent years developed what seemed like a mild case of short-term memory loss, which most people would fail to notice. Rosa had talked to me one morning about it.

"The funny thing is, Alice, Bertie hasn't really forgotten something; the memory simply has to be triggered. I find myself inventing short phrases or words which I emphasise after we've discussed anything. Then I use the relevant short phrase later, when the subject comes up again."

I had asked Rosa for an example.

"Well, let's say I'm hand-watering plants. I will talk to Bertie about hand-watering using a bucket. At the end of the conversation, I will look at him and say 'Bertie, buckets'. And from then on, if I say 'Bertie, buckets', he will head off and fetch buckets to the front garden. It sounds odd, but it has given us a better way of dealing with his loss of memory, if that is all it is. It might sound a bit cruel, but he seems so happy with the arrangement that I now use it for all sorts of things."

I couldn't help noticing that she seemed to put an emphasis on "all sorts of things", but then that radiant look on her face that she so often wore in the mornings took over and we moved on.

. . .

On the first Saturday morning after Rosa's admittance to hospital, I woke later than usual and immediately panicked, thinking that Bertie might still be confused about his wife's absence. I still hadn't formulated a plan that included him in a daily breakfast routine, nor knew whether or not that was necessary.

I did know that he usually stayed in bed for a while after Rosa got up. I knew that she sometimes took him a cup of tea in bed, but I had never bothered questioning her about it as I was usually heading out the door when she was still boiling the kettle.

My earlier conversation with Rosa had intrigued me. Nothing that I had learnt so far in my Psychology studies had touched on anything like what she spoke of, although it could be that Bertie was showing signs of early stages of a particular form of dementia that I didn't know about.

Now I would have the opportunity to observe Mr Bennett without interruption and I was excited at the prospect of having an unofficial client–patient situation here at home.

I headed for the master bedroom.

The door was slightly ajar so I knocked quietly, pushed it gently and looked in. Bertie was lying on his back with his arms out of the bed and folded on his stomach over his dark blue pyjama top. His eyes were closed so I thought it best to come back later, but as I began to pull the door shut behind me his voice called out.

"Alice. is that you?"

"Yes, Bertie. I thought you were asleep and didn't want to disturb you."

I put my head back around the door and saw him lift himself up on one elbow.

"Come in girl. Don't be shy. I wasn't asleep, just trying to think things through. Come and sit here. You can probably help me better understand about Rosa's situation."

He patted the bedclothes in front of him. I walked over and sat down.

"Well, I don't know any more than you do at the moment, but I would expect we will get a clearer picture later in the day, after you've visited her. The doctors will be able to update us, I'm sure."

Bertie grunted to indicate his satisfaction with my answer.

"How come you're still here, Alice? Won't you be late for classes?"

"It's Saturday, Bertie. I don't go to university at the weekend. I get to sleep in and do other stuff. Leisure time! I love it!"

"I hope you will stay on here with us, Alice. With Rosa away, I think I would be a bit lost on my own. I can look after myself pretty well except for grocery shopping. So long as there is food in the fridge and in the garden, I'm fine."

"Oh Mr B, of course I will be staying here. I so love this place and being with you both, and I so want to find out more about the two of you, particularly Rosa."

"Thank you Alice. We both love having you here."

Then Bertie began talking about his side of the family and I took the opportunity to look around their bedroom.

As I was about to comment on something he'd just said and was bringing my eyes back to look at him, they were drawn to a bulge in the bedclothes just slightly behind were I sat. My first thought was that the bedclothes had got strangely bunched up, but the more I looked, the more I had to accept that Bertie had an erection. I stared at it long enough for him to notice the direction of my eyes.

What Bertie said next – although I didn't realise it at the time – triggered enormous changes to my life, changes that would affect me for ever.

"Rosa calls that her 'Morning Glory' and sometimes her 'Wake Me Up'. She has it most days before she leaves the bed."

I looked up at his face, trying to establish the reality of the situation and what he had said. Had I misheard him? Was he talking about something completely different from what I was looking at?

"I think he's missing her as much as I am," Bertie said gently with a wry smile, sounding completely innocent and unselfconscious.

My head was full of possible scenarios. Should I excuse myself on pretence of getting breakfast, and leave? Was this a form of aberrant behaviour related to memory loss? It seemed nothing he said matched with any previous experiences in my life, and Bertie's speech and mannerisms did not appear to be inappropriate in any way.

I told myself that I must respond to him honestly, as he had seemed to express himself to me.

"I know Rosa loves you very much, Mr B, so I can imagine she would see everything with loving eyes. She knows she is a very lucky woman to have you as her life-long partner."

"Thank you Alice. Yes. We are so very happy together."

I was now getting over the initial shock of spotting Bertie's erection. A new thought – or was it an emotion – was gathering strength. I suddenly had a strong urge to see his erection.

I told myself that this was just so that I could learn more about the couple's relationship, and what might have made them so close and happy for the past fifty years. That was my feeble attempt at an intellectual rationalisation.

Before I could stop myself I was speaking, seemingly from a distance.

"Can I see Rosa's Morning Glory please, Mr B?"

There was silence for a long moment, then Bertie spoke.

"I'm not sure that Rosa would approve of that, you being her friend's stepdaughter, and so young and all. She's pretty liberal in her outlook but she might have a reason to say no.

"Remind me to ask her if I can show it to you when I see her later."

I took a deep breath and tried to analyse what Bertie had said. It seemed that he did not object; it was just that he thought Rosa might. And the openness of his thoughts about asking her first was beautiful, to say the least.

My head was buzzing. I now really wanted to see his erection. I would have to work with his simple honesty and his lack of guile.

"Mr Bennett! I really want to know why you and Rosa's fifty-year relationship has been so successful. I can get just so much from talking to her and looking at old photos, but it is not enough.

"You have exposed a very personal intimacy by telling me about your erection, and it seems to me perfectly acceptable that, as a mature, university-educated woman, I should find out more about the two of you via this intimate communication we are having. Please Mr B? Just a peek will do."

A long pause followed. Bertie's eyes were closed. Had he fallen asleep, I wondered?

"Very well then. Given the situation Rosa is currently in, and the possibility of an uncertain future, I agree that you should be able to investigate. Go ahead, Alice. Pull back the bedclothes and do your research."

Even though I think I looked calm, I felt sure an observer would have noticed a faint shaking in my limbs and, dare I say, a sparkle in my eyes.

"Thank you, Mr B."

For a moment I wondered which end of the bedclothes to lift.

"This end is where she starts," came Bertie's soft voice.

I felt like an amateur and I blushed. Then I leant forward, lifted the bedclothes up and back and uncovered Morning Glory.

Oh, what a sight it was. In simple terms it was very big, but it was by no means fully erect; rather it was standing at rest so to speak, and not looking to rampage anywhere soon. I was flabbergasted.

"It's very beautiful, Mr B."

"Thank you, Alice."

So now I found myself half lying on the end of the Bennetts' bed in nothing more than a light cotton dress and skimpy knickers, propped up on my elbows with my chin in my hands, staring at Bertie's massive cock and trying to appear objective and impartial.

In truth, I was experiencing little flutters in parts of my anatomy I didn't know could flutter, and, by the way, how dared this thing sit so still with a young woman staring at it close up?

Such was my real state of mind: chaotic, and with a growing feeling of excitement. I so wanted to reach out and touch it, and I had momentarily become oblivious to Bertie's presence.

Bertie's voice interrupted my reverie.

"I'm sure Rosa wouldn't mind you touching him now that you've come this far. Some mornings she can't help teasing him with her tongue, just for fun, before she climbs on. Other times she simply gets on with it."

My mind went into overdrive trying to process everything he said. Half of me wanted to explore all the possibilities of this situation, the other half was inhibited by the sexually repressed upbringing that most children experience. I think the correct term for my thoughts and emotions at that moment would be "conflicted".

"Thank you, Mr Bennett," I mumbled, not wanting him to know that I was truly-tongue tied.

I was eager to reach out and grasp Morning Glory for my very own. I had crossed all the barriers to arrive at that decision and the sexual flutterings throughout my body became more seriously rampant.

Taking hold of Bertie's cock with one hand was exciting. Adding another hand was more exciting, and when his beautiful member suddenly twitched and surged upward in my palms, I gasped audibly.

I heard a little gasp from Bertie too, which reassured that I wasn't the only one experiencing this.

I stretched out on the bed, moving up to bring my mouth close to the now growing throbbing penis that was giving me so much pleasure. I began by sticking out my tongue and touching the top of his member. It was then that I realised that I was crazily, happily randy.

Bertie's cock was still growing and what had been a big soft lump of sleeping penis was now changing, both in length and hardness. I dragged as much of it as I could into my mouth and left it there.

My eyes were closed. Lying in this blissful state, I began thinking of where I might go next, with Bertie's best wishes of course. Reluctantly I removed his cock from my mouth.

"Mr Bennett?"

"Yes, Alice?"

"Is this how Rosa lies on the bed when playing with Morning Glory? Or does she do things from a different position?"

"Well, she would start off where you are, but then she would turn herself completely around and put a leg either side of me."

This was very exciting information, and I experienced a sort of full body hot flush.

"And what did Rosa achieve by doing that, Mr B?"

"Well, mainly it was to ready herself for getting onto me. But she also enjoyed being able to wiggle her rear end at me, especially if she thought I had forgotten her and gone back to sleep."

Things were definitely getting better by the moment. My randiness now knew no bounds and I had a terrible moment when I thought I could rape Bertie, such was the intensity of my excitement.

"I think I need to get into that position too, Mr B. Please tell me if I'm doing it wrong."

"Fine, Alice. Just swing yourself around and back up towards my face. Just so long as you can reach everything you want. You are about Rosa's height so you should be fine. Oh, and how's the research going, Alice? Are you discovering more about us?"

That last sentence floored me. Was Bertie enjoying this as I was, or was he just an unfeeling automaton?

"Great, Mr Bennett. I'm about to swing round. And yes, Mr B, I'm learning heaps. And Mr B, can I ask if you are enjoying this?"

"I sure am, Alice. Rosa says it is good for me to have variety. She has her friend Maude over once a month. Maude lost her husband a couple of years ago. She's very lonely. Rosa gets me to give Maude a special something, which she loves, and that her husband used to do.

"Of course, Rosa is especially affectionate to women, as you will no doubt have discovered. I love her for it dearly."

I wanted to be left totally alone with Bertie's wonderful cock, but the information he had just delivered sent my brain into overdrive.

My God! So much to process.

I overcame the problem by letting lust get the upper hand, blotting out the rest of what he had said, at least for the time being.

I eased my body around and slid a leg over Bertie's torso. I was now up on my knees with all of my private parts on full view to him. I wondered if he would even notice. Whether he would or not didn't seem to matter any more. Overtly exposing myself to his gaze was a thrill in itself.

"You are a very beautiful young woman," came Bertie's soft rich voice.

And if I had thought he might not be interested in the view, imagine how it felt when his fingers slipped into the top of my undies and dragged them over my bottom and down to my knees. This caused a tiny orgasm and I felt a sudden wetness down there. I was in heaven.

"Thank you, Mr Bennett. And you touch me beautifully."

Bertie's cock was now so big and hard I could hardly get it into my mouth, and when I did, my throat could take only a third of it. But I was so happy with my lot, I simply stopped thinking and instead luxuriated in the pure uncensored sensuality of my situation.

Then, when I thought Bertie was just happy staring at my privates, he placed a finger on my wet vagina and wriggled it around. It was electrifying, but even more so when he gently pushed it into my swollen cunny and placed his thumb lightly on the head of my clitoris.

I pulled my mouth from his cock and gasped incoherently.

"Oh Bertie! Please don't stop."

"I will when you tell me you are ready, Alice."

What did Bertie mean? Ready for what?

"Ready for what, Mr B?" I panted.

"Ready for Morning Glory, Alice. Rosa goes from where you are now to putting my cock inside her. Once it's in, Rosa takes things really slow, hardly moving; then, as if by magic, she has her orgasm, sometimes more than one. Moments later she's off out of bed and heading for the kitchen."

I struggled to take in what he had said. Were things going too fast? Was I going to go all the way with this? Could things possibly feel better than they did at this moment?

I looked at his giant cock. It was a sentinel, a provider of security, but only to those who showed it love. How could I refuse it my love? It had led me to the state of ecstasy I was feeling right now. It deserved my love and affection. Yes, all the way was the only way.

"Ready, Mr Bennett."

Bertie's finger slowly exited but the fire in my cunny burnt on fiercely.

I don't really know why, but I waited. Moments like this should be savoured according to the tiny voice of my totally in-charge lustful self.

Then he licked, then kissed my private parts, which convulsed me so that I jumped forward and I found myself in a crouching position above his cock.

Until now, it hadn't occurred to me to think about how his cock would fit inside me.

Bertie's fingering had definitely caused me to swell and open up. Was that his plan? Is that why Rosa played and teased him each morning, to get him to help prepare her cunt for the final delight?

With one hand I took hold of Bertie, then I lowered myself and rubbed the head of his penis and around the top of the shaft with all my wetness.

What happened next I still can't believe. As my vagina spread itself over the top of Bertie's cock, my cunny opened up and I had a distinct feeling that it was sucking his cock in and upwards as, at the same time, I was lowering myself onto his superb affair.

Within moments his cock was housed, entirely filling me.

I simply stayed in this position, impaled with the source of my lust. Then I felt his cock pulsate once, twice, three times. I exploded. 'Morning Glory' indeed, dear Rosa.

"Thank you, Mr Bennett."

"My pleasure, Alice."

I slowly unsheathed Bertie's massive cock and lay still, my head between his thighs, while my body melted away into a semi-dream state. After a few long moments' rest I realised that there was still one thing that Rosa would do to complete 'Morning Glory'.

"Cup of tea, Mr B?"

"Great idea, Alice."

As I part walked and staggered to the kitchen in an extraordinarily blissful state, and with my hand joyfully nursing my pussy, I reasoned that researching Rosa and Bertie's fifty-year relationship could never get better than this. Or could it?

2

THE CODE

A UNIVERSITY COMMITMENT prevented me from visiting Rosa on that first Saturday. I was the faculty representative for my year at a university conference, and it wasn't until late that evening that I returned home. Bertie had already gone to bed, so I called Helen to see if there was any news.

"She is in good spirits, apart from not liking being away from home. The doctor says that she expects to keep Rosa there for at least a fortnight, as some of the tests required observation over that length of time.

"We left Bertie with her for a couple of hours while your father and I went to the new exhibition at the Gallery. Fabulous, darling, you must see it."

"Yes, I plan to."

"Gotta go, sweetheart. My show is about to start. Talk tomorrow."

I settled on the sofa with a cup of tea. The house was so peaceful, especially at night.

I tried to order my thoughts. What a day it had been, especially the way it had started. I sailed through the conference in a dreamlike state, not wishing to lose any of the glow that I felt from my early morning experience with Bertie. And interestingly, I seemed to have come to terms with my adventure with him.

I felt no guilt or shame, and I accepted responsibility for what had happened. My only concern was that I would not cause harm to either Bertie or Rosa or their relationship. He seemed fine about things, but I knew that I still had to deal with the likelihood that his wife would soon know about what had happened, and that this could be confronting.

I awoke on Sunday morning feeling refreshed and happy and decided that I would stay in bed for a time, at least until I heard Bertie moving about the house.

I felt comfortable with myself and in control. Life was very good.

Bertie was just clearing away his breakfast dishes when I arrived at the kitchen.

"A good sleep, Alice?"

"Yes, Mr Bennett, wonderful! And you?"

"Ah yes, I slept like a log. But don't tell my wife or she will think I'm not missing her."

"Helen says Rosa is there for a fortnight at least, so I hope you will make sure she knows that you miss her, Bertie."

Bertie smiled.

"She's worked out a routine with the staff so that she and I get quality time together when I visit, so it's not as though we're missing out on our cuddles, although we do have to be a little circumspect."

I looked at him closely to try to read the handsome weathered face for clues to what really was going on in his head.

"By the way," Bertie continue, I should tell you that yesterday I mentioned to her how well you were looking after me and how well we were getting on, if you know what I mean. She was amused and asked me to express her gratitude. She also said that she would like to see you on your own, and asked if you could call in after you finished at university tomorrow."

I was beginning to adapt to Bertie's forthright honesty about what anyone else might call sensitive issues, so this was not the bombshell it might have been earlier.

He had obviously told Rosa about my visit to his bed and now she wanted to see me alone. Had she genuinely expressed her gratitude, or was that just her way of dealing with it? Was she about to throw me out of the house?

"You will see her before I do, Mr Bennett, so tell her I'll be there around three thirty."

"Great! Now that I've worked out the bus timetable at last, I can get to her all on my own in less than twenty minutes. Isn't that wonderful, Alice? I'm a cleverer boy than I thought."

"You're a very clever boy, Mr Bennett. I've never doubted it."

And in more ways than you think, Bertie, I thought to myself.

I felt nervous as I walked to Rosa's room at the hospital. I couldn't help feeling guilty about my intimate moments with Bertie. In fact I was still confused about how I truly felt about it. Was I really looking for information about the success of the Bennetts' long happy marriage, at that moment when I asked Bertie for a peep at his erection? Far too late for analysis now, it's time for the reckoning.

A radiant Rosa greeted me from her bed.

"So glad you could come in, Alice, and congratulations."

I took Rosa's outstretched hand and leant down so that we could exchange kisses on both cheeks.

"Congratulations, Rosa? What have I done to deserve them?"

"You know very well what I'm talking about, Alice; stepping into my shoes when needed. Bertie told me everything, so let's not pussy-foot around. You did well according to him and I'm proud of you."

"Well, Rosa, you are being incredibly understanding and kind. What began as me wanting to know more about you and Bertie's very successful marriage suddenly took an unexpected turn. It should never have happened and I ... "

"Don't say another word, darling. Just as long as you are OK, I'm very excited that you and Bertie had that moment together and you might not like me saying so, but I fully expect it won't just be a one-off. Bertie is a rare creature. He can become very addictive."

I couldn't believe what I was hearing. Was this really my landlady speaking?

"But Rosa, such things are wrong for many reasons. I will not be going down that path. I would leave your house rather than risk the possibility of coming between you and Bertie."

Rosa's beautiful face suddenly took on a stern look, and she admonished me severely.

"Alice, the relationship between me and my husband is very different from most couples' relationships, and that difference is what has made it possible for us to fully enjoy each other over all these years. If you want to understand us more, then this is the first thing you need to know.

"Bertie and I no longer have any inhibitions about occasionally having sexual dalliances with other people. I practise it myself, and encourage him to express himself in that way as well, if and when he chooses.

"We have no secrets. However, we do not advertise any of these intimate arrangements to the people around us, simply in deference to other people's feelings. Now is that clear, darling girl?"

I stared at this very youthful sixty-seven-year-old with the sparkling eyes, and could think of nothing that could be said that would make any sense in the context of what she had said. Rosa had said everything. In fact, far more than I could ever imagine.

I did not reply and just sat holding her hands and looking at her admiringly.

"Once this other life with other people began, these relationships quickly started to follow a pattern. I very rarely spent time with other males, much preferring female company. And Bertie, never the extro-vert, only rarely spent time with other women he met, those I called 'his strangers'."

Rosa leant back on her pillow and giggled, obviously remembering something from the past.

"I was always disappointed in who he fell in with, and realised that he was vulnerable to exploitation by some not particularly nice or caring females.

"I took steps. It wasn't hard. I simply selected one of my girl-friends, one whom I deemed appropriate for Bertie, and brought her home. 'Keeping it in the family' Bertie called it. It worked very well. It protected Bertie from the sharp claws of those 'strangers', and because of my interest in the person I brought home it provided a deeper and more enjoyable interaction for all of us."

The researcher in me suddenly came to the fore and I asked Rosa a question.

"Rosa, at what point in your marriage did this change occur, and can I ask what caused it?"

Rosa looked thoughtful for a moment, repositioning herself beneath the bedclothes.

"As you already know, we married very early and our life together was wonderful. We had the children, Henry and Caroline; Bertie had a succession of promotions in his job at the museum; we bought the house and went on holidays every summer; and life continued the same, right up to my mid-forties.

"The children had left home, and it was around then that I came to the realisation that I was addicted to my husband, and as a consequence, what I had always felt as love was love no longer. I think now that it was what many women experience, in long-lasting hetero-sexual relationships.

"It doesn't much matter how supportive of her husband a woman may be, she has a need for a deeper, different kind of intimacy, and she eventually discovers that most men are biologically incapable of providing the sort of emotional support she craves. It's not men's fault; it's simply part of the evolutionary differences between men and women.

"We can often find an example of this simply by looking at the difference in friendships a woman can have with gay men, and those she experiences with straight men."

Rosa paused and reached for a drink of water. I topped up the glass again and she drank some more.

"This is thirsty work Alice."

"I am loving your story, Rosa. Please go on."

"Well, my first lesbian encounter was with my now longtime friend Maude. I hope you will meet her soon. I have told her so much about you, in fact so much that I think she is already in love with you, so be warned."

I think I blushed just a tiny bit, which Rosa noticed and seemed excited by.

"I will one day recount our first meeting, which you might like to hear, but now we should stick to the question of Bertie and our relationship.

"Having this new and first-time sexual encounter since getting married to Bertie caused an explosion in my heart and in my head. Maude and I couldn't get enough of each other, mentally, emotionally or physically, and for the first few months I was confused about my marriage and my relationship with Bertie.

"But then the unexpected happened. What started as me running away from what my husband represented now changed, and I was able to see Bertie in a new light. Suddenly I began to appreciate him for what he was, and not for who I thought I wanted him to be."

Rosa paused and took another drink of water. She gazed into the distance, seemingly looking for the right words to go on.

"Maude is twelve years younger than me, and bisexual. But it still came as a bit of a shock when she announced that she had met a man and thought that they might eventually marry. I knew she wanted children, but her announcement still came as a shock. I wanted to know if this meant we would stop seeing each other, to which she replied 'I hope not'.

"But of course we saw less of each other as her relationship with her future husband grew, and in hindsight this was a good thing.

"Meanwhile, I had a new confidence in knowing what I wanted, both sexually and emotionally, and being able to appreciate Bertie for what he was, rather than what I believed he should be, meant that I could now explore our sexuality more openly. It was then that I decided to ask Maude to visit us at home, although I wasn't sure how this would work out, given her new love interest, but it worked very well.

"I don't know who was the more nervous, Maude or me. We agreed beforehand that she would be helping me spice up my marriage, and with her enthusiasm for sexual encounters this, our first threesome, looked promising. Of course, fantasy is always simple in the imagination. In reality it can sometimes be stilted and unfulfilling.

"I had already informed Bertie that I had a close friend to whom I was physically attracted to, was coming for afternoon tea on Sunday, and whose company I thought he could also enjoy. He expressed interest and Maude came to the house. The only other thing I told him was that I knew she loved to have her breasts fondled. Maude had very large breasts and extraordinarily long nipples, especially when aroused. He seemed excited about that."

My head was full of large and small questions, but Rosa's story was too gripping for me to want to interrupt.

"Well, the three of us took tea on the sofa in the lounge. I played mother, running to and fro from the kitchen, while Bertie engaged Maude in conversation.

"It was a sunny afternoon and I had deliberately pulled the curtains over enough so that the room was not too bright.

"Bertie and I sat either side of Maude. And at a moment when she turned to say something to me, I leant forward and kissed her on the mouth. Then, while still glued to her lips I pushed her gently against the back of the couch, and as I did so Bertie's hand came across and began unbuttoning her blouse and exposing her breasts. Then he engulfed one of her enormous nipples with his lips and teeth and we were on our way."

Rosa stopped talking, and in the silence that followed I felt myself propelled along on Rosa's story to a point where I wanted to be there, on the sofa with all three of them. I couldn't stop myself thinking about it.

I gazed into Rosa's beautiful eyes and saw both a joy and a longing, and I understood.

Unable to stop myself, I stood up and moved closer to her, then bent and put my arm around her neck, drew her up, and kissed her on the lips. Her body shook and our lips remained stuck together, neither of us wanting to stop.

When I sat back down, Rosa held onto my hand.

"Thank you, Alice. What you just did was both brave and beautiful. I will never forget this moment. Always remember darling, kissing is everything."

I suspected that my face was probably a crimson colour and I felt my body shaking. I felt that same fluttering in odd parts of my body that I felt lying on the bed with Bertie.

"Thank you, Rosa. Yes, I will remember."

Just then there was a knock on the door.

"Come in," Rosa called.

A woman in uniform came in, a nurse. She looked to be in her late thirties or early forties. She was quite tall, even in her low-heeled sensible shoes, and she had what one could best describe as a full figure: in short, curvaceous. She looked striking with her red hair and green eyes, and she smiled most lovingly at Rosa. I instantly felt that they knew one another, very well.

"Christine! I would like you to meet Alice. Alice, this is Christine, senior nurse of this wing of the hospital. She is the only person here that can order me around."

Christine laughed, then turned and looked at me closely. Was she seeing my pink face, or had the blushing subsided?

"Hello, Alice. Rosa has told me so much about you. I think we might even know some of the same staff at university. I did some of my training in your faculty. But that was quite a few years ago. Are you enjoying yourself there?"

I took a deep breath to try to sort myself out.

"So pleased to meet you, Christine. Yes, I'm loving university, and from what I understand, you are Rosa's favourite around these parts. She has high standards, so you must be good."

"Just checking everything is all right with you before I head off for the evening. I'm off duty tomorrow, but will be back on Wednesday. I look forward to seeing you then. Try to stay out of trouble, Rosa, at least until I get back."

The two held hands and embraced and kissed, then Christine turned and gave me a beautiful smile. Her eyes ran slowly down to my feet and back to my face. It was a full body scan that I could not ignore and I felt myself blushing.

"I look forward to us meeting again soon, with Rosa's permission of course."

They both looked at each other and smiled and Christine disappeared out the door.

"She is a great comfort to me, Alice. It would be so nice if you both became friends."

I told Rosa that I hoped that could be so.

Rosa was getting tired, and I suggested perhaps it was a good time for me to leave so that she could get some rest. But Rosa said she had one more thing to tell me, and that it was important and asked that I stay longer.

"Certainly, Rosa. I'm always very happy to be with you."

"So, you know now how things changed for Bertie and me. By judiciously introducing him to other women friends, we established a new loving relationship which gave us both a freedom that we could never have anticipated.

"Bertie blossomed and I can only assume that, most likely, the new liaisons that I introduced him to were an important reason for it. But I also saw that he felt less pressure in his daily life, and I worked out that this was most likely because I was not hanging on his every word, or confusing him with my moods.

"He was at last free of a woman's need for him to offer deeper emotional sustenance. The support I received from him now seemed like a genuine interest in my day-to-day interactions with my friends and my general daily pursuits. The emotional stuff was, thankfully for him, now far away from his jurisdiction."

Rosa reached for more water, then smoothed the bedclothes in front of her absentmindedly as she sorted out what she was going to say next.

"Bertie and I had enjoyed a wonderful and varied sex life together, and our lovemaking activities had become delightfully fulfilling even though, understandably, over the years they had become a little predictable.

"So intense was my enthusiasm for our new-found freedom, and for the people we included in our threesomes, I wanted to be sure that our successful lovemaking moves would translate easily to every new situation with other lovers as successfully as they did for us as a couple.

"These ideas coincided with my first noticing that Bertie was becoming a little vague, occasionally disoriented, and sometimes downright forgetful. It meant that we would sometimes get mixed messages from each other when making love as a threesome. I figured out a plan of action.

"I have already told you about the shorthand phrases that I had introduced to Bertie in our daily domestic life, watering the garden with buckets for example.

"Now I turned my mind to developing short messages about our various sexual activities. I wanted to simply say a particular word or phrase and know that Bertie would follow the manoeuvre that we practised, at the time I spoke the words for that instruction."

Rosa stopped speaking and rested for a moment. I was trying to make sense of what she was saying.

Was Rosa talking about making a particular spoken code, an abbreviated set of instructions, for a specific sex act? Would that even be possible? Perhaps it would, but maybe only because the two of them had many years of practising each move. Regular and constant lovemaking must surely reinforce the memories of each activity.

"Coming up with a code also required that I have a key word, or trigger word, that prefaced each short instruction and that could be common to all the codes. The idea was that the coded instruction, having been carefully prepared, would cause recall in Bertie so that he simply 'got on with job', so to speak. Like heading off to get the buckets when I said, 'Bertie, buckets'."

Rosa thought for a moment, then started talking again.

"Many years ago, I gave Bertie a birthday card that he so loved, that he now has it fixed to the inside of his wardrobe. The card portrayed a black-and-white drawing of a French maid in a short skirt, stockings and suspenders, little shoes, a white pinafore and a cap.

"She was shown in that saucy pose men love, bent over with a lot of thigh showing, while she busily dusted with her feather duster, her head turned and a come-hither look on her face.

"There was a message on the front of the card: 'Fifi says *Joyeux anniversarie!*' Fifi was the obvious choice for the code trigger.

"And so it came about, over quite a long period, that we succeeded in developing shorthand instructions for whatever the loving sexual acts that we (I suppose I should say I) felt we wanted to enjoy. I loved it, and Bertie seemed more than happy with the arrangement.

"As time went on, I developed a long list: 'Fifi wants a spanking', 'Fifi wants her breasts touched', 'Fifi wants to suck you', 'Fifi wants over the couch', 'Fifi wants to share a bath' and so on and so on. And when I had a girlfriend visit, usually one of the three or four that I was very close to, and who showed enthusiasm for trying my husband's handsome cock, I simply added the word 'friend' to the instruction so that when we were in a *ménage à trois* Bertie would know which of us was to receive his attention. I might add that, for some reason, 'Fifi's friend wants over the couch' was very popular with visitors."

Rosa stopped talking. She seemed to be reviewing what she had said, or maybe she was daydreaming about a fun past event.

As was the case so often recently, I was having trouble sorting out my thoughts and my emotions. I seemed to have slipped into another person's private world and I still wasn't sure if I should be there.

I was also experiencing feelings that I had never experienced before most notably, a totally unexpected sexual attraction to a woman.

"Illicit" and "taboo" were words that came readily to mind whenever I tried to approach the situation with logic, but a sort of physical longing took hold of me when I began to visualise some of the things Rosa talked about. Suddenly, it wasn't difficult to push logic aside.

And I was still confused by my reaction to Rosa's own desires, which quietly reached out to me just a short time before, making me want to kiss her in a way that excited both of us and caused me to blush.

And there were all the unanswered questions that were filling my head.

Would I wait for a time when things had quietened down? When I thought Rosa had told me all, or most of the things she felt the need to talk about? And was this still simply a quest to know more about the Bennetts' fifty years of marriage and better understand their life together and their happiness?

Rosa was getting very tired, but she stirred, lifted herself up and reached over, and opened the drawer in the bedside cabinet and took out an envelope.

"I know I have passed on a lot of information that has probably shocked or confused you, but being here in hospital has made me realise that we never really know how much time we have left, and so helping you understand our lives better has accelerated my desire to pass these things on to you.

"I only hope you will not judge me or Bertie harshly, when you sit down to try to make sense of it all. At the end of the day, we have hurt no one and enjoyed ourselves immensely.

"I've managed to write a few things down, which will help you understand how Bertie's and my happiness has survived through the latter half of our fifty years.

"I should add that despite everything we've discussed, our relation-ship wasn't just about making love. It was as much about bringing up a family and making a home as it was about playing our erotic games in the bedroom."

Rosa proffered the envelope, which I took from her. On the outside, she had written, "Personal & Private: For Alice Harding's eyes only".

"As for you, young lady, you now face the dilemma of choosing an academic approach to what you have discovered about the Bennetts, or a personal and private response. Maybe you will find a way of doing both.

"Come and see me again in a day or so, and I will willingly answer the mountain of questions that I'm sure you will have. Now I'd better have nap, I suppose. Take care darling. I love you very much."

Rosa turned, fluffed up her pillow and wriggled down into the bed.

"Thanks, Rosa for everything. I will tell Bertie when I'll be in to see you again. It should be the day after tomorrow."

Rosa raised her hand.

"There is one more thing, darling. Whatever you get up to with Bertie, remember, he is highly addictive. Enjoy him but do not lose yourself in him."

I blushed and offered a naive smile.

"Under your guidance, Rosa, how could a girl go wrong?"

Rosa laughed out loud, blew me a kiss and rolled over.

"Sweet dreams."

3

FRIENDS WITH BENEFITS

I ARRIVED home from the hospital at around seven-thirty. Bertie had eaten his dinner and retired. There was a television in their bedroom, and I knew that he loved to watch documentaries, especially about things archaeological or scientific.

Just to be sure Bertie was home and okay, I walked up to his bedroom and listened at the door. Sure enough, the television was on and without opening the door I picked up the words "Tutankhamen" and "pharaoh". Since there was no need to speak to him, I headed back to the kitchen and made myself a snack. Then I locked up and headed along the veranda to my cosy little flat, intending to have an early night.

I showered, put on my pyjamas and lay on the bed. The silence was blissful, and I had to stop myself falling asleep on the bed instead of in it.

I rose to pull back the bedclothes, and against my better judgement picked up and opened Rosa's envelope, intending only to scan its contents briefly and read them properly later.

A good hour passed before I put Rosa's half dozen beautifully handwritten pages back in the envelope. Then I carefully hid the envelope under the fancy paper liner at the bottom of my underwear drawer.

Getting to sleep was not going to be easy after all. The information in Rosa's detailed and explicit missal had put an end to that. How could a girl get to sleep with Fifi's codes bombarding her senses?

I didn't get back to Rosa until the following Friday afternoon. Bertie had told her to expect me.

I'd thought she and I would be alone, but when I got there, a handsome women of around fifty-something, was sitting on the bed beside her.

"So glad you could get here, darling. Alice, this is Maude. Maude, this is Alice."

Maude stood up and put her arms out and came towards me, and we embraced. I felt her large chest pressing against mine, and I immediately felt a severe case of blushing come over me.

In my mind's eye, I replayed Rosa's description of her friend's first visit and her introduction to Bertie. I saw Bertie's hand unbuttoning Maude's shirt and his mouth covering her nipple, while at the same time Rosa kissed her passionately.

When Maude stepped back, she looked at my red face and announced that Rosa had obviously told me things and that she was glad she had, because now she wouldn't be a total stranger to me. I tried to focus.

"I'm honoured to meet you at last, Maude and yes, Rosa has talked a lot about you. All good things of course."

"In which case I must assume that you approve of me, Alice. That is comforting."

She and Rosa exchanged knowing looks.

"Alice darling, I think I mentioned that Maude usually stays a night with us once a month, when she comes down from the country. This way we get to spend time together and she can visit her sister and other friends the following day.

"Because I am stuck here longer than I thought, Maude chose to forgo her stay this time, so as not to inconvenience you or Bertie. I've told her that I'm sure you would want her to stay over on her next visit and continue the arrangement, but if this will inconvenience you in any way please say so. Its up to you, darling."

"Of course she must stay with us, Rosa. It might not be as homely without you, or the cooking up to your high standard, but if Maude is happy to muddle through with Bertie and me then she is very welcome. And I'm sure I can also welcome her on Bertie's behalf."

After Maude had thanked me and arrangements for her next visit had been confirmed, she left us and we settled down for a chat.

"Well, Alice, you must have questions, I presume? Oh, but before we start I should just reassure you about Maude. As you can see, she can seem a bit overpowering. If you find yourself in a position with her that you find uncomfortable, it is perfectly okay to say, 'No thank you, Maude' or, if you are worried you might offend her, then 'No thank you, Maude. I'm just not ready' is fine."

"Thanks, Rosa. That is reassuring."

"Now girl! Any questions?"

"A million! But firstly, as we were talking about Maude, can I ask what the special thing is that Bertie does for Maude? He mentioned it in passing, something special he did for her, but I thought it better not to ask him for details."

Rosa smiled; or was it a grimace?

"Well, Alice, while I enjoy a wide range of sexual activities and fantasies, there is something I've never wanted to try, and that is anal sex. Bertie mentioned he'd like to try it quite early in our relationship, but I firmly refused and nothing more was said.

"I told you that Maude had married, but she lost her husband only a few years later. Arnold was his name. Arnold introduced Maude to anal sex. She says she objected at the beginning but let him anyway, and over time grew to enjoy it so much she almost couldn't do without it. Losing Arnold meant the end of much of her special love life.

"Over a cup of tea one day, Maude confided in me that the lack of anal sex, or 'bottom play' as she preferred to call it, was her biggest love loss. I thought about it and decided that I would find a way to instruct Bertie, so that he and she could share this pleasure that so interested the two of them.

"It was a bit tricky, as I was trying to get Bertie to do something and absorb a coded instruction without my having to go all the way to demonstrate it. Also, we had never engaged in anal sex, so he had no instilled memory of the two of us in the act of doing it.

"Well, with a bit of effort and mishaps with lubricant bottles, and me saying, 'No Bertie' at the crucial moment, we sort of got there, and 'Fifi loves bottom play' became part of the code.

"Then came the moment of truth. Would it work with Maude?

"I have already told you about introducing Maude to our first threesome. Bertie already knew her. I knew he was impressed with the size of Maude's posterior, as he had excitedly commented on it later, at the end of our first threesome together.

"So when Maude visited us again a month later, I was keen on giving her, and him, this special present. And everything went like a charm.

"Firstly, I took Maude aside and told her that Bertie had this present for her, something which I knew she and Arnold enjoyed together. She immediately guessed what it was.

"I had already told her about the codes Bertie and I had developed, and she quickly wanted to know how, considering my unsympathetic view of 'bottom play', we had managed to succeed with the instruction, to which I answered sternly, 'With a great deal of difficulty'.

"I told her that if she would like to try it, I couldn't guarantee the outcome, but she only had to say, 'No, Bertie' and he would stop.

"Maude was beside herself with excitement but she ran hot and cold, constantly thinking up reasons why she shouldn't, then excitedly changing her mind and saying that she should.

"She was worried that Bertie might not want to do it, but I quickly reassured her that Bertie had already enthusiastically admired her 'beautiful arse' and when I told her this, she got visibly excited and agreed. In fact I'm sure she would have rushed off to find Bertie at that moment, except that he was out at the bowling club with his mates.

"Then she had endless questions. Would he want to take her over the back of the sofa, or on her knees on the floor? Should she leave her panties off? Would she be in charge of the lube? Where would I be during the event? And on, and on.

"I asked her to be quiet, and told her that she could have him in the lounge room or in her bedroom at a time that suited her. I then said that it was now four thirty and I expected Bertie in at around five o'clock, and that he would normally go straight to the bathroom and shower before dinner.

"We could all have a leisurely meal and a glass of wine, during which time she could chat to Bertie. A sort of familiarisation prelim, so to speak.

"I would then excuse myself, feigning a headache, and she could pick her moment to say the magic words, 'Fifi loves bottom play'. And I finished by telling her that the lube would be in the kitchen in the fruit basket near the sink.

"Maude suddenly got control of herself and took herself off to her room to shower and prepare for her 'little adventure'."

Rosa rested and I was ready to ask another question, but then I couldn't just leave things there and move on.

"So Rosa, did everything go well for Maude and Bertie?"

"Very well, Alice. It's been a regular monthly feature of Maude's visit and Bertie has settled into a routine to which he's added a few moves that were not included in the code instruction."

"What sort of move, Rosa?"

"Well, he enjoys having fun with that 'great backside' as he calls it. Spanking is a favourite fantasy of his, and it seems Maude delights in it also.

"Interestingly, Maude is a bit of a spanker herself, very much enjoying it with of some of her women friends who want to experience a bit of domination. It is interesting that she lets Bertie do it to her. Perhaps she picks up pointers?"

Rosa chuckled at what she had just said, as I attempted to file the information under its correct heading.

"Oh yes, there is something else about Maude I should probably tell you."

Again Rosa smiled with her knowing and wistful grin.

"Yes, Rosa? I'm building up such an image of this amazing woman that I suppose another tidbit won't hurt. What is it?"

Rosa looked at me oddly, seeming to assess my ability to cope with what she was about to say.

"I'll only say that Maude has a giant clitoris. Very large clitorises are not common, and they are much enjoyed by the women who have them. I've never seen another like it."

My mouth fell open. Rosa had rocked my world for the umpteenth time.

"Thank you for that, Rosa. I'll just pop that information in with all the other stuff, in what is fast becoming the Fantastic Story of Maude file."

Both of us laughed and Rosa took a drink of water from beside the bed.

We joked about a few things and then Rosa said there was something she had forgotten to put on her written list.

"In the spare bedroom there is a small wardrobe which is locked. You will find the key in the bottom drawer of the vanity basin in the bathroom.

"The wardrobe contains my dress-up fantasy clothes, a complete french maid's outfit, a girl's school uniform, a tweed skirt that goes with the button-up shirt and woollen cardigan, heavy lisle stockings and sensible brogue shoes. Oh yes, and there is a pair of horn-rimmed glasses there somewhere.

"This last outfit is our librarian or schoolmistress uniform. Bertie joyfully calls 'her' his most challenging seduction.

"I do so enjoy playing this austere professional no-nonsense fantasy lady. She seems to lend herself to playing hard to get. It's also the only time I wear the old whalebone corset, which Bertie can never find his way into, and I have to help him while at the same time admonishing him, as the librarian would, telling him in a loud voice: 'If you don't be a lot quieter and behave yourself, I will have you removed'."

I burst out laughing. Rosa had provided a strong image of their fantasy and I treasured it.

"There are four drawers, a couple of drawers for underwear and delicates, stockings in different lengths and colours, suspender belts and fancy garters and bows. The bottom two drawers contains panties, slips, negligees – oh yes, and the lovely old-fashioned corset along with three corselets in different colours. There is also a beautiful pair of silk pyjamas and a cotton pair fashioned on old-style bloomers.

"There is a collection of shoes that might interest you. I find very high heels no longer suit my age bracket, but there are a few pairs of high heels. You might have fun trying them on. Bertie has a foot and shoe fetish so he has always enjoyed me wearing heels, especially with ankle straps, and even the low ones I wear today.

"Oh yes, and I forgot to mention that there is a box on the floor of the wardrobe full of sex toys, mainly different types and sizes of dildos, even tiny ones for bottom play. You are most welcome to look through and try on anything that takes your fancy, 'fancy' being the operative word."

Rosa laughed her slightly wicked laugh, and I joined her.

"Oh, and there is something else you will see that I should warn you about, at least in regard to Bertie.

"A girlfriend gave me a present, a complete nun's habit. An aunt who was a nun had given it to her when she was clearing out her closet and my friend, Lola who was visiting, had asked if she might have it.

"Lola had been a day student at a girls' convent school and had vivid memories of hearing the older girls talk about Sister so-and-so having favourites amongst the boarders.

"Much of the girls' talk might well have been exaggerated fantasy, but it certainly excited many of students, including my friend. She loved the idea of a particular nun whom she had a crush on leading her away from the dormitory to a secret room and removing her nightie and having her way with her."

Rosa stopped talking. She was obviously remembering a past adventure and she smiled that special smile.

Again, I was being swept along on vivid images of sexual taboos, and I loved it.

"And is it the nun's habit you wanted to warn me about, Rosa?"

"Ah, yes Alice. It is. We were just settling down for the evening. Bertie was out finishing something in the greenhouse and I had just showered in preparation for going to bed. I was finding hangers and a place in the wardrobe for my new nun's outfit, when I suddenly had an urge to try it on. I had realised that there were more bits and pieces than I had imagined. The headgear alone was made up of four different items.

"I eventually got it all together, and when I looked in the mirror I was pleasantly surprised. I imagined I looked just like the famous actress Audrey Hepburn in 'The Nun's Story'.

"I had no stockings or shoes or even knickers on, but I heard Bertie heading along the passage and thought I would surprise him and get his opinion. After all, we needed to share our fantasies, and I had no idea what he thought about a woman dressed as a nun.

"I hopped out the door and called out, 'Darling, what do you think of this?' And when he turned around, I pirouetted to show off the costume.

"Well, things happened very quickly, and to this day I cannot remember anything being said by either of us, although there were moments when I almost pressed the alarm button and called 'No, Bertie'. But I didn't.

"Bertie took two giant steps towards me, grabbed me by the throat and pushed me up against the wall. Then he lifted my nun's habit and held it up with the hand holding my neck, while with his other hand he unbuckled his trousers and let out his cock. Then he spat violently onto his hand and wetted his member, and a moment later spat on his hand again and shoved it up between my legs.

"Then he took me like he never had before. I think I could describe it as 'violently'.

"He poked my vagina with a total disregard for our usual procedure, whereby I or both of us would normally part my pubic hair and wet my lips in readiness for entry. Instead he forced himself through, painfully dragging hairs and skin in along with him as he drove forward.

"Suddenly he was in right up to the hilt and I was about to scream because I was in pain. My vagina was very dry, not having had the benefit of foreplay, so having Bertie inside a dry vagina was, to say the least, uncomfortable.

"Then, after only a few moments, during which Bertie pushed me about, he ejaculated and I was filled with lubricant, and my immediate crisis was over.

"And then it was all over. The whole event had taken less than two or three minutes.

"Bertie took back his member, hoisted his pants and headed off back up the passageway without a word or second glance. I let myself slide down the wall, sat on the floor and cried.

"In all our sexual interactions, and however rough or demonstrative they might be, Bertie had always shown his loving side, always giving at least a sign that he really loved me.

"Even when I rewarded him for something by letting him give me a heavy spanking, we would always end with a tickle and a laugh, and kissing. What had just happened was totally unlike him.

"I went to the kitchen and made a cup of cocoa and sat thinking about it for ages.

"It occurred to me that perhaps Bertie had not seen the nun as being me dressed up, but as someone else. Perhaps he had thought it was a real nun? I knew religion was one of the few things Bertie regarded as truly evil. So was this a violent act, a reaction against some deeply felt moral dilemma? Hardly possible, I thought.

"I decided it was more likely to be related to something going on in his head that I did not yet understand. Was there really a mental problem developing other than simple forgetfulness? The change to his mental state that I had only lately begun to notice was a mystery to me, as it certainly still is today.

"I went and got into bed beside Bertie. He rolled over and cuddled me and kissed me, and asked if I was all right because I was so late coming to bed. Then he wished me goodnight as though nothing had happened."

Rosa stopped talking and I saw her brow was still furrowed and she wore a worried expression. I quickly spoke, to move her on from that subject.

"And so that was the end of the nun theme then, Rosa?"

Rosa focused on my face and smiled.

"Well, actually no, darling. I did put it on a few weeks later, when Lola who had given it to me, visited and we spent the afternoon in your flat.

"It was an immediate hit. I told Lola to wait while I went to wash in the bathroom. When I came out and announced that Sister Carmel was stepping in, in place of her friend Rosa, she could not believe her eyes.

"I ordered her to come and stand in front of me, then I began removing her clothes. When she was standing in just her little bra and panties I asked her to kneel down, tilt her head so that I could see her eyes, and told her to open her mouth wide. Lola dutifully fulfilled my wishes.

"Then I told her to put her hand under my habit and caress the calves of my legs, which she did eagerly. Then I commanded her to run her hand slowly up my stockinged legs. She looked up at me with bright excited eyes and gasped as her hand touched the swinging head of the very large strap-on I had hidden there.

"I lifted my habit above the rubber penis and took hold of it and pushed it towards her mouth, dragging her head towards it with the other hand. Lola shivered with lustful excitement and instantly became my lesbian convent schoolgirl slave.

"From then on, all she ever wanted when she visited me was more of Sister Carmel."

I was transfixed by Rosa's erotic story. The way she told it was so real that I suddenly shook and noticed the wetness between my legs. Was Rosa's simple story able to make me into a bisexual woman in just a few minutes?

I stood closer to Rosa's bed staring at her as she licked her dry lips. Her beautiful face, atop a view of her breasts standing firm beneath her nightdress, was so alluring I could no longer keep myself from her.

I put out my hand and lifted her chin, then bent down and kissed her gently.

I then pushed my lips against her mouth with more force and offered her my tongue, wanting at that moment, to also be Sister Carmel's schoolgirl slave, and as I did so my hand lightly touched a nipple through the fabric of Rosa's nightie.

I felt Rosa's hand reach out to the back of my knee and wander up my leg to the bare thigh, where she paused and caressed my skin.

Then she moved on and touched the damp crotch of my panties. She pulled the crotch to one side and her fingers lightly fondled me, and I shivered. She left the hand there for only a few moments, then slid it back down my leg and away, and we ended our delicious kiss.

"Thank you, darling Alice. You are very brave."

I looked at her lovely face, even more illuminated by what we had just done.

"I hope you come home soon, Rosa, and when you do I hope you will introduce me to Sister Carmel. I am desperate to meet her."

"As soon as I get in the door, sweet girl. Even Bertie might have to wait."

We adjusted ourselves and rested for a moment, then I sat back on the bed, and we talked on for ages. Everything Rosa said was another revelation, and I filed the information away for future use.

But there was still much to be learnt.

———

University life was a totally different world from the one I led at home, and I enjoyed it immensely. I loved studying Psychology and also loved the social life on campus and spending time with my few special friends.

I had two particular friends whose company I regularly enjoyed. People sometimes joked and called us the three musketeers. We were each very different.

Freya was a couple of years older than me, around thirty-one or two. She was very tall and very thin and with her bobbed hair and delicate features could easily – if she had been a tad shorter – have been mistaken for someone much younger. She had a gentle nature and a gentle voice to go with it. She seemed never to get angry or really upset about anything. She told me once that she was resigned to the fact that men did not rush to engage her in conversation or ask her out. She thought that being so tall probably frightened them. Then she coyly added that having such tiny breasts might not help either.

Angela couldn't have been more different. Quite overweight and displaying more curves than anyone could imagine, she was talkative, giggled a lot and enjoyed eating. Though she was super intelligent, she often showed a lack of common sense when assessing a suitor, and was too often setting herself up for a less than satisfactory relation-ship. She was younger than me by about a year.

As well as often lunching together during the week, we regularly caught up at a nearby cafe on Friday afternoons to chat about the week past and the weekend ahead.

On this particular Friday I suggested that, as it was Angie's birthday early the following week, I would like to invite her and Freya for a cake and champagne afternoon at my place the following day, to which they excitedly agreed.

It was their first visit to my home. They enjoyed the tour of the house and then we settled into my flat, each of us with a full cham-pagne glass and all sitting around a large platter of savouries alongside Rosa's wonderful two-tiered cake plate with the silver serving handle projecting above and loaded with cream cakes and French patisseries.

Angie wore her usual stylish but very appropriate nineteen-fifties brightly coloured vintage summer dress, with a hand-knitted shawl around her otherwise bare shoulders and over her voluminous breasts. Her hair was teased and pinned back to carry a very large red artificial flower on the side of her head. She wore a lot of makeup, most notably a bright red lipstick, with which she exaggerated her Cupid's bow of a mouth.

Angie had suddenly become obsessed with reaching the age of twenty-eight and still not having a regular boyfriend.

"Oh dear, what will become of me? In another couple of years I'll be an old maid like you two."

Freya and I both yelled and remonstrated with her; then I topped up our glasses and we energetically nibbled from the delights on offer, relaxing in the sometimes crude banter mostly heard from younger students when let off the leash.

As the afternoon progressed and a second bottle of champagne was opened, the conversation drifted to more sensual subjects: our views on crotch-less panties or what each of us thought was the most sexually attractive thing about a man etc, and lots of ribald laughter ensued.

It was at this point that Freya suggested that each of us should tell the story of her most exciting sexual encounter.

This caused a sudden silence as each of us reviewed the suggestion and thought about what we would or could say.

The idea was great, but to expose ourselves with such a personal and, until now, private event needed close consideration.

"What if our story is so private that we couldn't possibly reveal the event?" I asked.

Angie thought the idea was great, and was very keen to participate.

"We don't need to give real names or times or places. It is what happens that matters. The tricky bit is only who will go first."

Angie burped and hiccupped and took another sip from her glass.

After much to-ing and fro-ing accompanied by Angie's excited and nervous giggles, and with Freya's sudden blushing fits as she thought of some moment in her past, it was decided that Freya would be first to tell her story.

Occasionally, you might find someone calling out at a moment in the story that excites them. It will most likely be Angie, who gets emotionally moved very easily.

FREYA'S STORY

I was working as a nursing aide at a large city hospital before I enrolled at university. I mostly worked night shift, and enjoyed the quietness and the lack of hustle and bustle. The work was easy; just checking on patients through the night. Some patients were just in overnight for minor surgery, while other more serious cases where often heavily sedated and only required their life support equipment to be monitored.

This particular night was very quiet. Only half the beds were occupied, and only one of the special care rooms contained a serious case.

Kat, the aide I was to replace, met me as usual. It was two o'clock in the morning, and she said everything was under control, and the patients were all sleeping comfortably. Then she took me to the special care room, and we stood outside while she gave me the details of the case and what we were expected to do.

She said that the Director of Nursing had indicated that, at the moment, it was unclear whether the patient would last through the night. She explained that he had been brought in unconscious, having survived a very nasty motorbike accident. He was now on life support, but it was also important to keep his temperature down. For that reason, staff were asked to spend a little time every hour or so swabbing his body with a sponge and cold water.

Now that she had outlined the duties for my shift, she took me in to see the patient. The man was huge and he was hairy and probably in his late thirties. His eyes were closed and he was eerily silent. Only a single dial beside the bed confirmed that he was breathing. He lay naked, but for a sheet covering his lower half.

I thanked Kat and she prepared to leave, then she stopped and turned and looked at me and smiled and in a hushed voice provided a final piece of information.

"Just one other thing I should tell you, Freya. He has tattoos, as do most of the bikie patients we get admitted. But he does have a special one."

I asked her what was special about it.

"He has a honey bee tattooed on the end of his penis. One of the day staff said that when he first came in, he had a partial erection, probably caused by a rush of adrenalin or a sudden hormone surge in the moments leading up to the accident. She said that the bee had its wings extended but later, when the erection subsided, it appeared to have them folded."

I was looking at her in amazement and she laughed.

"Thought I should tell you, just in case you thought it was a real one and started madly beating him with a fly swat."

We both laughed nervously and then she left me to it.

I shut the door behind her and turned to look at my patient. He looked so gentle, so serene. His long blond hair and strong square chin made him look like a sleeping Viking chieftain, the sort we might see in a movie or picture book. His huge muscular arms could have easily swung a sword to cut off his rival's head and limbs. But now his arms rested beside his body and his giant empty hands faced upwards.

I lifted the patient record sheet from the end of the bed and read his name, Odin Amundsen. Definitely a Viking, I mused. His ancestors might easily have known mine way back when so many girls would have been named Freya.

I collected a sponge and a bowl of water and started the task of keeping the giant cool. I began with his brow, face and neck. His skin was taut and leathery. I could have been wiping down a leather skirt, or a snakeskin handbag.

As I prepared to move to his chest, I had a sudden desire to kiss him, so I leant forward and lightly touched his lips with mine. But then I wanted more, and pushed my mouth harder against his lips. It gave me a beautiful feeling and I suddenly felt very happy.

I sponged his broad shoulders with one hand while I burrowed my fingernails into the forest of hair on his chest. Swabbing Odin was suddenly feeling exciting, and I began to concentrate on each moment with loving attention.

I had not had a lot of experience with men. I probably should say I'd had none. Well, that's not quite true. There was a moment after school one day, when Danny Roberts walked me home via the park and asked me to sit down with him on a grassy bank beneath a giant Moreton Bay fig tree.

Danny had kissed me and I liked that. Then he'd put his hands where my breasts are but as you all know, I'm more than a bit size challenged in that area. Then he'd slid his hand up my skirt and begun exploring under my knickers with his fingers. That wasn't unpleasant, but then he'd unzipped his trousers, and placed my hand on his penis. Suddenly I got frightened and yelled "gotta go, Danny" and stood up and ran away.

"Oh no! Go back Freya!"

As I grew older I began to realise that, being so tall and thin and with no boobs to speak of, I wasn't going to get men rushing to me with offers of a romantic date, or with bunches of flower's or chocolates. It wasn't that I didn't like men, but I did find that I seemed much more attracted to girls and, thanks to you two, I eventually discovered love and happiness.

"Stick to the story, Freya, or we might have to grab you."

As I said, I experienced a growing feeling of excitement as I swabbed Odin. I began to have thoughts about things I could do, quite rude things, and that made me more excited.

I went back to Odin's face and kissed him again. I even ran my tongue across his closed lips. Then I moved back down, just below his chest where the long hair stopped and his shorter belly hair began. I looked at his hand lying beside him and only inches from the edge of the bed and where I stood. His bed was quite high but because I'm tall, it didn't seem unduly so.

I reached out and slid my hand beneath his and lifted it. I had a sudden thought: I can have his hand if I want to. I looked at his long, thick fingers. For all I knew, or rather didn't know, about men's penises, any one of Odin's fingers looked capable of doing what a penis did.

With my other hand I lifted up the hem of my nurse uniform, exposing my panties. Then I took Odin's hand and placed it between my legs and rocked it slowly to and fro. Then I took hold of his index finger, pulled my panty crotch to one side and placed the tip of his finger against my wet pussy. It felt wonderful.

"Push it in quickly, before he wakes up."

I about to, but then I remembered the story of the bee and I put his hand back and went and drew back the sheet, all the way to the bed end.

Oh my goodness! Probably through lack of experience, I've never thought a lot about the size of men's penises. Odin's penis looked very large, even though it was resting, and at its base was a coconut-sized bunch of testicles nestled inside a mass of blond hair. And sure enough, there was the honey bee neatly tattooed on the big reddish brown bulb at the top of his penis that stood up through this nest of blond hair.

Looking at his manhood was so invigorating, and I desperately wanted to have it, to own it. I wriggled my hand down into the hair to find the base of his penis and when I did, I clasped it tightly and closed my eyes. I found myself shaking just a little, but didn't know why.

And now I knew what I most wanted to do in the whole world. I still had an hour before I was to be relieved for my tea break. I locked the door.

I had entered a state of being that I did not understand, but did not want to stop. I took off every piece of my clothing and footwear. Then I climbed up onto Odin and flattened and pressed my body against his.

I felt so calm, and what began as excitement morphed into a sort of ecstasy and I sighed and shut my eyes.

I must have lain there for a good ten or fifteen minutes, most happy with my lot. I thought how nice it was to lie on top of a person. In fact, to this day lying on someone is one of my favourite loving positions, even if I'm fully dressed and not feeling especially sexual.

"As we know, and so dearly love you for it Freya."

As I just said, some time had passed and I was feeling sleepy. Then I imagined I felt something between my legs. I managed to not flinch or respond. Yes, something was definitely moving slowly up between the tops of my thighs, pushing my flesh gently aside as it did so.

"Oh my god! He's a zombie. Run Freya, run!"

I was mesmerised. I couldn't move. I didn't want to move. I wanted whatever it was to keep coming up towards my crotch.

So much rushed through my mind. I couldn't take it all in. I lifted my head slowly, opened my eyes and looked at Odin's face, but nothing about it had changed.

Then, without planning to do so, I found myself moving my legs apart, and edging down to meet whatever it was coming up towards me. I had already felt a tiny orgasm and I knew that I was wet and getting wetter. Suddenly, whatever it was pushed against my vagina, which opened like a flower and spread its wetness everywhere.

I now knew exactly what was happening and I didn't want it to stop. I started to move down again and as I did so, I opened up and sucked in Odin's penis head, but I kept on moving down along his huge shaft. Further and further down I wriggled, and Odin came further and further up into me.

I began to sob. I wanted Odin to put his giant arms around me and fasten me permanently to his body. I wanted to run my hands through his long hair and stick my tongue into his mouth. I wanted him fully alive.

I stopped crying, and settled down and rode my Viking ruler's manhood as if I was riding a galloping horse. I desperately wanted to feel him come inside me, and he did.

At first he frightened me with his bellowing roar. But he only roared once, when he sent a torrent of sperm into my helplessly lustful and soaking little vagina.

I heard myself calling out "Yes Odin, yes!"

I lay still for a long time, but all was quiet. Odin didn't move or make another sound. I heard a bell ringing in the distance and knew that my time was up and that someone would be looking for me. I dragged myself off of my Viking lover and stood up.

I looked at his penis, still standing tall, sticking out of its luxuriant blond nest. And there was the honey bee, wings spread wide, drinking from the hole in Odin's penis.

I quickly cleaned Odin and swabbed his belly and pulled the sheet back over him. Then there was a knock on the door and I called "coming, just give me a moment please."

I threw on my clothes and headed out the door.

"How is he?" asked the nurse who had looked after him the night before.

"Nothing seems to have changed," I answered, trying not to look at her, and thinking that I must look dreadful.

"He can't last much longer. He just didn't seem to want to go. Like he was waiting for something," said the nurse.

I stared at her.

"Do you believe he will die?"

"The doctors and surgeons think so. It's a brain problem. It's no longer connected to his body, or something."

I turned abruptly and hurried away, unable to get my mind around it all. Had I simply imagined everything? Had it not really happened? But what was leaking from me now was proof that something had happened, something beautiful and amazing.

I got to work early the next night. I'd spent the whole day wondering and daydreaming. Dreaming that Odin would recover and throw me on the back of his big motorbike and we'd ride off into the distance. But that was not to be.

"They found him dead early this morning. Strange, though! He had his one good eye open, and a most angelic smile on his face," said a nurse going off duty.

"And the girl that found him said he had an amazing erection and that the bee tattoo was truly beautiful."

When my night shift finished, I went to Odin's room. It was not occupied so I sneaked in and locked the door and lay on the bed, and cried and cried, and I imagined that I was the wife of an ancient Viking god.

So now you all know why Freya always wants you to let her lie on top of you, and why you make her so happy when you do.

I love you both. Thank you.

———

We have heard Freya's story. Now we discover Angie's account of passion.

ANGIE'S STORY

You might recall that before I started at university, I worked as a teacher's aide and doubled as a youth worker at a city senior high school.

I had moved to the city at age sixteen to live with my Auntie Betty, Mum's younger sister, and had worked mainly in low paid jobs. Getting a position at the school was a step up.

One of the youth worker tasks that I particularly enjoyed was going on school camps. It meant that I got away from my crazy aunt, whom I loved dearly but who could be quite demanding. It also gave me an opportunity to work in a responsible and serious work environment.

The school owned a couple of holiday camps, one in the mountains the other in bushland that fronted a beautiful beach. I got to know them both very well.

As a member of staff, I was involved in the planning of student activities. This also involved getting the students up early and organising them for bush walks or beach trips, or whatever.

Most times everything was good and the kids were great. Occasionally there would be a couple of kids, or I should perhaps call them young adults – usually sixth formers – who could prove tiresome and shirk their rostered duties, or disrupt some well-planned activity. We tactfully tried to sort these students and put them into roles where they couldn't easily cause problems.

My story begins with a planned combined canoeing and bushwalking trip. Everybody knew what tasks they had been allotted. The weather was perfect, and at nine fifteen we congregated at the centre of the camp, then moved off towards the jetty and the canoes.

It was at that moment that one of the staff noticed that two of the boys were missing, and I was sent to find them and hurry them up.

I headed up to the rows of tents. It was very quiet, as everyone had already headed to the beach. I approached the tent of the two missing students, Ray and Kevin. As I drew close I thought I heard a sound. I walked around to the back of their tent and peeped through the mosquito netting of the small back window.

Ray and Kevin were laying on the floor with their trousers pulled down around their ankles. Each had a hand on the other's cock and both were rubbing and tugging furiously. Instead of immediately leaving, I stood fascinated and watched until the two ejaculated, then I quietly left, my mind swirling.

I reported back that the boys couldn't be found and they were both marked down for detention when they were back at school the following week.

The thirty or more students on the trip had a great time. It was interesting observing them. Some seemed so young while others were quite adult. All were entertaining and often I smiled watching what they were up to.

One girl, Judy Somerville, was the girl who had everything going for her and commanded attention wherever she went. Not only was she tall and shapely; she was also beautiful to look at and spoke confidently on all matters.

If Judy Somerville had a problem, it must surely have been that she was what some boys would call a "cock tease". She knew that she reigned supreme over all the other girls in the school and that she was the most desired female on the campus. And if that wasn't enough, she had a more than adequate bosom, about which the boys could never pass up the opportunity to make a comment.

One wanted to be sympathetic towards Judy, but it just was not possible.

"If I could just get to strip Judy and lie on top of her, it would sort her out for good."

"Yes, darling Freya, I'm sure it would."

Judy had a couple of girlfriends but they were only there to bathe in her glory and enjoy her occasional largesse as a wealthy benefactor. Judy Somerville's parents were well-to-do, and she made sure that everyone knew about it.

She had a boyfriend who sometimes picked her up in his father's expensive European sports car. She was unattainable by any of the lads at our school.

After school one day, I called out to our school camp naughty boys, Ray and Kevin, as they headed off for the mall. I said that I had a few hours paid work for them at my house and asked them to get there as soon as school finished on Friday. When Kevin, the cheeky one, replied "We are expensive Miss," I replied "So am I, but everything is negotiable. Just be there."

Friday came. The two lads knocked on my door and I showed them in. I told them to follow me, led them to the lounge and asked them to sit on the sofa. They were out of their comfort zone, and a bit self-conscious.

I don't think male students take too much notice of a woman's clothing, being usually fixated only on her anatomy, clothed but preferably naked. I was wearing a very tight dress that accentuated my prominent backside, a very low cut top, stockings and high heels and lots of lipstick, and had put on perfume. Hopefully they'd notice that I looked a little different from the way I looked at school.

First, I told them to each move aside and make a space for me on the sofa, as I had something to tell them. I sat down between them, making sure my skirt rose above my knees. Then, on pretence of needing to switch something off in the kitchen, I stood and walked slowly away from them, towards the swing door.

Immediately through the door I turned, and looked through a crack on the side. Both boys were grinning and nodding, and Kevin made a gesture with his hand indicating he was doing something rude with himself and with me.

I smiled to myself. Bingo! They've noticed. I came back and sat on the sofa.

"Now boys, it's your lucky day."

"How come, Miss?"

"Well, how will I put this? I'm sure you both have fantasies. In fact I'm certain you both fantasise about Judy Somerville, for instance?"

There was a stunned silence.

"Oh, and in case you are wondering why I invited you, you are here to help me with my fantasies. Yes, girls have fantasies too."

The two stared at me with a wide-eyed look of disbelief.

"And just in case you both feel disinclined to share my fantasy with me, I should tell you one important thing. I saw you wanking each other in your tent at camp last month. So if you don't do as I ask, I could put out the rumour that you two are wanking each other, and that probably has something to do you with you not being able to get girlfriends."

The two young men stared at me then at each other. Kevin turned to me.

"Oh no Miss, you can't do that. We don't do it much, Miss. Please don't tell anyone."

"Good, Kevin. Now tell me, when you were both tugging on each other, what was your fantasy at that moment? Ray, you go first.

"Gees Miss, do we really have to do this? This is so embarrassing. We came to work in your shed Miss, we should get started."

"Kevin, you are the cheeky one. Tell me what you were thinking about. Were you thinking about Judy Somerville? Were you fucking Miss Somerville in your head, while Ray was giving you the hand job?"

Kevin pulled a face.

"That bitch should be fucked. She's such a bitch."

Then Ray added his thoughts.

"Yeah Miss, every bloke at school wants to fuck her. She's so sexy and good-looking."

"So Kevin, if you had Judy Somerville here right now and you could do anything you wanted with her, what would you do? Tell us, Kevin. What is your fantasy about the gorgeous Judy? You can say whatever's in your head."

The two boys each looked past me, and at each other and grinned.

"Well, Kevin?"

"I'd first give her big backside a good whack. In fact, I'd push her over the back of this seat, drag down her pants and spank her till her bum turned red and she screamed for mercy. That's what I'd do, Miss."

"That sounds very exciting Kevin. Thank you. You're next, Ray. You suddenly have the most desirable Judy Somerville in front of you. What would your fantasy be? How would you handle the dear girl? Would you woo her with kind words, or would you have something else in mind? Tell us, Ray."

Big Ray coloured up behind his youthful chin stubble.

"Well, Miss, I'd start by pulling her top off, Miss, then I'd bite and suck her tits, then I'd pull out my stiffie and make her suck it, Miss."

The two exchanged looks and grinned. Then Kevin spoke.

"Yes, Miss, we would show her what's what."

I eyed the two and notice that one had a bulge in his pants while the other was touching himself in the same place.

"Now boys, would you like to hear my fantasy? Are you both ready? Remember, I said you are here to help me."

Both boys were suddenly more forthcoming.

"Yes, Miss, whatever you want, Miss."

"Here we go then. This is *my* fantasy."

Two sets of eyes stared at me and I noticed that one lad had a hand moving awkwardly on his trousers.

"My fantasy is that I am really Judy Somerville, and that I am suddenly trapped alone in this room with the two of you."

As I spoke, I placed a hand on each lad's trouser front and let my fingers search for signs of life. There was an audible gasp from Ray, and Kevin wriggled.

"Judy Somerville is getting a little excited, sitting beside two of her most enthusiastic admirers, and she notices that things are happening inside their trousers. She reaches out, unzips each of you and gets out two cocks. Having one in each hand makes Judy very happy, and very horny."

I was unzipping the lads as I spoke. Kevin's cock sprang out of his trousers and I untangled Ray where his cock was caught up in his underpants.

"Oh Miss? Your fantasy is fantastic. What next?"

"Yes, what happens?"

"Judy is very excited. She has a lovely cock in each hand and she moves her hands gently up and down. Judy Somerville is getting more and more excited until she can stand it no longer, and tears off her blouse and brassiere and exposes her boobs to her admirers."

I let go of the boys at this point and removed my top and bra. Then I closed my hand around their erections once again.

Both lads were red-faced, and stared at my breasts.

"Now Ray, Judy's breasts are all yours. Suck them while you can."

I let go of Ray's cock and put a hand behind his head and pulled him to my chest. He immediately opened his mouth and gorged himself on my nipples, moving rapidly from one breast to the next and back again.

Kevin gazed at what was happening. His jaw was slack and his mouth was open. I let go of him and unzipped my skirt, lifted myself and slipped the skirt down and away. Kevin's eyes bulged. Then I slid myself down on the sofa a little, and lifted my legs in the air.

"Judy wants Kevin to smack her bottom while Ray is sucking on her big titties. Please get down on the floor and make Judy happy, Kevin."

Kevin practically fell off the sofa onto the floor. He knelt and stared in awe at my backside and my stockinged legs and my heeled shoes.

"My fantasy, Kevin, so do as you are told. Take Judy's panties off please. Oh, and when you've got her panties off, Kev, she would love you to kiss her wet pussy."

I really didn't need to say or do a lot more.

The boys where fired up. I was suddenly without skirt, pants or bra and two energetic young men where feeding on me, like crocs on a herd of wildebeests crossing a river, and I lay back to fully enjoy it. I was in 'bad boy' land and I loved it.

Occasionally I would ask for a little something like "Judy wants you to play with her tits, Kevin darling" or "Judy wants you to suck her clitoris, Ray."

"You're doing a fantastic job, boys. Please try not to blow your load yet, though, because Judy will want you to do something else with your cocks soon."

I judged that time had arrived.

"Back off a moment boys, Judy wants to turn over."

I moved down and knelt on the floor. The boys held their cocks and watched lustfully.

"Look at her arse and her stockings, she's so beautiful Kev. I've only seen that in porn videos," Ray croaked.

I loved the compliment.

"Now boys, Judy would like you to fuck her. Take it in turns. She can suck one of you while the other is in her slippery cunt."

The boys were good. They had managed (I suspect with great difficulty) to hold on until the moment when Judy told each of them separately to empty their balls in her.

We ended the day with me back on the sofa with a stocking round my ankle and a shoe missing, being gently licked and touched as one of the boys played with my suspenders while the other gently rubbed the end of his now flaccid cock against my open mouth and lips.

I complimented the lads.

"Thank you, Kevin; thank you, Ray. You have satisfied my fantasy perfectly. And I hope you both enjoyed yourselves."

"Oh yes Miss, you're the best. We loved your fantasy, playing Judy, but it was the real you who was really fantastic Miss Angie."

I thought I noticed that Kevin had a more sensitive look in his eye and his manner had changed.

"Miss Angie?"

"Yes, Ray?"

"I'm in love with you now. Bugger Judy Somerville."

"Me too," murmured Kevin.

"Hmm, buggering Miss Judy Somerville? Now that's a fantasy I will definitely think about."

The boys exchanged knowing smiles.

"Glad to help in the garage any time, Miss Angie."

That is not quite the end of the story. After some time away on holidays I returned to the school. I hadn't been back more than a day when Kevin and Ray met me outside the school gates.

"Hello, you two. Not getting into too much trouble, I hope?"

They both laughed.

Ray started to talk.

"Miss Angie! We wondered if ... ?"

"Come on, spit it out, Ray."

"What he wants to say Miss, is that we would be very happy to help you clean up the garage anytime you feel like it."

I laughed. This seemed vaguely like a proposition, or was 'cleaning up the garage' a euphemism for a schoolboy orgy?

"Well, boys, I'm not against the idea, but I should tell you that last time my crazy Aunt Betty, whom I live with, was away and so I had the house to myself. Now she is back."

A downcast look crossed their faces.

"Mind you, Auntie is a randy bitch. She would love to have some young cock around the house."

Both lads straightened up and smiled.

"Is she as beautiful as you, Miss?"

"Probably, but in a different way. It might be just what you young blokes need, a mature woman who knows what to do with what you've got in your trousers."

Kevin and Ray laughed heartily.

"I think Judy Somerville would also enjoy having her aunt there to take care of one of you while Judy handles the other one. Do you think you're up for a double act, lads?"

"God yes, Can we really do that, Miss Angie?"

"Leave it with me. I'll check with Auntie. In the meantime, you both have a tentative booking for Saturday afternoon.

"Oh yes, and by the way, I think Judy and her aunt might enjoy a good buggering, so save yourselves. You'll need all the strength you can muster."

———

We topped up our glasses for the umpteenth time. Both Angie and Freya had told their stories and had now settled back side-by-side on the sofa, and I kicked off my shoes and adjusted myself in the big armchair opposite them.

It is probably important to remember that we had just opened our second bottle of champagne, so the personality changes in all three of us that became evident through my recounting of my story were more likely made by the effects of the champagne overriding our inhibitions.

Who knows if anything would have happened between the three of us, if we had all been properly sober?

ALICE'S STORY

Being a twenty-nine-year-old educated and liberated woman in the modern world doesn't automatically give you a wide experience when it comes to love and sex. In fact, there have been times when I've backed away from situations and later wondered if there was something wrong with me, and that perhaps I was frigid.

You will find it believable then, when I tell you that my recent experience with Bertie on the Bennetts' bed had been my most momentous sexual experience. Nothing that I had done previously came anywhere near it.

I naturally changed the physical address in my story and made out that it had occurred two years previous to when my Morning Glory adventure had really happened. Bertie was now called Harry and Paula was the name I chose for Rosa. Doreen was Maude.

You may remember that the story takes a turn when I first notice the bunched-up bedclothes in the bed.

"I must mention to you at the outset that the main character, Harry, is a very fit older man, aged almost seventy. He appears to be suffering early onset dementia, although he hasn't yet been officially diagnosed. His delightful sexy wife Paula is a few years younger and has just been admitted to hospital, having suffered some sort of turn. She is expected back sometime within the month.

"I am renting a bedroom attached to the back of their house and I will be starting at university in a couple of weeks. I will study Psychology and I'm already mad keen to discover new things about people. It is probably the reason I am fascinated by the seemingly very successful fifty-year marriage of my landlords.

"We start when Paula has only just been admitted to hospital. It's Saturday morning and I have woken up wondering if I should take some responsibility for her husband's wellbeing so I go to check on him.

The door was slightly ajar so I pushed it gently and looked in. Harry was lying on his back with his arms out of the bed and folded on his stomach over his dark blue pyjama top. His eyes were closed, so I thought it best to come back later, but as I began to pull the door shut behind me, his voice called out.

"Alice? Is that you?"

"Yes, I thought you were asleep and didn't want to disturb you."

"Come in girl. Don't be shy. I wasn't asleep, just trying to think things through. Come and sit here. You can probably help me better understand about Paula's situation?"

He patted the bedclothes in front of him. I walked over and sat down.

"Well, I don't know any more than you do at the moment, but I would expect we will get a clearer picture later in the day, after you've visited her. The doctors will be able to update us, I'm sure."

Harry grunted to indicate his satisfaction with my answer.

"How come you're still here, Alice? Won't you be late for work?"

"It's Saturday, Harry. I don't go to university at the weekend. I get to sleep in and do other stuff. Leisure time! I love it!"

Then Harry began talking about his side of the family and I took the opportunity to look around their bedroom.

As I was about to comment on something he'd just said and was bringing my eyes back to look at him, they were drawn to a bulge in the bed clothes, just slightly behind were I sat. My first thought was that the bedclothes had got strangely bunched up, but the more I looked, the more I had to accept that Harry had an erection. I stared at it long enough for him to notice the direction of my eyes.

"Paula calls that her 'Morning Glory' and sometimes her 'Wake Me Up'. She has it every day before she leaves the bed."

I looked up at his face, trying to establish the reality of the situation and what he had said. Had I misheard him? Was he talking about something completely different from what I was looking at?

"I think he's missing her as much as I am." Harry said gently with a wry smile and sounding completely innocent and unselfconscious.

My head was full of possible scenarios. Should I excuse myself and leave on pretence of getting breakfast? Was this a form of aberrant behaviour related to memory loss? It seemed that nothing he said matched with any previous experiences in my life, and neither Harry's tone nor his mannerisms were inappropriate in any way.

I told myself that I must respond to him honestly, as he had seemed to express himself to me.

"I know Paula loves you very much, Harry, so I can imagine she would see everything with loving eyes. She knows she is a very lucky woman to have you as her life-long partner."

"Thank you Alice. Yes, we are so very happy together."

I was now getting over the initial shock of spotting Harry's erection. And a new thought – or was it an emotion – was gathering strength. I suddenly had a strong urge to see his cock. I reasoned that it was just so that I would know more about the couple's relationship, and what might have made them so close and happy for the past fifty years. No doubt that was my attempting an intellectual rationalisation.

Before I could stop myself, I was speaking, seemingly from a distance.

"Can I see Paula's Morning Glory please, Harry?"

There was silence for a long moment, then Harry spoke.

"I'm not sure that Paula would approve of that. She's pretty liberal in her outlook but she might have a reason to say no. Remind me to ask her if I can show it to you tomorrow, when I visit her later."

I took a deep breath and tried to analyse what Harry had said. It seemed that he did not object; it was just that he thought Paula might. And the openness of his thoughts about asking her first was beautiful, to say the least.

My head was buzzing. I now really wanted to see Harry's cock. I would have to work with his simple honesty.

"Harry! I really want to know why you and Paula's fifty-year relationship has been so successful. I can get just so much from talking to her, and looking at old photos, but it is not enough. You have already exposed a very personal intimacy by telling me about your erection and it seems to me perfectly acceptable that, as a mature, university-educated woman, I should find out more about the two of you, via this intimacy. Please Harry? Just a peek will do."

A long pause followed. Harry's eyes were closed. Had he fallen asleep?

"Very well then. Given the situation Paula is currently in, and the possibility of an uncertain future, I agree that you should be able to investigate. Go ahead, Alice. Pull back the bedclothes and do your research."

Even though I think I looked calm, I felt sure an observer would have noticed a faint shaking in my limbs, and a sparkle in my eyes.

"Thank you Harry."

For a moment I wondered which end of the bedclothes to lift."

"This end is where she starts," came Harry's soft voice.

I felt like an amateur and I blushed. Then I lent forward and lifted the bedclothes up and back and uncovered Morning Glory.

"Oh my God" exclaimed Angie. "I don't believe it! He's going to let her see it!"

What a sight it was. In simple terms it was very big, but it was by no means fully erect; rather it was standing at rest so to speak, and not looking to rampage anywhere soon. I was flabbergasted.

"It's very beautiful, Harry."

"Thank you Alice," he replied."

So now I found myself half lying on the end of my landlord's bed in nothing more than a light cotton frock and skimpy knickers, propped up on my elbows with my chin in my hands, staring at Harry's massive cock and trying to appear objective and impartial. In truth, I was experiencing little flutters in parts of my anatomy I didn't know could flutter and, by the way, how dared this thing sit so still with a young woman staring at it close up?

"I want to see it too. Please Harry? Please?" Angie screamed.

Such was my real state of mind: chaotic, and with a growing feeling of excitement. I so wanted to reach out and touch it. I had momentarily become oblivious to Harry's presence.

Harry's voice interrupted my reverie.

"I'm sure Paula wouldn't mind you touching him, now that you've come this far. Some mornings she can't help teasing him with her tongue, just for fun, before she climbs on. Other times she simply gets on with it."

"Christ! What an amazing man Harry is. He seems so innocent," Freya commented in her super soft voice."

My mind went into overdrive trying to process everything he said, and what I was doing there, lying on his bed.

I think the correct term for my thoughts and emotions would be "conflicted".

Thank you, Harry, I mumbled, not wanting him to know that I was truly tongue-tied.

I was ready to reach out and grasp Morning Glory for my very own. Having crossed all the barriers to arrive at that decision, the sexual flutterings throughout my body became seriously more rampant.

Taking hold of Harry's cock with one hand was exciting. Adding another hand was more exciting, and when his beautiful member suddenly twitched and surged upward in my palms, I gasped, audibly.

"Oh God yes! Go girl! I can feel it too. Yes, I can." Angie called out.

I heard a slight gasp from Harry, which was reassured me that I wasn't the only one enjoying this.

I stretched out on the bed, moving up to bring my mouth close to the now growing throbbing penis that was giving me so much pleasure. I began by sticking out my tongue and touching the top of Harry's member. I realised that I was crazily happily randy.

I looked over at Angie and was shocked at what I saw. Angie had pulled up her skirt and had parted her legs and was just about to put a hand inside her panties. She had done nothing like this ever before, when she was with us.

"Oh yes please, yes!" she screamed.

Harry's cock was still growing and what had been a big soft lump of sleeping penis was now changing, both in length and hardness. I dragged as much of it as I could, into my mouth and left it there.

My eyes were closed. While lying in this blissful state I began thinking of where I might go next, with Harry's best wishes of course. I reluctantly removed his cock from my mouth.

"Harry?"

"Yes, Alice?"

"Is this how Paula lies on the bed when playing with Morning Glory? Or does she do things from a different position?"

"Well, she would start off where you are, but then she would turn herself completely around and put a leg either side of me."

This was very exciting information and I experienced a sort of bodily flush.

"And what did Paula achieve by doing that Harry?"

"Well, mainly it was to ready herself for getting onto me. But she also enjoyed being able to wiggle her rear end at me, especially if she thought I had forgotten her and gone back to sleep."

"I would wriggle my rear for Harry until the end of time. He is a darling," came Freya's soft response.

I looked over at her and saw how radiant her face looked. Freya was eagerly looking down at Angie who was now rubbing herself and pouting and frenetically running her tongue around her Cupid bow lips.

I was puzzled as to how a simple spoken story could have such an effect on my two friends. But then I thought how much the event I was describing had affected me at the time.

Things were getting better at every moment. My randiness now knew no bounds and I had a terrible moment of thinking I could rape Harry, such was the intensity of my excitement.

"I think I need to get into that position too, Harry. Please tell me if I'm doing it wrong."

"Fine, Alice. Just swing yourself around and back up towards my face. Just so long as you can reach everything you want. You are about Paula's height, so you should be fine. Oh, and how's the research going Alice? Are you discovering more about us as a couple?

"Great, Harry. I'm about to swing round. And yes, I'm learning heaps. And Harry, can I ask if you are enjoying this?"

"I sure am, Alice. Paula says it is healthy for me to have variety in my life.

"She has her friend, Doreen, over once a month. Doreen lost her husband a couple of years ago. She's very lonely. Paula gets me to give Doreen a special something, which she loves and that her husband used to do. Of course, Paula is especially affectionate to women, as you might discover. I love her dearly."

"Oh! She must be bisexual then. How exciting."

In amazement, I watched as Freya too, parted her legs, and I saw her hand disappearing up her skirt.

What was happening to my friends? Was the mixture of an erotic tale and champagne causing this?

I wanted to be left totally alone with Harry's wonderful cock, but the information he had just delivered sent my brain into overdrive. My God! So much to process.

I overcame the problem by letting lust get the upper hand, blotting out the rest of what he had said, at least for the time being. I eased my body around and slid a leg over Harry's torso. I was now up on my knees with all of my private parts on full view to him and I wondered if he would even notice.

"Please let that happen to me. Please! I want to be looked at too," gasped Freya.

She had now lifted her skirt. She was staring at me with a stupe-fied expression on her beautiful face with occasional sideways glances at Angie who had repositioned herself on the floor, legs apart, and totally exposed to us both.

Whether he would or not didn't seem to matter any more. The thrill of exposing myself to his gaze was a thrill in itself.

"You are a very beautiful young woman," came a soft voice.

And if I had thought he might not be interested in the view, imagine how it felt when his fingers slipped into the top of my undies, and dragged them over my bottom and down to my knees. This caused a tiny orgasm and I felt a sudden wetness down there. I was in heaven.

"Oh God! Oh God! Please Harry. Look at me now. Please!" Angie's hand was moving rapidly on her exposed and swollen clitoris.

Freya and I stared at Angie, then at each other.

"Thank you, Harry. And you touch me beautifully."

Harry's cock was now so big and hard I could hardly get it into my mouth, and when I did, my throat could take only a third of it.

But I was so happy with my lot, I simply stopped thinking and instead luxuriated in the pure uncensored sensuality of my situation.

Then, when I thought Harry was just happy staring at my privates, he placed a finger on my wet vagina and wriggled it around. It was electrifying, but even more so when he gently pushed it into my swollen pussy and placed his thumb lightly on the head of my clitoris.

I pulled my mouth from his cock and gasped incoherently.

"Oh Harry! Please don't stop."

"Oh Harry please don't stop!" parroted Angie.

The world was being turned upside down in front of my eyes, and Freya was becoming front and centre stage. I was both stupefied and strangely elated.

Freya was now removing her dress and I stopped talking to watch this most elegant statuesque woman.

Then she removed her tiny bra and dragged her knickers down over her thin legs and round her ankles and stepped out of them.

She turned towards me and, dressed only in her little white socks, came over to me, bent and lifted my face to hers and kissed me passionately, thrusting her tongue into my mouth as she did so.

When we stopped kissing, Freya looked at me with her beautiful innocent eyes and said, "Please touch me, Alice. Touch me anywhere."

But she hardly needed to ask. My hand was already sliding up the back of her wonderful long legs, towards her tiny firm buttocks, and my other hand joined it there and together they fingered her wet little pussy. My mind was reeling and I suddenly felt very wet.

Then she turned abruptly and left me and walked over to Angie and bent down and began to undress her.

Angie sighed but managed to whisper. "Please go on Alice. I'll die if you don't."

"I will when you tell me you are ready Alice." What did Harry mean? Ready for what?

"Ready for what, Harry?" I panted.

"Yes, Harry. Ready for what?" echoed Angie, clasping Freya's leg.

"Ready for Morning Glory, Alice. Paula goes from where you are now to putting my cock inside her. Once it's in, she takes things really slow, hardly moving, then, as if by magic, she has her orgasm, sometimes more than one. Moments later she's off out of bed and heading for the kitchen."

I struggled to take in what Harry had said. Were things going too fast? Was I going to go all the way with this? Could things possibly feel better than they did at this moment?

I looked at Harry's giant cock. It was a sentinel; the provider of security, but only to those who showed it love. How could I refuse it my love? It had led me to the state of ecstasy I was feeling right now. It deserved my love and affection. Yes, all the way was the only way.

"Ready, Harry."

Harry's finger slowly exited but the fire in my cunny burnt on fiercely.

I don't really know why, but I waited. Moments like this should be savoured according to the tiny voice of my lustful self.

Then Harry licked, then kissed my private parts, which convulsed me so that I jumped forward and I found myself in a crouching position above his cock.

Watching Freya bent over Angie while undressing her was much more exciting to me than my story, especially as Freya's beautiful bottom and almost hairless pussy were only a short distance from my face.

Why had I never seen Freya in this way before?

Suddenly Angie let out a short scream as Freya liberated her large breasts and bent down even further and sucked a nipple into her mouth.

Then Freya dragged the now naked Angie away from the sofa and laid her out flat on the floor so that she could lie on top of the girl who was now blubbering incoherently and heaving her large body first this way then that.

"Yes, Freya, please. Do it to me, Freya. Please!

"Will I go on with my story?" I enquired quietly.

"Yes, please," they answered in chorus before Freya started her slow shagging movement and Angie began to scream "Yes, yes, yes!"

Watching what my friends were doing on the carpet in front of me was having a profound and exciting effect on me, and I almost forgot where I was up to in the story.

Until now, it hadn't occurred to me to think about how his cock would fit inside me. Harry's fingering had definitely caused my cunny to swell and open up. Was that his plan? Is that why Paula played and teased him each morning, to get Harry to help prepare her cunt for the final delight?

With one hand I took hold of Harry then I lowered myself and rubbed the head of his penis and around the top of the shaft with all my wetness.

"Oh, Freya? Please! Don't ever stop."

What happened next, I still can't believe. As my vagina spread itself over the top of Harry's cock, my cunny opened up, and I had a distinct feeling that it was sucking the cock in and upwards as at the same time I was lowering myself on to his superb affair. Within moments his cock was housed, entirely filling me.

I simply stayed in this position, impaled with the source of my lust. Then I felt Harry's cock pulsate once, twice, three times.

I exploded. "Morning Glory," I called out loudly.

"Thank you, Harry." I whispered.

"My pleasure, Alice."

I slowly unsheathed Harry's massive cock and lay still, my head between his thighs, while my body melted away into a semi dream state. After a few long moments' rest, I realised that there was still one thing that Paula would do to complete Morning Glory.

"Cup of tea, Harry?"

"Great idea, Alice."

As I part walked and part staggered to the kitchen in an extraordinarily blissful state, and with my hand joyfully nursing my pussy, I reasoned that researching Paula and Harry's fifty-year relationship could never get better than this.

I threw off my clothes and got down onto my knees and crawled over to my two friends. Our friendship had just been changed forever and I wanted to be a part of it.

I straddled Freya's mesmerisingly thin long white legs and lowered my crotch gently towards her slowly heaving buttocks, so that she brushed against my clitoris as she moved up and down.

I didn't want to interrupt the happily shagging pair; rather I wanted to simply enjoy the closeness and intimacy that our three naked bodies could share.

Surely this was Bertie's "Morning Glory" with extras.

When eventually we slowed then stopped our lovemaking and began to cool down, I suggested in a timid whisper that we all go and get into bed. Silently and without looking at one another, we climbed in.

Snuggling into a soft warm bed with my new loves on an overcast and windy day was sublime.

We all kissed each other in the shadowy evening light, and gently, perhaps even shyly, touched and explored each other. Then slowly we drifted off to sleep.

As we nestled down, Freya's angelic voice uttered the words, "Happy birthday, Angie."

4

LOVING IT!

My life had moved in a different direction over the past six weeks. I had simply carried on each day without realising how it had changed since moving into my flat.

I had gone from living an almost celibate existence to having sexual relations with both Bertie and Rosa Bennett and both of my university friends Angela and Freya, with the possibility of a romantic liaison with one of Rosa's friends in the future.

I needed to sort myself out, prioritise; decide how I really wanted my life to work. I had always leaned towards being a neat, orderly and studious person. Would the lifestyle I now embraced change me? Was this really the life I wanted?

Rosa's stay in hospital had been extended for a possible further five weeks, following unsatisfactory results from her medical tests. She had already been away from the house for three weeks, and in that time I had increasingly taken advantage of Bertie's favours.

I would sometimes get into bed with him on a Friday night, after studying quite late. Usually he was asleep when I slipped in beside him, but he often rolled over and embraced me and kissed me and murmured "goodnight sweetheart."

I wasn't sure whether he thought I was Rosa. Perhaps in his mental state he simply didn't register who I was, but I didn't care. I loved being with him like that. It was a freedom from pressure, knowing that I was not expected to act in a certain way or do anything other than be myself. It made me feel so beautifully secure and grown up.

I would very gently caress his back and shoulders, then put my hand around his waist and rub his chest and belly. Finally I would find his big soft cock and his testicles and brush them lightly with my fingertips, knowing I would be having all of it at "Morning Glory time" when I awoke on Saturday morning.

I instinctively knew that I loved this man, but whether or not this was the same as being "in love" hadn't occurred to me. I had not bothered to differentiate between love and infatuation.

Rosa was now also my lover. Although we had not spent much time together, we had expressed our desire to intimately explore each other. I had grown to love her, but it was still her wonderful mind that impressed me most at that time. The kissing and touching were just a bonus and another way of getting to know her.

She had also introduced me to her constantly on-heat friend Maude. Maude would be coming in from the country for her regular monthly stay over at the Bennetts' place some time soon. And from what I understood, there was every indication that she would be keen to know me better, no doubt only after she had enjoyed her regular session with Bertie.

I found Maude's likely interest in me strangely exciting. I asked myself: who was I to deny an attractive spirited woman in her mid-fifties, with spectacular breasts, large buttocks and super shapely solid legs, and not to mention a most enviable and lewd reputation, the opportunity to share herself with me?

That birthday party at my unit for my close university friend Angela had taken all three of us in a new direction.

The most significant thing to come out of it was that I was now totally in love with Freya and it seemed that this loving feeling was mutual. Angela sensed it immediately and joked about whether she would wear all red at our wedding, so that she would get more attention than the bridal couple.

Often during a lunch break at university, I would meet with Freya. If Angie was unable to join us, we would find a quiet picnic table in the park and hold hands as we shared our packed lunches, eyeing each other meaningfully.

Sometimes Freya would kick off a shoe and with her long leg reach across under the table and find my legs. When I felt her touch me I would wriggle forward on the seat and then she would slide her foot up under my skirt and rest it on my crotch. I would kiss her hand passionately and we stayed like that as passers-by walked on, oblivious to our carrying-on.

As you can see, life now was indeed very different from what it had been only a few weeks earlier. My search to better understand the reason for the Bennetts' successful fifty-year marriage had led me into a vastly different world, one that was richer but very likely more dangerous emotionally.

Everything that my talks with Rosa threw up proved inspiring and offered me a new window on the world. Yes, most of it was probably of a sexual nature, but there was much more to her than that. She and Bertie seemed to have made the breakthrough to a better way of living, simply by overcoming the tyranny of orthodox coupledom.

When I quizzed her about what triggered the changes in the first place she said that, while it was in a large part due to that mid-life dark cloud that rolls over most of us at some point, she must give credit to Bertie's earlier questioning of the way in which humans functioned.

Bertie had been in the army and had served abroad during the Vietnam war. After his return home, he happily went back to his post as a senior researcher at the Museum.

He had always found this work satisfying, but now he also

embarked on another personal research project at home. He studied different eastern philosophies, but not out of a desire to learn about myths and gods, or architectural or political history. He was more interested in how cultures addressed the simple day-to-day problems of life.

He discovered ancient Chinese Taoist writings and these, along with early Middle Eastern texts, contained references and advice about men's and women's sexuality.

His main discovery was that a man should not ejaculate every time he had sex. Holding back your *chi* resulted in benefits to both men and women. A man remained healthier because his biological resources, and subsequently his strength, were conserved and not easily depleted.

Another benefit was that a man could make love over a much longer period. Men of yesteryear who followed this practice of not ejaculating whenever they made love, and who kept a harem or had more than one wife, were supposedly able to comfortably satisfy all of their partners and make love right through the night, should they choose to do so.

When Bertie first began to implement this idea in their love life Rosa was dubious, to say the least, but he convinced her that certain things were different for a man. Over time, he not only perfected the art of holding back his *chi* and not ejaculating, but he also discovered that he did in fact have small internal orgasms, "a succession of most pleasurable *petits mals*," as he told his wife.

This situation was enhanced a few months later, when he went on to master other techniques from old Tantric and Indian yoga texts: in particular, an ability to get an erection whenever he chose to – surely a man's ultimate "on demand" achievement.

Rosa found that she was able to explore their sexuality differently, now Bertie was offering himself "on demand", as he called it.

I have already described how Rosa developed a code using the trigger word *"Fifi"*, by which she could instruct her husband to perform particular sexual manoeuvres; and you know that she wrote down these codes.

One evening, not long after my quick initial reading on the day she gave it to me, I sat back and read Rosa's code list in detail.

Every code had a number beside it. Most codes had notes printed below, messages such as the one under "Fifi would like her feet played with": "B prefers high heel shoes or sandals with a strap or straps."

And under "Fifi would like bottom play," the message: "B sometimes forgets to have lube on hand."

Then, just as if she were presenting a menu in an Asian restaurant, Rosa provided an indented list of her suggestions for what she referred to as "side dishes". For example "No.7: Fifi would love you in her stockings", could have as an add-on "No.5: "Fifi wants her breasts touched."

I don't know if it was my recent flurry of sexual activity, or the accumulation of emotional feeling that now seemed forever bubbling below the surface, but I found myself fighting off the urge to respond to Rosa's codes, a strong desire to sample something from the Fifi code catalogue.

Hardly an hour went by, on any day of the week, that I didn't think of Bertie in an imaginary sexual encounter. Simply thinking of this remarkable man made me decidedly horny and wanting to be with him.

These feelings wore me down, and eventually I could stand it no longer, and I gave in. On a weekday afternoon, I returned home early and prepared myself for him.

Sneaking in the back way, I went straight to my flat and showered. Then, totally naked, I sat down at the dressing table and applied face makeup, experimenting with lipstick colours as I went.

I thought about what I was about to do. Even though I had been with Bertie a number of times, each had been a Morning Glory during which I half kidded myself that I was helping both him and Rosa get through a tricky period of separation.

What I was about to do was different. Using Rosa's Fifi codes, I would solicit Bertie.

I couldn't help trying to imagine how a man might feel on going into a brothel to engage a prostitute. Wasn't I going to do just that very same thing, with only minor differences? I put these thoughts out of my mind, turning instead to the joyous task of dressing.

I had brought a few things from Rosa's wardrobe. Everything I needed was here in my flat. Keeping things simple was always Rosa's advice, unless you were deliberately wanting Bertie to work hard for his benefits. I chose to wear neither a bra nor panties.

A woman is forever impressed by the way gorgeous film stars in old movies roll on their stockings and keep their seams straight at the same time. However good or bad one may be at it, it is always fun.

Putting on a suspender belt and stockings feels just a little naughty. It's as though, deep down, you know they are a cultural symbol of femininity, sexuality and intimacy, and they may just take you to a moment of anticipation, excitement and adventure.

I chose a black pleated skirt fastened with a zip at the back. Then I added a short-sleeved blouse with four large buttons down the back. Then came the shoes.

I do love shoes, but I don't have a budget that allows me to spend much, other than on serviceable footwear. Now I could choose, from Rosa's shoe collection, between heels with a single strap and buckle, heels without any fastening, or a slightly lower-heeled shiny black patent pair with a thin strap secured with a button. I chose the latter.

I checked myself in the full-length bedroom mirror, then went back to the dressing table to look for a pair of earrings, but at the last moment chose not to wear any. "Keep it simple," came Rosa's voice from somewhere. Oh no, Rosa's watching me, I thought and smiled.

All I needed now was Bertie.

On the way to the kitchen, I peered into the greenhouse in case Bertie was there but he wasn't, nor was he in the vegetable garden, nor around the corner in Rosa's front garden. I went into the house.

Bertie was just coming into the kitchen. He was drying his hair with a towel.

"Alice! You're home very early!"

"Yes, Mr Bennett. I felt like coming home and spending a little time hanging out with you. I hope that's okay?"

"Hanging out? Now let me see if I can interpret this youthful phrase into something I can understand."

Bertie laughed heartily, which I'd never seen him do before.

"I assume that we do things together while 'hanging out'. Well, that shouldn't be too hard. I do so enjoy your company, so anything you may have in mind, I'm sure I will enjoy."

I couldn't believe my good fortune. Bertie was all mine. The problem was that I could feel myself becoming tongue-tied. How on earth would I be able to say the code?

"By the way, Alice, you are looking very beautiful this afternoon. There is something different about you. Your lipstick perhaps, very alluring. If only I was a bit younger, dam it, I'd be trying to pluck up courage to ask you for a date. Yes, indeed I would."

And that was all I needed. Confirmation that this man was hungry to be with me, even without using a code.

"Thank you, Mr Bennett. I would love a date with such an attractive man and, if I might make a suggestion, "Fifi would love you in her stockings."

The silence probably wasn't as long as it seemed. Bertie moved towards me, smiling his gentle, wondrous smile.

"How lovely. That would be very nice Alice. Come with me."

For a moment I was terrified. What had I done? Bertie seemed so normal. Somehow I had got it into my head that once the code was uttered, Bertie would become a silent automaton. Why had I thought that? Could it be that he was really just going to be who he really was, and not my imagined man, seemingly hypnotised and responding only to a predefined trigger word?

"Yes, Mr Bennett."

Bertie leant forward and gave me a brief kiss on the lips, then took my arm and led me into the lounge room, seating me first, and then himself, on the sofa. My heart was pounding, mostly with excitement but also with a smidgeon of fear.

The curtains were pulled to keep out the afternoon sun, so as the evening advanced, the room was full of shadows and only a small amount of light came from the kitchen via the passageway.

"I must confess to you, Alice, that I'm a little nervous. Strange, isn't it? This is our first time together away from the bedroom. I want to touch you, but I don't want to frighten you."

I was suddenly overwhelmed by Bertie's sensitivity and I realised that maybe he needed a tiny bit of help. I turned towards him.

"Mr Bennett, you are a wonderful kisser and I so want to be kissed by you and touched by your strong beautiful hands.

"Please, Mr B, kiss me."

With that, I reached around and pulled his neck down towards me and fastened my lips to his. As our kissing became more intense, I reached for his hand and placed it on my dress, at the top of my leg.

Bertie's sails suddenly found the breeze and our boat sailed.

He moved his hand up from my leg to my shoulder and pulled the top of my body forward and down a little so that he could reach my back and unbutton my blouse. Then while he kissed me, he slowly pulled the arms of my top down from my shoulders exposing my naked breasts.

"I adored your breasts from the moment I caught glimpses of them beneath your frock that first morning, when you backed up to me on the bed. I so wanted to touch them then. Now I can, at last. Thank you sweet Alice."

Bertie gently caressed them and played with my nipples, then he leant forward and sucked and nibbled the nipple on my right breast. The feeling was electrifying and I gasped. While he was doing that, I slipped my hand inside his shirt, touching his nipples and drawing my nails through the thick hair on his chest.

Then he unexpectedly unzipped himself and in a moment exposed his member. He took my hand and placed it on his upright cock. I rolled my fingers around it and held it tight. I shuddered fully for the first time.

Bertie's whispering about how much he secretly admired my breasts, while confidently putting my hand exactly where he wanted it, assured me I was indeed with the wonderful man who had taught me how to enjoy his Morning Glory.

He left my breasts and lifted my skirt up well above my knees. He sat looking at my stockinged legs then gently put out his hand and touched my knee. He ran his hand down the back of my leg to my ankle, where he spread his fingers all the way round it and squeezed it, then he let a finger move down to touch the top of my foot below the shoe strap. I realised that I was breathing and gasping quite heavily.

"You are so beautiful, Alice. I want to have every part of you all at once."

Bertie unlocked my fingers around his cock and stood up. He quickly took off his trousers and underpants. Then he knelt in front of me. Taking a stockinged leg in each hand, he lifted them up high, high enough to reposition me on the couch so that my bottom was partly hanging over the edge.

He gazed down on the bare tops of my legs and my exposed private parts and breathed an audible sigh of appreciation.

"So much beauty," he whispered.

Then he placed my legs so that they hung from my knees down over his shoulders, with my feet dangling down his back. Then he touched my bare upper leg and lifted the top edge of my stocking. He placed his cock at the spot where his fingers were, lifting the top of the stocking over the head of his member while gently sliding it up into the stocking. In a few moments his cock was completely ensconced in the stocking. I could feel it and I trembled.

Almost immediately, as had happened so often before, Bertie's cock jerked backwards and forwards, signalling to the world that even in its silk cage it was available for all purposes to do with love.

I was enjoying this relaxed and erotic male fantasy. I was a part of it, yet could view it as though from a distance: as a voyeur.

Then Bertie found my hand, flattened it out and placed it over his stocking-covered cock.

"Stroke it for me, Alice."

"Oh, yes, Mr Bennett."

As he spoke, he reached forward with his other hand and put a finger into my mouth.

"Make it wet for me, please."

I licked Bertie's finger slowly, staring at his face and showing him my tongue. Then he withdrew it from my mouth and moments later I felt his hand brush my clitoris. Then he pushed the finger I'd sucked, slowly into my cunny, and as I felt his big cock pulsate under my hand I gave a tiny scream thrust myself upward, and came.

"Oh how I love you Mr B."

My tiny voice seemed to come directly from my vagina, and I felt a wetness on my cheek as I shed a tear. Was this a release of tension? All this wetness and Bertie's undivided attention made me feel so very special.

Then he began to undo the suspender on my other leg and, when the stocking was released, dragged it upward till it hung somewhat loosely, just below my knee. He took his finger out of my cunt and my hand away from his cock. He laid my hand on my crotch, pushing it gently backwards and forwards, suggestive of me pleasuring myself.

He removed his cock from the stocking on my right leg and slipped it up into the unfastened stocking on the left leg. He could now rub it against my calf while his balls nestled in the hollow at the back of my knee.

"Oh, Alice. You have such beautiful legs," he whispered.

"Thank you, Mr Bennett. And what you are doing to them is truly beautiful."

I was loving every moment of Bertie's attention, but I reminded myself that I had planned more.

After he had been rubbing against the back of my leg for quite some time, and I rubbed him through my stocking, and had enjoyed more tiny orgasms, I spoke.

"Fifi would love you inside her, Mr Bennett."

Nothing happened at first and I thought he might not have heard me. Then he removed himself from the stocking and nuzzled his cock in under my hand. The very large hood pushed gently inwards, and my cunt willingly opened up ahead of him.

Bertie looked down at my face and smiled, then he spoke.

"One day, sweet Alice, I would like to fuck your mouth, right between those bright red lips. But we'll do that another time."

Bertie's fantasy momentarily carried me away and I shivered at the thought.

"You can have whatever you want, whenever you want it, you darling man," I whispered.

What I said caused him to pulsate and his giant cock moved up into me even further. Even though I had had him right up inside me during our morning lovemaking, this position made it seem different. I figured that, in the mornings, I was on top and in charge. Now my cunt was there for him, and in whatever way he wanted me.

Bertie hoisted me up and lifted both my legs by the ankles so that I could see them perfectly, waving in the air. I had always believed that my legs where acceptably shapely, but suddenly I could only think vainly, how beautiful they were. His beautiful cock was giving me a superb feeling of pleasure so that I was constantly on the verge of coming. Suddenly I screamed and came two or three times in rapid succession. Bertie remained still while I recovered, then settled back into shagging me again.

My imagination came into play and I had a vision of my beloved Freya lying like this beside me, with her long thin legs in her white little-girl socks that she always wore, and wearing her tiny white high-heeled sandals, her feet high in the air alongside mine.

In my fantasy, I saw Bertie shagging her while she and I kissed and touched each other. Then I saw an image of him shagging me while Freya held his balls and the base of his shaft hard up against me, and with that I came three times.

Bertie was having a wonderful time. No doubt he felt some pride each time I came. He loved kissing my legs and my feet and shoes. I envied him; I, too, wanted to make love to my beautiful legs.

Then I remembered there was just one more coded instruction I wanted to give and, from what I had recently learnt about Bertie from Rosa, he might not want to do it.

But I really wanted this.

"Fifi wants you to come inside her, Mr Bennett."

There was quiet and Bertie stopped moving his cock in and out of me.

"Are you sure about this, Alice?

"Yes, dearest Bertie, of course I want it. Is there a reason I shouldn't have it, Mr B?"

"Only that I choose to ejaculate very rarely and because of that, when I do, I can become very self-centred, selfish and even forceful, and forget where I am. I would never want to hurt you, Alice."

"Mr Bennett, how sweet you are. But I want to experience you totally, you beautiful man. Fuck me silly if you want to. I will never blame you for anything that happens."

Bertie became quiet. He went back to kissing my knees and calves, and bent down low to lick the bare flesh above my stockings. Then he reached forward to put his mouth on my breasts and suck my nipples. He put a hand round my neck and pulled my head forward and kissed me, and thrust his tongue into my mouth. I cried out and orgasmed.

I didn't know what to expect next. I luxuriated in what he did while admiring my legs and feet, still waving high above me, and I rotated each foot slowly, first one way then the other.

Then I felt him wetting a finger in my cunny. He lifted me up a little higher and I felt his hand around between my buttocks. I felt his wet finger at my tiny bottom hole, and suddenly it was inside me moving around very slowly. This was something I had never expected, and knew nothing about.

I decided to relax as best I could and just go with it. Then, just as quickly, Bertie removed his finger.

It was as though he was claiming ownership of every part of me before fucking me. I found the idea appealing and I experienced still another excited shudder.

Ever so slowly, Bertie started moving his cock in and out of me.

The vision of Freya lying beside me with her legs in the air came back to me and I decided, there and then, that somehow I would bring her into my secret world. It was risky, but I was besotted with both her and Bertie. I wanted her to have what I was having and I wanted to share it with her.

Bertie's orgasm came quite soon. I don't know why I thought he would take a long time. But that he came soon was a good thing because his violent pounding of my cunt, and his pushing me all over the sofa and twisting me first this way then that, could not have gone on much longer.

When he came, the earth did move. His reaching right into me and unloading his enormous volume of sperm was like nothing I had experienced then, or was likely to, for the rest of my life. Later, in bed, right through to the early hours, his cum dribbled out of me.

After Bertie ejaculated, he did not withdraw. He remained in me for a long time while spasms ran through his body. His cock remained firm and his spasms provided me with the longest constantly active bout of orgasms I was ever to experience.

"I love you Mr Bennett," I whispered.

"I love you too," came his reply.

My life had definitely changed from what it had been before. Could this be how it was to be, always? Was I now a fully fledged bisexual woman? Did it mean that I could never return to a normal life, entering into a relationship with just one man and having his children?

But I was enjoying the change, wasn't I? And the heavens hadn't fallen in. In fact it was quite the opposite. They had opened up.

Indeed, it seemed that I had fallen into heaven.

Since Angie's birthday party and our erotic girlie romp, our coffee breaks and lunch times together at university went on much as before, except we now smiled at one another with a more meaningful look.

Occasionally one of us would say something that acknowledged our new-found intimacy and it would usually lead to a fit of giggling, even blushing. All three of us were obviously happy about what had happened and no one had regrets.

Angie enjoyed our "liberation", as she called it. She would say whatever came into her head and as both Freya and I now habitually stared longer at Angie's bust as she arrived at the table, she would announce quite happily, "It's nice to know that someone wants to touch my tits" or, "You will each have to let me pick something from your lunch boxes if you want me to let you play with them."

There was a new and deeper respect for one another, even in our banter and the subsequent hilarity. Our sexual liberation was refreshing, and it added a welcome element of frisson to our lives.

As yet, we had not talked about getting together again, although there was some sense of anticipation. It seemed that we were all a little self-conscious. Perhaps we were both self-conscious and a little shy.

Freya casually mentioned one day that she looked forward to modelling her newly purchased old-style bloomers for us. I suddenly thought to mention that we would be getting a special visitor to our house in a couple of weeks. Her name was Maude, and I was certain the two of them would love to meet her.

When Angie asked why I thought they would want to meet her, I made up a story so as to protect Rosa and Bertie. I told them that Maude was a friend of an older relative, Judy, the Black Sheep in our family, and a cousin of my father.

"I have long known that Judy was gay and quite active. I had met Maude at a garden party given by Judy for her twin nephew and niece's twenty-first birthday, and found her interesting. Admittedly Maude was showing me a lot of attention, but of course I let her know that I wasn't the least bit interested."

I smiled at Angie and Freya.

"That was long before certain unnamed girls had their sleep over, and me with it."

The two girls giggled.

"When I asked about her later, Judy smiled and said that it wasn't just Maude's amazing bust and extraordinary nipples that excited both men and women; she had another secret surprise to be enjoyed by all. And when I asked what it was, Judy said, "Best you find out for yourself.""

"Sounds interesting, Angie, don't you think? I'm game to meet her if you are," said Freya.

"I'll be in it. I'm starting to think I've got a nipple fetish anyway," said Angie.

"Tell us the date Alice, so that we can be sure to be there," Freya asked.

"OK. Maude arrives on Friday the twenty-second for two nights so lets have a meeting of the Feeling Sweet Club on Saturday the twenty-third at two thirty."

Both girls laughed.

"Hey! Aren't we supposed to democratically choose the name?" Angie asked.

"Change it any time you want. I think we all agree though, that it was very sweet?"

"That must make me a sweetmeat," said Angie.

"I've never ever felt sweeter," added Freya, eyeing me lovingly.

5

FEELING SWEET CLUB

I WAS EXCITED about getting together with the girls again.

Even though I had Bertie and my beautiful weekly 'Morning Glory', the erotic feelings I felt with my girlfriends were very different, and I loved it.

There was something special about being with them. There was a sort of camaraderie, an understanding that you could be whatever, and whoever you wanted to be, with nothing needing to be hidden or disguised.

I was secretly excited too about the arrival of Maude. We had only met once, but the vibrations I had got from her had been electric.

I was determined to be coy with her, hold out, and enjoy her attempts to seduce me.

And if I could resist her advances until Saturday afternoon, that would be perfect.

Rosa told me on a recent visit to the hospital that it would be Maude's fifty-fourth birthday on the Sunday when she was staying with us. That was good news, and made the plot I was hatching with the girls at our lunchtime meetings even better. A birthday surprise, no less.

When I returned home on the Friday night, I avoided going

straight into the house and instead, sneaked around to my flat, where I showered and put on fresh clothes before heading in to make dinner.

At the last moment, I chose to wear the schoolgirl skirt that I had brought over from Rosa's dressing-up collection.

Rosa had mentioned some time ago, that Maude was especially attracted to older schoolies, both boys and girls. It was her taboo fantasy that she rarely got to enjoy.

I added knee-length white socks, a blue blouse and a pair of regular school sandals. I looked in the mirror and was pleasantly surprised. Could I really be mistaken for an eighteen-year-old I wondered vainly?

I had just put the vegetables in the steamer when Maude arrived in the kitchen. Her hair was still a little wet from the shower, and she wore a light top coat over whatever was, or wasn't, underneath.

I assumed that she had spent the afternoon with Bertie enjoying her usual fun and games with him, her "something special".

I had gone through a moment a few weeks earlier, thinking that I would be jealous of anyone other than Rosa spending time with Bertie and I had a few days of feeling frighteningly possessive of him. During talks with Rosa, this feeling dissipated. I think it was my sudden appreciation of what Bertie's Taoist philosophy truly meant, by asserting that all people are a lot healthier and happier loving more than just one person.

"Darling Alice. There you are. I was terrified you might not be coming home tonight. I was so looking forward to seeing you."

I turned from the stove and took a step towards her, putting out my arms to embrace her. She in turn hurried over and lovingly embraced me.

"So lovely to see you again, Maude. At last we can have some time together."

Maude stood back and looked me up and down, smiling.

"What a fabulous outfit, sweetie. Deep down I knew you were really just a schoolgirl. I love it."

Maude put her hand out and touched my skirt, then moved closer and put a hand under my chin, leaning forward and kissing me on the lips.

This was my opportunity to lead her on a little bit. It felt like a naughty thing to do, but hey, a girl likes to be pursued sometimes.

As our lips touched, I reached my arm around her waist and let my fingers run down over her bottom. At the same time, I pushed my lips more firmly against hers.

Maude trembled ever so slightly. She gently extended her tongue and nudged my lips, and I let her tongue in, then offered her mine and we tongued each another. While this was happening, Maude placed her hand on my bottom, cupped one of my buttocks and squeezed it.

I realised that what I had planned as just a "come on" risked getting out of hand. I felt myself getting horny and wondered when and how I would break away from this totally enchanting woman.

I could not stop myself sliding a hand down inside the front of her skirt and reaching down to touch her between the legs. She was not wearing panties, but that shock discovery was nothing to what I discovered next.

Sticking out from the mass of Maude's pubic hair was a warm soft something.

"That is my very large clitoris, darling Alice. Don't be afraid," she said.

She was now gently licking my neck.

"A rare beast amongst women, but a treasure to those who have one. Please hold it for a moment, darling girl. It will adore your young fingers."

I was now definitely losing all sense of what I had planned and was simply going with the flow.

Just when my fingers were about to close on this "rare beast", there came a rude awakening.

The steamer on the stove erupted behind me at the same time as we heard Bertie come through the passage door behind Maude.

We both hurriedly turned to address the demands of the moment and I felt a sudden devastating fall to earth, or perhaps more simply put, a cruel clitoris interruptus?

Bertie accepted that I had not been able to get to the butcher, saying that fish fingers and steamed vegetables from his garden were just fine. The fruit salad and ice-cream pleased him, even though he said he never ate ice-cream for health reasons. Maude seemed OK with everything, not expressing an opinion one way or the other, and I could not get Maude's amazing clitoris out of my head.

Bertie managed to engage Maude in a conversation of sorts. He told her about the vegetable garden drought management course he was doing through the University of the Third Age, and she attempted to show interest.

I loaded the dishwasher and cleared the table. When I asked who would like coffee, both of them declined.

"I'm going to have an early night. You two could play cards, perhaps. The pack's in the sideboard in the lounge."

Amid loving "Goodnight Bertie, sleep tight" farewells, Bertie disappeared back down the hallway.

Maude and I stared at each other; then she rose from the table and turned towards me

"Sweetheart, you might need to rest. I know you've probably had a very busy week. Oh, but I do have a small present for you in my room. Why don't you pop down and get it, after you've finished here? It'll only take a moment."

We eyed each other carefully for signs that would tell us what the other was thinking. I stepped forward and put my arms around her and she responded in a like manner.

"I'll be there in just a few minutes, Maude."

Then I put my face close to hers and she closed her eyes and slowly kissed me on the lips. I put my tongue between her lips and she shivered.

"Won't be long. Oh, and Maude?"

"Yes darling?"

"When we are alone together, would you mind if I called you Auntie? I love your name, but calling you Auntie would make me feel closer to you, more connected."

Maude looked at me with shining, smiling eyes.

"I love that idea. From this moment on, call me Auntie. And I have a similar request. I would sometimes like to call you my little girl. Would that bother you, Alice?"

I pulled her closer to me.

"I would love that too. I so want to be your little girl, and any other pet names you might think of."

"And sometimes, when I'm excited and feeling particularly bad, I might call you nasty names like 'little bitch' or 'lazy hussy' or 'my sexy slave' or maybe even a 'dirty little slut'."

"Whatever makes you happy, Auntie. Call me whatever you like. I will love it."

When I got to Maude's bedroom, we had both forgotten about her present. I rushed to her and embraced her and we kissed passionately.

Maude then took my arm and directed me to the big armchair in the corner of the room. She sat down and made me sit on her knee.

"Oh, my little girl. I've so longed for this moment. Now you are mine, I don't know where to begin."

I kissed her lips and again offered my tongue, which she immediately sucked. Then I let go.

"I am so happy to be your little girl, Auntie. Please do anything you want. I will love it, whatever you do."

We started kissing once again. Then I felt Maude's hand lift the hem of my skirt. She put her fingers down into my right sock and then the left one, feeling around my calves, then behind my bare knees. Then she moved her hand up my leg until she touched my pubic hairs.

"What a naughty girl you are. You are not wearing your regulation knickers. I've a good mind to tell your mother."

"Please don't Auntie, I only took them off in the hope that you would touch me where your hand is now, or you would find it easier, if you wanted to see my bottom. Please don't tell."

I could see now how an authoritarian older woman and a fantasy discipline scenario could work for me.

Maude saw that I enjoyed playing the subservient schoolgirl, and that it worked for me as well as it did for her. Perhaps that was why I responded the way I did to Rosa's story of Sister Carmel?

"Well, girl, we'll see if you can be good and obey my orders. Now, unbutton my blouse."

Maude's hand gently caressed my wet pussy. Then she pushed her hand further under me, and a finger searched my bottom for an opening, and when she found it her wet finger slipped in remarkably easily. I gasped.

Then I turned towards her and began to undo her buttons until her blouse fell open, exposing her huge black lace brassiere.

Maude let go of me and reached up and removed her blouse exposing her white shoulders. Then she leant forward and reached back and unfastened her bra, then slipped the shoulder straps down off her arms.

"Now little girl, take Auntie's bra off and throw it on the floor."

I reached up and lifted the bra away from Maude's breasts and threw it away as she asked. Then I stared at her breasts. What an incredible sight they were.

Maude suddenly put her hand behind my head and pushed my face onto a hard nipple.

"Now you can suck Auntie until she tells you to stop. Suck me, you naughty little girl."

Oh, how beautiful Maude's breasts were.

I suddenly remembered Rosa and Bertie on their first contact with Maude as a threesome. I thought of how I was sucking on something that Bertie or Rosa had touched and sucked.

Having Maude's finger in my bottom was more exciting than I

would ever have expected. She gently and slowly pushed her digit backwards and forwards, and I began to feel a pleasant sensation there.

Maude's nipples were huge and I would gladly have stayed sucking and nibbling them all night, but in my mind's eye there was something more that I wanted to know about, the rare secret, resting between Maude's legs.

But how to get to her clitoris when she was so firmly in charge presented a problem. But then all was solved.

"I'm going to spank you, Alice. I've wanted to from the moment I met you, so let's roll you over and place you across my knees and let you feel the slap of my hand on your lovely young bum."

I assisted by lifting myself and turning around and bending over, so that Maude could position me across her thighs. I had noticed earlier that she had removed her stockings to shower. I had long wanted to study Maude's strong, thick but shapely legs ever since I met her at the hospital, and now I was lying on them and observing them up close.

Alabaster is the description too often given to describe a woman's skin, and yet this description of translucent whiteness, applied to Maude's legs and thighs, could not have been more accurate.

As Maude gazed at this girl's bottom and private parts, I gazed at her legs and thighs. Her skin was taut and shiny. Large as they might be, her legs were indeed divine.

I could not see through the darkness beneath her skirt, but I knew that not a great distance away was the object of my desire. And oh, what a beautiful odour issued from below her skirt. The sweet smell of her preferred bath soap mixed with her wet sex enthralled me.

"Now, young lady. Have you ever been spanked?"

"No, Auntie. And I'm a little frightened. Will it hurt me much?"

"It might. We shall see. I will spank you until your buttocks are a nice pink. Are your ready, girl?"

"Yes, dear Aunt. Please do it. I shall try not to cry."

The first slaps did indeed sting quite a bit, but slowly they became less painful and more enjoyable as my stinging bottom became first, an irritation then very hot, and then pervaded the lower half of my body and became exciting.

After a few minutes, I braved my aunt's wrath, and began caressing her inner thigh, working my hand and fingers up towards her pubic region.

"Your are a naughty little girl, taking advantage of your poor aunt's leg while she is so busy on important business."

I paused while Maude slapped me harder a couple of times, then my fingers continued along the alabaster high road to heaven. And then there it was.

Her clitoris was hard and strong and bursting with excitement. It stood to attention, just like a small boy's cock might stand when he played with himself. I quickly established ownership by wrapping two, then three fingers around it and squeezing it gently.

Maude stopped her spanking and lay back gasping. I felt her trembling, and I knew that I was now in charge.

"Oh you darling girl, please don't stop touching it. Your fingers are like magic. Do you like, it darling? Do you want Auntie's clit for your very own? Would you like Auntie to fuck your sweet lips with it, your mouth, your pussy, your bottom? Oh you darling girl. I adore you."

I was in heaven once again. I was indeed holding the key to Heaven's Gate.

"Auntie! I'm in heaven, Auntie. This is the most beautiful thing in the whole wide world. Can I lick it, Auntie? Can I hold it in my mouth? And will you please do those things you just talked about, Auntie, please?"

Maude slowly moved me off her lap and around so that I faced between her legs; then she pulled open her dressing gown, took my hair in her hand and drew my face up to where my hand was holding her.

"Suck your Auntie, my sweet child. Enjoy yourself and I will enjoy you."

I brought her clitoris up to my lips and stuck out my tongue and licked it. Maude shook all over, and as she did so the effect of her spanking me, and me holding her clitoris, caused me to orgasm, and I felt an extreme wetness in my vagina.

I must have lain there licking and sucking Maude for a good twenty minutes. During that time she orgasmed a number of times. Sometimes they repeated as multiple orgasms, and each time she came, I did too.

Eventually, the lateness of the hour and simple exhaustion made us stop. I sat up beside her and we cuddled and kissed and strangely, we both wept and sobbed like heartbroken lovers. But, oddly, we both really enjoyed doing so. Cathartic might be a word to best describe those crying moments together.

As I was straightening myself and preparing to go to my flat to sleep, I remembered to mention the arrangement for the next day.

I told Maude that I was having a couple of student friends over in the afternoon and we had agreed to give my guest, Maude, a little birthday party. Would she honour us with her presence? Maude managed a faint happy smile.

"Of course, darling. I'd love to. Are they nice girls?"

"They are the best, dear Aunt. In fact you had better get plenty of rest. Anything could happen."

We both laughed.

"Oh, and one final thing. My friends know nothing about Bertie or Rosa, and for the moment, I prefer it that way. So please avoid mentioning the Bennetts if you would."

"I can see Rosa has taught you well, young lady. Goodnight darling."

"Goodnight Auntie. Meet me in the kitchen at three o'clock. Love you."

Angie and Freya arrived at two thirty and I told them my plans for Maude's birthday. They giggled but agreed to do what I asked.

A couple of days earlier I had brought over Rosa's box of sex toys and popped it in the bottom of the wardrobe. After a moment's hesitation, I invited the girls to look in the box.

"My God! Where did you get all of these?" Angie asked innocently.

I had already planned my answer and replied nonchalantly.

"I rescued them from a maiden aunt's house when I went in to clean up after she had been put into care. She never asked about them. I've put them all through the washing machine a couple of times. I thought we might be able to find a use for them."

Both girls laughed and looked at me to see if I was joking. Freya picked up a large strap-on dildo.

"If we only knew what they used it for!" she said in an exaggerated innocent little-girl voice.

We all laughed. Then Angie announced in her version of a little-girl voice. "Well, Freya. I would be happy to work with you on this project. Together I'm sure we'll find a use for it."

The stage was set and it was time to go and get Maude. I had a silk scarf in my pocket to blindfold her with, along with something else I had found in Rosa's box which I intended to use.

Maude was waiting in the kitchen when I got there. She looked at me lovingly and pouted her lips.

"Hello darling. Don't smudge my lipstick. I'm both nervous and excited. Do I look all right?"

I kissed her very gently, breathing in her perfume and smell.

Maude had her hair pulled back in a bun, which suited her pretty but strong face. Her makeup was minimal and her frilled high-necked blouse accentuated her enormous bust. Her tight black woollen skirt showed all the curves of her beautiful legs along with that magic backside which Bertie so loved. She wore black stockings and black high heels. She was, indeed, a living doll.

"You look stunning, Auntie. Now I should tell you that Angie and Freya have a surprise for you, which means when we get to the door of the flat, I will cover your eyes with this scarf before we go in. Please don't be nervous. The girls are already in love with you."

. . .

At the flat door, I wrapped the scarf around Maude's head.

"There. Can't see, I hope?"

"Not a thing, Alice."

Then, as I put my arm around her and gently moved her arm around to her back and held it, I fetched her other arm around to join it.

"What are you doing, darling?"

"Just adding the final ingredient to your birthday surprise, Auntie."

And at that moment, a click sounded as I fastened Rosa's handcuffs on Maude's wrists.

"Goodness, Alice. Am I going to be your prisoner? I hope you know where the key is."

I opened the door and led her into the flat. This was the moment we had been waiting for. I removed the scarf and she let out a tiny scream.

As prearranged, the girls appeared to be making love on the floor. Angela was naked except for a bra and panties and white knee-length stockings, and she had her legs in the air and Freya, naked except for her tiny bra and little white socks, was lying on top of her in her favourite position.

As soon as they knew that Maude had seen them, they jumped up and bounded over to us, laughing and calling out. Freya stared deep into Maude's eyes.

"Happy birthday, Maude. So very pleased to meet you."

Both women put out their arms and wrapped them around the stupefied Maude.

"I'm Freya and this is Angela, or Angie. We've heard so much about you. Welcome to the Feeling Sweet Club. Alice is hoping you will agree to become a member."

At first Maude was unable to speak, then in a whisper she said, "I think I've died and gone to heaven, and the angels are all delicious."

As this was happening, I stood behind her. I lifted up my dress and threw it off and stood in just my panties and long white socks. Then I stepped around to confront her and stand with the others.

Three semi-naked young women looked lovingly at Maude, each putting out a hand to touch her.

"What darlings you all are, and thank you for inviting me to join you. Now, sweet Alice, if you would be so kind as to unlock these handcuffs, I will be lewd and have one of you beauties right now."

We all laughed and Angie squealed.

"Me first, I hope. And Maude, would it be all right if we called you Auntie? Freya and I both have pleasant memories of naughty aunties doing naughty things with us when we were teenagers. And you can call us whatever you wish."

"I would love you all to call me Auntie. Now Alice, I'm getting a little desperate. Unlock me you little vixen."

I interjected.

"Sorry, Auntie, but you are not going to have any of us, not yet at least. *We* are going to have *you*."

Her jaw dropped. "But I don't understand."

We all marched poor Maude over to the sofa and sat her down. Angie and Freya sat either on side of her.

"I think we should start here," said Freya, reaching for the top button on Maude's blouse.

"I agree. This woman has even more bust than me. I want to see if it's really all her own work." Angie started unbuttoning from the bottom.

"Oh, my god. What is happening to me? You're all mad! This is against the law. I'm being forcibly held against my will by three young sex fiends. What on earth will become of me?"

As the girls opened Maude's blouse and leant her forward to more easily remove it and then unfasten her bra, I got very close to her face, and kissed her. Then I slowly put my hand under my right breast and pushed the nipple into her mouth. She gasped with delight.

"Against your will, Auntie?"

I heard Angela scream and Freya say "I don't believe it." The two of them were staring at Maude's extraordinarily large nipples. Large and like ripe black figs, blue-black and with a smoky grey sheen, set in an areola the size of a child's tea-set saucer.

I watched as Freya moved a hand towards the nipple closest to her and Angie, mesmerised, moved her face closer to the other one.

Maude started to breath deeply, snorting as she tried to hang on to my breast while coping with the anticipation of what the girls were about to do to her. Her giant nipples stood straight out, long and thick, the size of the first joint of her index finger.

"How heavenly, Auntie. We are going to enjoy ourselves and suck you until you wet yourself with cum," Freya whispered.

Then they both swallowed Maude's nipples in unison and she moaned and bit me. I quickly changed to my other breast and she feasted on me again, sucking and gurgling like a baby.

I took advantage of the two girls' obliviousness to everything around them, and touched and played with each one's breasts: Angela's big, bosomy, double-handful-sized bouncing beach balls and my darling Freya's tiny pink buds.

I unfastened Freya's little bra and removed it.

I became aware of a hand sliding up the inside of my thigh and looked down to see Freya reaching for my pussy. Almost immediately, she began to fondle it, and moments later I came on her fingers.

Maude released my breast and spoke quietly, not wanting to interrupt the nipple-loving girls below.

"Please let me go, darling. I promise to be good. My fingers are aching for want of touching the bodies of these beautiful girls. Please, please let me go."

"Angie! Freya! Will I release Maude now? Can you cope with her onslaught?"

No one spoke for a moment or two. There was just the sound of sucking and sighing.

"If she becomes difficult, we could put the cuffs back on her."

Angie's voice was a mixture of words and sucking noises. It seemed that neither girl could get enough of Maude's nipples.

Perhaps it would be good to make some changes. I wondered what it would be like when they discovered her clitoris.

"Okay! I'm setting you free, Maude, on condition that we take off your skirt."

Maude beckoned to me to come closer so that she could whisper in my ear.

"It would be nice, Alice, if you took the hand of one or other of the girls and put it where they will discover my clitoris. The other one will soon discover it, and if you free me, we can move on."

I unlocked Maude's handcuffs, then I unzipped her skirt at the side and, without interrupting the girls, slid it down over her feet, lifted her legs out and threw it away.

The white tops of Maude's beautiful strong legs were exposed and her legs filled her black silk stockings, demanding that all hands caress them.

What I hadn't expected to see was that Maude was wearing crotchless panties, and there, protruding through her mound of pubic hair and the panties, was her amazing key to Heaven's Gate.

Then I kissed Angie on the back of her neck, nibbled an ear and took her hand in mine. Angie left Maude's breast and turned to see what I was doing and when she looked down to where I was taking her hand, she gasped.

"That can't be real," she whispered.

And when I gently rested her fingers on Maude's secret, Angie burst into hysterical sobbing.

Freya now turned to see what was happening, and in seconds her hand slipped beneath Angie's.

"Auntie! This surely is a miracle. A little penis all of your own."

Freya was the first to reach it, as Angie was still recovering from the shock, wiping her eyes and wanting to blow her nose.

Maude was rolling her wrists around to get back her circulation. She looked at me sternly and whispered that she would not forget this affront, and that my next spanking would result in my not being able to sit down for a week.

Freya's tongue now began licking Maude's clitoris and Maude leant back on the sofa and groaned, closing her eyes, and resting a newly liberated hand gently on Freya's head.

. . .

I thought the two might like a little space and I knew that I did, so I put my arms around the still sniffing Angie and whispered in her ear. She took my hand and we moved over to the big armchair across from the sofa and I sat her on my knee.

I had long felt that I was not seeing enough of Angie, probably because I thought so much about Freya. Now I had an opportunity to make love to her and enjoy her sweet sexuality.

I whispered to Angie that, now Auntie was free to do her own thing, I was free too, and wanting to relax with her. I asked her if she would oblige me by lying on the floor on top of me, just as Freya had lain on her that first time we were together. I said that, as well as liking the idea of being underneath her, I would also be able to touch her all over.

We hugged each other and kissed, then Angie got up and found some spare pillows against the wall and laid them on the carpet. Then she took my hand and I lay down and she lay on top of me.

We both giggled as our breasts tried to work out where they should be, then I pulled her down tightly onto me, and kissed her passionately at the same time. Then I reached out and put both hands over her sumptuous backside, and pushed it down so that our pussies rubbed together.

We both gave a tiny gasp. Then Angie began to grind herself on me before she changed to a slow fucking motion.

"I love you Angie," I whispered.

"I love you too, Alice. You have changed my world. Thank you so much."

"Oh, and Angie. Would you please put on a one of those strap-on's later and fuck me?"

"Oh yes I will, you naughty thing. Hard?"

"Yes please. As hard as you like."

I squeezed my hand between our tits and began to caress Angie above a nipple and below her neck. She pushed her mouth against mine.

"And Angie, you can have first pick from my lunch box every day next week."

There was a sudden scream from the sofa and then we heard Freya's voice, not her usual soft-spoken voice but a very agitated high-pitched one.

"Let me go, you randy bitch!"

Angie and I had been oblivious to what was happening there, but now we sat up and looked.

Maude was holding Freya tight around her chest as she lay belly down across Maude's lovely legs, which were pressed tightly together.

Below her knees, Freya's skinny legs were waving frantically and one of her socks was about to fly off.

"You and Angie put her up to it, so that you could abuse my poor little titties, didn't you? Now I've got my hands back you are going to find out just what they can do."

"No! No! We knew nothing about it. Alice didn't tell us. Oh, oh, ouch. Stop! Please! No more!"

Maude was certainly enjoying herself, but being spanked like this was a totally new experience for Freya.

"Oh my God, poor Freya. Is Auntie really hurting her?"

We both watched as Maude's hand came down hard on Freya's tiny bottom and she writhed in pain. She was helpless against the heavy arms of Maude.

"Maude loves to spank bottoms, especially those of young boys and girls. It is one of her favourite taboo fantasies. I'm pretty sure she will get her hands on your derrière before too long, Angie. The truth is, Maude got to mine last night. It hurt at first, but then things seemed to change and suddenly it was delicious and made me doubly horny. Relax and you will enjoy it, you beautiful girl."

As we watched the activities of the two on the sofa, Angie began to touch her breasts.

Then she looked at me and we grabbed each other and fell back on the carpet, kissing passionately. Angie then threw her leg over me and hoisted herself up on me. I grabbed her buttocks and pushed them down hard and she began to ride me with added vigour. I whispered in her ear.

"I want to spank you one day, darling."

Angie shivered and pushed her wet cunt harder against me. It was delicious. From across the room, I heard Freya calling softly, "Yes! Yes!" Suddenly things became very quiet over on the sofa and I opened one eye and peeped.

The spanking had stopped. Freya was still lying over Maude's lap, but her eyes were closed and she was very still.

Freya had pushed herself up on to her knees beside Maude's leg and her rear was thrust high so that Maude could inspect the results of her hard work, which she measured by the depth of the shade of pink or red of Freya's buttocks.

I saw Maude's satisfied smile. Her eyes were bright and her tongue constantly licked her lips. Then she spoke quietly.

"Beautiful Freya. Now that wasn't so bad was it, darling?"

As Freya whined and mumbled about being sore, Maude licked two fingers and placed them carefully in Freya's cunny and when she did so, the girl shook and moaned, and ran her hand up and down Maude's leg. Then she began to lick Maude's thigh, moving upwards towards Maude's crotch, and Maude in anticipation slowly opened her legs wide, fingered her suspenders to adjust her skewed stockings, and nestled back down on the sofa to be ready for Freya's arrival at the key to Heaven's Gate.

As the afternoon headed into evening, we continued to pleasure one another and ourselves.

Angie did indeed fuck me hard with the strap-on dildo, while the other two watched and caressed each other.

Freya came over and kissed me passionately on the lips as Angie added more lube and pushed on in, and Maude couldn't resist running her hands over Angie's bottom, in anticipation of what she planned to do to her, as soon as the opportunity arose.

As we all relaxed our well-exercised bodies on the bed, Maude asked in a gentle voice if the members would accept her into the Feeling Sweet Club.

After a few moments, Angela replied. "What do we think, girls? Should we allow her in?"

"Only if she teaches us spanking, so that we can all spank her," murmured a sleepy Freya.

"I believe we should make her a member. I suspect Auntie could teach us a thing or two. She does seem to know her way around a gal's parts. And of course, there is the small matter of her very beautiful body."

Everyone laughed and Maude became the fourth member of the club. We kissed each other to celebrate. As I fell asleep, squashed between Freya's tiny bum and Angie's beautiful tits and belly, Maude, whose arms were around Angie, murmured to herself, "I think I might have to get the Feeling Sweets to buy a bigger bed."

6

A NOT SO WICKED STEPMOTHER

I WAS a little surprised when I received a text from my stepmother Helen, asking if she could visit me at home after university on a day to suit.

On the rare times we met, it would be for me to offer shopping advice before she went off to buy presents for the family. Other times we just had coffee and cake and talked about her closest friends, Bertie and Rosa, or films that we had seen or planned to see.

I texted back that Tuesday would be good, as I would be going home early to swat for an exam. I suggested two in the afternoon and she confirmed that she would be there then.

Helen's husband, Frederico Alves, was really my stepfather. He had married my late mother, Susan, after she became a widow. I was fifteen years old at the time, and I lived with the two of them until I left to go overseas when I was twenty.

I had very pleasant memories of that time, and I looked up to Frederico in some ways as our saviour. My mother had certainly been very happy with him in the latter part of her life. I had already moved out when she quite suddenly passed away after only a short illness. She was very young, just forty-nine.

. . .

Helen arrived on time and I invited her to over to my flat where I was studying. I had prepared nibbles and had the coffee machine set to go.

We embraced and kissed each other on the cheek and settled down, she on the sofa and me in the big easy chair opposite. I was genuinely pleased to see this lovely woman, and she appeared to feel the same way about seeing me.

"Well, Helen. I'm wondering what brings you here. There seems to be a hint of mystery somewhere. Has Frederico been beating you?"

We both laughed. Freddy was notoriously kind and thoughtful, the sort of man who caught moths or spiders in the house, and carefully escorted them out the back door. The idea of him lifting a hand in anger was unthinkable. Now that I thought about it, there were moments in my early teens when I had a sort of crush on my stepfather, and I was adamant that I would one day find a man just like him.

"Well, he hasn't yet. You most of all, Alice, know how thoughtful and considerate he is."

"Indeed I do. I can confess to you now that before I got my first boyfriend, I had decided that when I grew up I would find a man just like Freddy."

We both laughed.

There was a sudden quiet moment, and I could see that Helen was showing signs of unease.

"Is everything all right, Helen? Are you worried about something."

Helen's face changed and she looked more relaxed.

"Worried is not quite how I would put it, but I do have a little problem, Alice, and I have an idea you might be able to help."

"Oh! Now I'm really worried. Tell me about it, Helen."

I was taken with Helen's lovely green-painted leather low-heeled sandals with the small coloured wooden bead decoration. Her shapely and attractive bare legs were crossed and she rotated her foot first one way then the other. I had to make myself look away. I realised that she had observed me observing her and I tried really hard not to blush.

"I spent some time with Rosa last week. We had a very deep and meaningful discussion, and she opened up and told me a lot about her and Bertie's relationship. She mentioned that you knew that I had lived with a woman, and that you were very accepting of it. Later I thought about that and decided you were the person I should be talking to in fact, particularly you."

Helen paused and looked a little uncomfortable.

"Please come over here and sit beside me, Alice. It feels like I'm at the doctor's or something, with you way over there."

I went and sat beside her. She was obviously agitated and having trouble working out how to tell me something, so I took her hand. She squeezed it appreciatively.

"I am hoping that you will understand what I'm about to say. But firstly I should mention something that I remembered you saying the night of Frederico's birthday party last year.

I giggled. "Oh Helen, I was a little tiddly that night. I hope I didn't say anything offensive, or embarrass anyone?"

She laughed a more relaxed laugh.

"No, Alice you actually said something that gave me strength."

"I did? Please tell me more."

"We met in the passageway near the kitchen, where a doorway leads off to the laundry and the driveway. I was standing waiting for a friend, who had gone out to their car, to come back in.

"You came along, slightly unsteady on your feet. You uncharacter-istically put an arm around my waist and put your face up close to mine and said, 'You are so beautiful. If only I had the courage to swing both ways.' Then you took your arm back and wandered off."

"Oh my God, Helen, did I really do that? I don't remember any of it. Are you sure it was me?"

She giggled at my embarrassment. I looked at her face. She was smiling and her eyes sparkled and she looked at me intently. Helen lifted up her legs and crossed them the other way and suddenly her other foot was turning and moving provocatively.

"Yes, you did and you made my heart soar. I needed to have more courage in my life, and the strength to do what I really wanted to do. Which brings me to the reason why I am here. I just pray you will understand, and bear with me till I finish."

I squeezed her hand and nodded an assurance.

"I have desperately missed the sort of love I once had with women friends. I love Freddy dearly, and he is a wonderful lover, but it doesn't stop me having this half-empty feeling deep down. But I cannot deceive Frederico. I cannot have a secret lover. It would destroy me and us. So I've thought of a plan to involve him in a loving, sharing arrangement. And this is where I need your help, Alice."

She stopped talking and looked at me to see if I was hearing her, and understanding what she was saying and I sensed that she was feeling awkward and acting like an adolescent in love.

She was about to go on but I spoke first.

"Helen, if you will let me kiss you on the lips first, the rest might become a little easier than you think."

The look on Helen's face was one of incredulousness followed by a surprised happiness that shone like a light.

Before I could move towards her she had thrown herself onto me and our lips became glued and stayed glued seemingly for ever. Then I slowly offered her my tongue and she trembled and met my tongue with hers. When we finally pulled away, we sat looking happily into each others eye's.

"Helen darling, I hereby declare me as your first new lady lover. Please say you accept me as that?"

"Yes, yes, yes, sweet Alice, I accept you as my lover with all my heart."

We kissed again then I moved her back to where she was first sitting.

"Now my new love, tell me your plan for getting over the Freddy problem."

But Helen didn't want to do that straight away. She had other ideas.

"At this moment Alice, I only want one thing, and that is you. Please allow me to touch you. I have been so empty for so long. Suddenly, I want to feel a love that only you can give me."

She reached over and began to unbutton my blouse, and I began to drag her top up from inside her skirt. We were both braless and in just moments we were bare-breasted.

We alternated between kissing each other on the lips, each caressing the other's neck kissing each other's breasts and gently biting each other's nipples. I swung my leg over her, and kneeled facing her. We cupped each others breasts in our hands and rubbed them against our own. Then I stood up, and taking Helen by the hand, led her to the bedroom.

"I want to take all your clothes off, Helen, and mine too."

For the next hour or more we cavorted naked, every which way, on the big bed and sometimes on the floor or in the armchair beside the bed. We laughed and we sobbed.

Sometimes the enormity of Helen's long isolation from other women overwhelmed her and she cried like a child. And when she had cried enough, I would slap her on the bottom, and tell her that I so wanted to spank her hard but now wasn't the time. She laughed out loud.

"Oh the times I've ached for a good spanking. Make it your number one task, my darling, when next we are together."

We exhausted ourselves, but still couldn't stop wanting more of each other. And when we thought we'd done enough, one or the other would round onto her knees, and push her bottom and pussy towards the other's face and wriggle, midst peals of laughter and licking.

Our first encounter was a truly beautiful time, and we would forever cherish the memory.

"So part two of the story, Helen, is what to do about Freddy and how I might help you with that."

We had dressed, and were back in the lounge having reheated coffee that we had abandoned earlier.

"So I'll not beat about the bush, Alice. I would like you to sleep with your stepdad. And before you list all the reasons why it's not possible, let me ask you: was there ever a time when you all lived together that you fancied Frederico, or perhaps had fantasies about having him as a lover?"

"Oh, Helen, what a dilemma. Yes, of course I had a crush on

Freddy, probably within a few months of him getting together with Mum.

"As I got to know him, and stopped being angry with him for having stolen my mother from me, I caved in, and from then on hung on his every word. He sensed my interest and handled me with the utmost care.

"I remember, at around age sixteen, deliberately not locking the bathroom door, running down the hallway naked when I thought he was about to come along, and hitching my school skirt up high when I came home and I knew Mum would still be at work, and he would be alone in the study.

"Nothing ever worked. He was just bloody perfect."

She laughed loudly.

"Just as he is now."

"Are you saying what I think you are saying Helen? That you would like me as your lover and you want to share me with your husband? And this could be the easiest path to follow, given he already knows me? And it will give you peace of mind, and the freedom you want? So are you only here to fix your problem, and I just happen to be a part of the package?"

Helen looked horrified.

"Alice! No! You are the woman I have most ached for, for a very long time. You could just as easily say that I only want to share you with Freddy, so that I can have you as my lover."

We fell silent for quite a long time.

"Freddy, has occasionally mentioned you with great affection. Despite what we might think about him, I know for sure that you have not gone unnoticed, and he has feelings deep down, like most men, that he will not allow himself to admit. And I believe that, understandably, he would have hidden any of these feelings or fantasies in deference to his love for your mother.

"Now that his world has changed and we are together and alone, I believe it would be a healthy thing if he put some of those taboos aside, just as you and I have done today."

We fell silent again. Then I mentioned the Bennetts, and Rosa and

Bertie's happy marriage, and how things changed for both of them when Rosa admitted to herself that she needed female love as well as Bertie's love.

"Bertie's research into early Chinese philosophy relating to the increased health and happiness of people who love more than one person, might be the key to all this.

"And yes, dearest Helen, I would go to bed with your husband, and yes, for mostly selfish reasons, one being that I get to have his wife as a lover. If, then, he and I grew closer through our lovemaking, so be it. And if Bertie happened to hear about us, he would rejoice and say that we all were better off because if it."

Helen reached out and took my hand and I leant over and kissed her.

"I think that Rosa and Bertie are the ones who might more easily influence Frederico, and however successful or not a would-be seducer might be, I think a direct approach at this point would not work.

"Does Rosa have an inkling of what you have in mind, Helen?"

"Yes, darling, our conversation was thorough and far-reaching."

Helen gave a funny little smile that made me curious.

"Rosa was very happy that you are looking after Bertie so well."

Helen watched as I coloured up in the deepest possible fit of blushing, and she smiled.

"My God, you're a sexy little bitch. Come here."

Helen pushed me off the sofa and on to the floor and lay on top of me.

We just stayed there lovingly grinding our pussies together and with our mouths glued and our tongues wildly thrashing about inside each other's mouths.

There was much sighing and moaning, as we expressed our delight in having discovered each other at long last. Finally Alice whispered in a mock child's voice.

"And Mummy dearest?"

"Yes, darling?"

"You are the most sexy wicked stepmother ever."

. . .

Most weeks over the next few months, I met Helen on a midweek afternoon. She told me how Freddy had started spending time with both Rosa and Bertie, and that he had said how impressed he was with their understanding of life.

Helen suggested, and I agreed, that I should visit her and Freddy for a meal regularly, under the pretext that I was in the midst of a very intense study period, and needed to go somewhere to relax. I had a firm booking for their house on a Saturday night.

Helen told Freddy that I had expressed a wish to connect with my past and that naturally, he was the major part of that. This meant that I would get to see Freddy in a relaxed and non-threatening family setting. He enjoyed my visits, and both Helen and I did too.

It was on one of my twice weekly visits to Rosa in hospital that she announced out of the blue, that she thought it was nearly time for me to sleep with Frederico. My prayers that I might lose the ability to blush had not been answered and Rosa laughed heartily.

"The sooner you three are happily involved in a loving situation together, the better."

"It's going to be a long drawn-out process, Rosa, and it might never happen. Freddy is such a good man. He won't do something if he thinks it's morally wrong."

"Ah, yes dear. But I believe he is on the brink of change. Bertie told me this week that Frederico now accepted that he and Helen should see other people for reasons of physical and emotional health, just as long as it was done with sincere love all round."

Rosa smiled her beautiful smile.

"Bertie mentioned that it might also be fun, but Frederico brushed that aside. But when Bertie casually asked your stepfather if he had a possible romantic liaison in mind, a particular person maybe, Freddy got flustered and said that he was very attracted to someone who was very close to him, but who was much younger and who might therefore not be willing to become romantically involved.

"Now we all know who that is?"

I watched Rosa's face as she contemplated the situation.

"I think I will ask Helen, when she comes in later, to consider broaching the subject with Freddy and to tell him that she too was leaning towards Bertie's philosophy, but would never do anything unless she and Freddy had first agreed on a course of action and did it together. And then she should go on to mention how wonderful it would be if they could find someone as caring and lovely as Alice."

"It certainly wouldn't do any harm Rosa, I suppose," I answered, with a self-conscious giggle.

"I understand you and Helen have turned the corner and are getting on really well. I'm so glad she found you. I hate to think what might have happened if she hadn't. And I so admire her, wanting her husband to be a part of everything she does."

I blushed and wondered just how Helen had described our getting together. Rosa was obviously very keen to see all three of us become lovers.

I felt we were running out of visiting time and that I should get Rosa talking about other things.

"Maude's visit was a success, Rosa. She managed to seduce me and gave me my first ever proper spanking, and I must say I loved it."

"Oh, darling, how wonderful. She will get a surprise when I see her next and tell her that I hear she's been having her way with you on my home turf and that I will claim spanking rights on you the minute I get out of here."

We both laughed.

"Come home soon, Rosa, and spank me as hard as you like."

"That's given me even greater incentive to get better, dear Alice."

"Rosa, I know we don't have a lot of time, but can I show you what Maude sent me in the post?"

"You certainly can, dear. I hope it's rude."

I stood up and moved right up close to Rosa, where she lay on her bed. Then I lifted my skirt and displayed the new crotchless panties.

"Oh my goodness, aren't they wonderful? But that hussy Maude has a lot to answer for, and I will plan something truly bad for her. Meanwhile darling, I'll just give you a tiny touch up, which will give this old lady a delightful flutter."

Rosa put her hand between my legs and gently caressed my clit, hidden away in its auburn fluff. I trembled a little and bent down and kissed her passionately.

"Oh darling, I feel so much better already. I'd run home with you right now if I could."

I was happy with the way things were. Freya and I were as passionate about one another as we'd ever been, and Helen continued to be my delightful wicked stepmother.

There was a tiny moment when things involving both of them looked as though they might go awry.

I had told Helen very early in the piece about my loving relationship with Freya. But it wasn't until a few weeks after Helen and I first made love that she brought up the subject of other relationships.

"Alice! I've got this nagging problem with us. You will think I'm being childish I know, but I've realised that I'm feeling jealous of Freya."

"Oh Helen, that's awful. You know that I love you very, very much. And you are always the first to acknowledge that we can love more than one person. You must not be jealous, sweetheart. We must fix this."

Helen stared at her feet and her shoulders were drooped sadly. I sat beside her and held her hand.

"I know I shouldn't be, darling, but it niggles at me. What can I do?"

"Whatever it takes, we'll do it together. I do have one idea which I've wanted to suggest, but thought it might be too soon."

"What is that idea, darling? Please tell me."

I paused for a moment then told her my idea, with my fingers crossed that she wouldn't get upset.

"I feel that you are now as much a part of me as Freya is, and increasingly I want to share you both with each other. I feel that we would benefit by including the three of us in our lovemaking.

"I believe, too, that if I'm not mistaken, you and Freya will fall in love in the same way as the two of us did. If that happens, bingo, jealousy goes out the window. And, there is another thing, your desire to be open and honest with Freddy. I know you would have no trouble finding other lovers. However, you might not want Frederico to think you had been secretly looking out for them. My solution would involve me bringing and introducing Freya to the two of you.

"Bringing Freya to dinner on a Saturday evening and seeing how the two of you reacted to her, and her to you, would be a start."

By this time, Helen was staring at me, obviously interested. Then her face took on that seductive and mischievous smile.

"Is she really tall and thin with tiny breasts?"

I had obviously broken through, and Helen was responding genuinely and with humour.

I reached out and pulled her face to mine with one hand, while the other hand tippy toed up under her skirt. She wriggled in anticipation and pushed her lower half down into the sofa and forward. Our passionate kissing session hinted that we might have just sorted the jealousy problem.

"Yes, Helen, she is a delight. Now, why am I thinking that maybe I'm the one that will end up getting jealous?"

My birthday was coming up and Helen and Freddy were planning a little party for me at their place.

Freya had by now been to my stepparents' house for dinner, just the once, prior to my birthday. It had gone well and I knew that she had won both their hearts.

I could see that Helen was desperate to know her better or, to put it more accurately, get her hands on her. And in the good spirit of things Helen had whispered, "I understand now how you feel the way you do about her darling. She is gorgeous. Thanks for letting us meet her."

Equally besotted though less expressive was Frederico.

Freddy engaged Freya in a conversation about attitudes people had about those who had a different take on life. He was obviously fishing for a clue to where she was in her head and discovering if she was really my lover, as Helen had explained to him, and not simply a university chum.

When Freya came over the next day and she had unpacked her little case, and we had put on our pyjamas and were sitting up in bed holding our obligatory Sunday night mugs of cocoa, I asked her what she thought of the two of them.

"What you are really asking me, darling wife-to-be, is, could I fuck them."

I laughed out loud, trying not to spill my drink.

"I could certainly enjoy Helen. She is a very sensuous woman. I can't work out why you weren't both licking each other years ago. What took you so long? Frederico is lovely, and yes, I would happily let him have his way with me, well, at least once.

"As you know, I'm not so much into men, probably because they've never shown a lot of interest in me so I don't have much experience. If Frederico was properly enamoured with me, I could probably get besotted and go right off and bonk him on a regular basis."

"Freya! I do love you so much and you do make me laugh. I just hope that I don't wake up one day, ridiculously jealous and hurt. You are such a delight."

Freya took my mug and hers and put them on the bedside table. Then she pushed me down under the bedclothes and lay on top of me.

She put her hand to my face and opened my mouth with her fingers. Then she leant forward and poked her deliciously long tongue into my mouth.

With our hands holding each other's buttocks through our thick pyjamas, she rubbed herself on me, licking my neck then moving down to my breasts.

"We belong to each other, darling Alice, so stop being silly."

It was party night, and Freya and I arrived at No 17 Eros Crescent as things were getting well and truly underway. Not that there was a big guest list.

Angie was there. She had brought a cousin with her, a nice man whom I remembered her saying was gay. Hayden, I think she said his name was. Freya stood with them while I went to find Helen and my dad.

Helen was just leaving a conversation with two couples, neighbours who lived either side of them.

"Ah! Here we are, the party girl herself. Alice, these are our neighbours Hilda and Charlie, who live at number nineteen, and Harold and Mary who live at number fifteen."

"Hello, Hilda and Charlie and hello, Harold and Mary. So glad you could come."

Harold seemed to be already a bit tipsy and Hilda tottered a little as she turned towards me and grinned rather grotesquely. They wished me a happy birthday. Then Helen and I wandered away to a quiet spot near the study. I had told Helen on her last weekly visit that Freya was excited about seeing her again.

"In her words, she found you sensuous and alluring."

I feigned displeasure.

"Oh dear, who's getting jealous now?"

Helen laughed and looked around to see if we were being watched. Then feeling that it was safe enough to put her arms around me she kissed me passionately.

I had also mentioned how Freya had said she lacked experience with men but thought Freddy was "beautiful" and she could be tempted to try being a little amorous with him, just to see how things went.

"Well, I'm excited. And please, please, don't feel threatened Alice. I know she loves you and so do I. And it was your idea to share."

We smiled and held hands, and looked longingly at each other.

"Now I have a message from your stepfather. He wants to meet you in the spare bedroom at ten thirty, to give you his present. It's a big surprise and he's put a lot of effort into it, so please don't keep him waiting."

"No worries, wicked stepmother. But don't think I won't be watching you."

We both laughed and headed off in different directions and I rejoined Freya, Angie and Hayden.

"Did you find them, Alice?"

"Yes, well I found Helen at least. She said dad has a surprise gift for me and I had to meet him in the spare bedroom at ten thirty. It's probably a complicated bookshelf from Ikea that he wants me to help him put together, or something like it."

Freya looked at her watch.

"Wow! Lift-off in just ten minutes for you dear lady. I will float around down here, most likely continuing my discussion about kitchen decor and utensils with Hayden. Hey! Hayden might like to help Freddy put your present together."

"Well, I have a feeling that you, the love of my life, are going to find that a certain 'sensuous and alluring' woman will be hunting you down, and to make an Ikea analogy she will be waving her Allen key at you and giving you the 'follow me' treatment."

Freya laughed and looked at me, but spoke with concern in her voice.

"Alice! I will leave this house this very minute if you are feeling threatened by Helen. You know you suggested this and we both know that we can both survive it and enjoy it. Now tell me that me snogging your stepmother is not going to threaten us in any way. Damn you! I love you so much."

I looked at Freya and we kissed.

"How about me?" came a voice behind us.

Angie stood smiling broadly at the two of us and each of us in turn leant forward and kissed her.

"Is that it? Well, I suppose it might keep me going until someone grabs my tits. I don't think cousin Hayden will be up for it. Perhaps I should get him in a corner and ask to see his cock?"

We all fell about laughing.

"Now that I think about it? Hmm! It might just work."

Freya and I chuckled as Angie wandered off to find her cousin.

"Hello, Freya and welcome."

Helen's voice sounded happy and relaxed.

"Hello Helen. Nice to be here."

Freya gave me a deep and meaningful look.

"May I kiss Helen, darling?"

"I think the sooner you two start kissing, the more relaxed I'll feel. It's the anticipation that gets me confused."

Both Helen and Freya laughed and clapped. Then Helen stepped forward and put both hands around Freya's face and kissed her.

"Feel better now that your two biggest loves have kissed, my sweet Alice?"

"Yes, I am. Now just get on with it. Meanwhile I think I'm expected in the spare bedroom, and I'd guess it will be to put a giant bookshelf together, or some amazing thing that Freddy has discovered that he thinks I need. See you both later. Hopefully!"

As I turned to leave, I noticed Helen looking at me with a joyous smile on her face and I wondered what she was thinking.

Going up the stairs and along the passageway, I managed to put my petty reservations about my two lovers aside. What was done was done, and I knew that everything would work out.

Instead I got myself in the mood for surprise presents, remembering birthdays of my childhood, rocking horse, tricycle, a table tennis set, then a real pony. They were highly anticipated and exciting moments. But I guess you only really got proper surprises when you were very young.

I reached the bedroom door and knocked, just so that Freddy could check who was coming in.

"Who is it?"

"It's me, Alice."

"Come in, Alice."

I pushed open the door and looked through the dim light provided by the bathroom door being open, and the mirror lights being on.

Was Freddy really working in the dark?

Suddenly I saw him. I don't think I have ever had such shock. It was the ultimate "Oh my God" moment.

"Helen said that this is what you most wanted for your birthday, but I'm having a little bit of trouble keeping it up. She got it up for me a few minutes ago and I've worked on it myself, but I think I'm probably nervous which really doesn't help. Sorry, sweetheart."

I was speechless, gobsmacked, and totally unprepared for any of this. Freddy lay naked on the bed. He had a big satin bow around his neck and a smaller satin bow around his erect, or semi-erect, penis.

"Freddy! I just don't know what to say. I ... "

"I hope you are not offended, darling. I told Helen that her idea was a little bit over the top, but she convinced me that this was something that you and I should have shared long ago. I do so hope you will accept my apologies, and forget this ever happened, if it's all too much."

I could see Freddy's enormous discomfort, and his rapidly disappearing erection confirmed this.

I ran all the possible scenarios through my head, looking for a sensitive response, but I had no similar experiences to go on. In the end I trusted myself just to be myself, and it worked.

"Freddy! You've always been my hero, but never more than at this moment. I can't tell you how impressed I am with the trouble you've gone to."

I moved over and stood beside the bed, and looked down at his face. He smiled the same smile I had fallen in love with as a sixteen-year-old.

"That is so kind of you, Alice. But I'm not sure what I should do next?"

I realised that this was the moment that could forge a wonderful relationship change with Freddy, one that would bind us together forever. I went and sat on the edge of the bed and took hold of his hand.

"Freddy! I'm going to take care of everything. I am so happy to see your cock at long last. I have had a crush on you since I was around sixteen. Helen was right. It was what I jokingly said I most wanted for my birthday."

I bent down and kissed him on the lips and gently rubbed his chest. Then I moved my hand down to his belly, and finally to his manhood.

I removed the bow. His now withered cock hid in my cupped hand. I bent and kissed it.

"Freddy! It's okay if you don't have or can't get an erection. Just holding it like this is a beautiful thing."

"You are so sweet, Alice. I can't believe we are doing this."

I moved my head down to inspect his scrotum and licked him gently. Then I asked him to move so that I could cover him with the quilt.

"I know where you are, Freddy. I don't want you to freeze," I laughed.

"Hmm yes! A frozen non-stiffy might not be a good thing."

I sat there for little while with my hand under the quilt.

"Freddy?"

"Yes, darling?"

"I want to take off all of my clothes and lie down beside you. Would that be okay?"

I still had Freddy's cock in my hand under the cover and I felt a tiny tremble. It was so sweet.

"Alice, that would be one of my oldest fantasies come true. Please let me watch you take your clothes off, darling. I would love that."

I stood up and realised that I was about to experience the full male gaze and that I could enjoy the power it gave me.

As I thought about it, memories came flooding back from my years with Mum and Freddy.

I remembered fantasising that Freddy would see me changing out of my school uniform, that Freddy would see me running naked from the bathroom or taking off my swimsuit when I came in from the pool. And when I was older, I fantasised that he would watch me through the partly open bedroom door, when I rolled on my stockings and slipped on my first pair of high heels. I had been waiting a long time for this.

"Freddy?"

"Yes, darling."

"How come you never once tried to see me without my clothes on when you must have known I had a serious crush on you? And why didn't you hug me in a special way that would have told me that you wanted me? Why did you not come into my room to have a chat? How come, Freddy?"

There was silence.

"Sweetheart, I am sorry that it caused you such anguish, but I'm not sorry about the way I acted. You didn't know how much I was affected by being your stepdad. Having you around was like having a beautiful younger version of your mother living in the house.

"I did catch glimpses of you getting dressed, and even naked a couple of times. But I so loved your mother. I was able to channel any thoughts that I had about you, into your mum's and my love life. In an odd sort of way, Alice, you might say that I made love to you for years. Unfortunately, you never knew."

On hearing this, I collapsed in a torrent of tears and went and got under the quilt with him. He rolled over and cuddled me and held me tight.

After about ten minutes, I turned my face up towards his. He kissed me gently on the lips.

"Can I be Mum now Freddy? Helen wouldn't mind, she has suggest we be lovers already."

"No, darling, you can't be Mum. But you can be the new love in the life that Helen wants us to share. We will explore each other, and sometimes I will remember moments when I was a bad stepfather, watching you through edge of the door as you changed out of your school uniform and especially seeing you pulling down your regulation knickers; and being excited when I first saw your fluffy pubic hair; and seeing you slip into your pretty lacy panties. My God, how beautiful you were."

I stopped sniffling. I looked up at him and smiled.

"Thanks, Freddy. I'm surprised I didn't know you saw me, but that helps me a lot. Knowing I wasn't being ignored is so gratifying.

"I don't want to talk any more, Freddy. I just want to kiss you and make you watch me taking off my clothes, just for you. I love you so much, so do as you are told."

Freddy laughed. I reached up and glued my mouth to his while I held his now obviously happy cock in my hand.

I put on a small bedside light, and stood not far from the bed.

For a moment I couldn't work out where I should begin, then I reached down and slowly lifted my dress up over my legs, the suspenders and panties and up over my bra, over my head, and threw it across the room.

I could see Freddy watching me and I felt a joyous sensation deep down. Since I was sixteen I'd prayed for a moment like this.

Then I unbuttoned the suspender on the stocking on my left leg and slowly peeled it down to the ankle. I unbuttoned the strap on my high-heeled sandal, slipped it off and put it beside the dressing-table stool. I repeated this with my right leg.

I then reached behind my shoulders and released the fastener on my bra, slipped it off and threw it on the pile along with my dress. I stopped to touch my breasts and cup them and inspect them and point them at Freddy. I realised that Freddy was moving.

I could see that he had removed the quilt and was naked as before. He was holding an erection and slowly moving his hand up and down. Watching Freddy do that made my pussy quiver, and I felt a loving feeling of desire for him.

I slipped off my panties and turned around and bent over, pushing my bottom towards him, then turned and walked to the edge of the bed.

"Freddy?"

"Yes, Alice?"

"I give you my fluffy pubic hair, to have and to hold until death do us part."

Freddy smiled happily, reached out for my hand and wrapped it around his cock.

"It gives me great pleasure to accept such a privilege. And now, sweet Alice, I would like to invite you to climb on top of me."

We were so happy. I threw my leg over his belly and bent forward and we kissed. Then I turned around and presented my rear to his face and moved his hands, putting my mouth over his cock and making it mine.

Having the tip of his beautiful penis in my mouth made me want to cry again. I recalled my teenage memory of wondering what Freddy's cock would feel like, and what I might do if ever I had access to it. That moment had arrived.

I also made a mental note of what a horny little teenager I was, and wondered if my mother ever thought about what was on my mind, or worried about me.

I had delightedly licked and sucked Freddy for ten or fifteen minutes, and his cock was now rock hard and pulsating.

"Freddy?"

"Yes, sweetheart?"

"I'm going to celebrate now."

"How will you do that?"

"It being my birthday and our first time together, and me being a modern woman, I'm going to shag you, Freddy. Later, you can be on top and shag me. Love you Freddy."

I heard Freddy sighing and breathing deeply. I turned about again so that I was facing him, then I put the end of his member against my wet vagina and Freddy slipped in.

Home at last.

When I had left Freya and Helen alone, it didn't take the two of them long to find each other. Helen asked Freya if she would like to see the fish pond with its newly installed lighting.

"It is quite beautiful in the dark."

"Love to Helen. Show me the way."

Almost before the two even reached the pond they began touching each other, tentatively putting their hands around each other's waists and rubbing their fingertips innocently on each other's backsides.

Moments later, Helen backed Freya against the door of her painting studio and kissed her passionately. Freya hung back a tiny bit, anticipating and looking forward to the onslaught of Helen's obviously strong desire for her.

But she wasn't expecting Helen's next move. Helen pulled her forward and swung her round to face the door. Then the seducer pulled up Freya's skirt.

Helen had wanted to see and touch Freya's extraordinary long thin legs and tiny buttocks from the first moment she had met her. Now there was nothing to stop her

Helen moaned with pleasure as she discovered the gentle Freya's delightful big silk knickerbockers, her latest fashion statement. Helen slipped her hand first up one leg and dragged the knicker leg up to expose the full length of Freya's beautiful leg, then she pulled down the waist to find the tiny bottom, and put her hand on it. She shivered and felt wet between her legs.

Helen's lust was potent. She was wildly excited and Freya appreciated it, joyfully sharing in the lustful anticipation.

Freya found the door handle and turned it, and went into the studio. Helen followed and guided her towards a sofa bed, just made visible by the lights of the fish pond shining through the window.

Freya turned to face Helen.

"I want you to make love to me, Helen and I desperately want you to take you clothes off and for me to lie on your naked body and shag you. I will undress you while you do what you want to do. I want you to touch me everywhere, Helen."

Helen sighed and began to undress Freya. It didn't take long. A skirt and a blouse, a tiny bra and her bloomers all came off, leaving her in her socks and her little white sandals.

And while Freya slipped Helen's dress over her head, then stopped to stare at her beautiful breasts, Helen vented her lust on Freya's tiny breasts and nipples. And when Helen paused for breath, Freya pushed Helen down on the bed and spread herself on top of her and with their mouths joined, she shagged her seducer to their first orgasms together.

"Oh my God, Freya, you are such a beautiful woman. I will want to make love to you again and again."

"Please let's do that Helen. I will want much more of you, too."

Helen and Freya stopped only because Helen suddenly remembered that she was supposed to be the hostess to the party guests.

When the two women went inside the house, they discovered that there were only two couples still there and Helen was shocked at what was happening.

The husband of one couple had passed out, as had the woman from the other couple.

What was a surprise was that the two who had not got drunk to the point of oblivion had discovered each other and moved into the study, where they lay on the floor.

The buttocks of a very large woman were heaving and her fat legs were flaying about as in a soft voice she whispered, "Give it to me, give it to me Charlie, more, yes, that's it, more, fuck me you gorgeous bastard," followed by another quiet voice saying, "Oh Mary. I love you Mary. Here, have some more, Mary".

Helen looked shocked.

"Well, I would never have expected that sort of behaviour in our house. If that is not being neighbourly, I don't know what is."

Freya giggled.

"There must be something in the air, Helen?"

They both laughed and kissed.

"I think we should check on the other newlyweds, Freya. Are you game?"

Freya grinned.

"Let's do it."

Helen quietly pushed open the bedroom door and ushered Freya in ahead of her. They closed the door and stood in the dim light.

Alice's naked rear end was rhythmically rising and falling as she rode on Freddy's penis. Both were making gentle gasping and groaning sounds and seemed in no hurry to finish or change their positions.

The visitors turned to each other and whispered.

"Thank the lord. It worked."

"I think we should pay them a little visit, Helen, and encourage them. Don't you?"

"Yes, at this moment I want to tell Frederico how much I love him. It's been a long journey getting him to this point. You might want to say encouraging things to Alice, Freya?"

Freya turned and put her arms around Helen.

"I do, but first, a big thank you for tonight, Helen. I hope we get a longer time together soon."

"We will, I promise."

Freddy opened his eyes and smiled as Helen touched his cheek and lowered her head to kiss him.

"Congratulations, darling, you did it."

"All thanks to you, my dear wife, and to our most understanding Alice, who successfully took me in hand at a crucial moment."

Freya took a handful of Alice's hair and gently lifted her swaying head. They stared lovingly into each other eyes, and Alice puckered her lips indicating she wanted to be kissed.

"I do so love you, Alice. It looks as though you are really enjoying Freddy's cock. I envy you, my love."

As she was talking, Freya was caressing Alice's bottom, then let her hand slide down to feel Alice's wet vagina and then the enormous root of Frederico's big cock. Freya sighed.

"Oh, darling, I would really like some of this inside me. Ask Freddy later, if one day he would do me the honour of having me."

Alice looked up at Freya with a distant look in her eyes and smiled.

"Don't stop touching me, darling. Get ready, my love. I think Freddy is about to come."

Helen moved down to join Freya behind Alice. She knew her husband intimately enough to be able to whisper "Any moment now."

Freya and Helen embraced and kissed passionately as Frederico yelled out and thrust himself up into Alice's welcoming cunny, filling her with his sperm.

Alice stopped moving her body and held her breath, and when Freddy came a second time she screamed and came with him, shaking and calling loudly, "Oh yes, Freddy, yes Freddy, at last my love!"

Alice's ongoing orgasms were contagious, and Freya and Helen embraced and cried out "Yes, yes, yes!"

Then the girls fell on each other, kissing and rubbing and touching, and calling out to Alice who was sobbing uncontrollably.

Alice had waited a long, long, time for this moment and she knew she would never forget it.

"Thank you, Freddy, my darling man. I love you."

7

EXORCISING ODIN

MY RELATIONSHIP with Helen was vastly different from the one I enjoyed with the ethereal Freya.

Being with Freya and her ghostly charms was like making love in the presence of God.

She seemed on the one hand unattainable, yet when you touched her and when she gave you her body and whimpered as you folded her in your arms, you experienced a state of religious bliss, an other-worldliness, and like any truly spiritual believer I could not envisage a life without her.

My love for Helen was very different. Our relationship had evolved into something more than being just sexual playmates, although we were indeed that as well. We had once speculated about our mutual love for Freddy, and wondered whether this connection could be part of the reason for our closeness.

Every encounter with my delicious stepmother brought us closer, to the point that it seemed as though we were each making love to ourselves, only the experience was a thousand times more sensual. It was, I suppose, a weird form of self-love.

Our interactions when we met became almost automatic, but it suited us. Helen would arrive, we would look lovingly at each other and then fall into each other's arms and kiss passionately, slowly tonguing between each other's lips and mouths.

Then we might giggle and join hands and go to the bedroom, where we would remove each other's skirt and top or frock, sometimes chatting about mundane events. We would kiss each other a lot on the lips and the neck, or bend down to kiss a knee or lick a thigh, partly with lustful enthusiasm, but also sisterly and matter-of-factly, comfortable in knowing that we could go to a high point whenever we felt like it.

This feeling of just being together was underpinned by an awareness that we were the same in so many ways. We each touched the other as we would touch ourselves.

Our breasts figured largely in our loving routine. Helen called mine slightly larger than pert, and I described hers as a little less than buxom. We touched and played with them constantly. Hardly a moment went by without one of us kissing, or sucking, or caressing the other.

It was our regular Wednesday afternoon date. Helen and I had deliciously mooned about for an hour or so before I got around to talking about Freya.

Helen and I now comfortably accepted her as the lover of both of us. We even discussed her charms and her welfare as if we were her parents, or guardians, as well as her lovers.

I said I expected to hear from her later, and couldn't help wondering how she was going and if she would accept Freddy's invitation. Helen expected a call as well.

"She seemed very keen one moment, when we came and saw you and Freddy together, but I sensed that she also had reservations."

Just then, Helen's phone rang. It was Freya.

"Hello darling. Are you okay? Yes, I'm with Alice. Just wait while I put us on speaker phone."

Helen switched the phone so that we could all talk and hear each other.

"Hello, sweetheart. Wonderful to hear your voice. I'll see you tomorrow at uni, but we were just talking here about Saturday night dinner at Helen and Frederico's. I was suggesting we bring a Thai dinner. Are you happy with that?"

"Sure thing, Alice. Now I'm glad I've got you both together. It makes things easier."

Helen leant forward to speak.

"It makes what easier, Freya?"

"Well, I don't want to go into it much over the phone, but what I want to say is that I want to try making love with Freddy, but I want both of you to be with me while we are doing it. Please say you will, both of you?

"Of course we will sweetheart, if that is what you want."

I looked at Helen, nodding my head as Freya continued.

"I want you both to distract me. I am terrified that I will slip back into my last and only lovemaking moment with a man, and want Odin back. It will kill me if I can't shake him off. Alice? When I hang up, please tell Helen my story. I gotta go to class now. I love you both desperately. See you on Saturday, Helen. Kisses all round. Bye!"

Helen looked at me amazed.

"What is this about, Alice? Please tell me."

I proceeded to tell Helen Freya's story of her moment of love with her Viking bikie. She listened very intently, occasionally nodding her head in sympathy and understanding.

"Oh, the poor darling. I had no idea."

We were quiet for a moment.

"Helen, you will no doubt know, and enjoy as I do, how Freya loves to lie on top of us, and how she has that divine sexy movement with her hips that we love.

"However, I've only recently worked out that what Freya is really doing, is not having us, but being had by us. That movement is her remembering being astride Odin's giant penis."

"My God, I believe you could be right. You never quite get the feeling that she is trying to push into you, do you? Yes, it is as though she is actually having you, and you think that in her imagination she is back at that moment with him? Oh, the poor darling, she must have suffered so after he had gone. God, that is awful."

"Not only that, Helen. You will sometimes see her wipe her eyes afterwards, although she does try to hide that. I believe she cries for him while she's doing it."

I had suddenly become teary, and when I looked at Helen we both dissolved in tears and cried for our darling Freya.

Helen unbuttoned her shirt and pulled me onto her breast, and we sobbed and blubbered some more. Then Helen reached for my breasts, tears streaming down her cheeks.

"Please darling, I need you too."

A Thai meal was the right thing, and our Saturday evening meal together at Helen and Freddy's house at Eros Crescent was wonderful, and made even better with the good conversation and humorous banter.

Frederico was in good form, avoiding some of his pet topics, usually the sort that men like to use to show off their knowledge to one another. Subjects like the origins of Guinness stout, or ways of keeping planes in the air.

Helen had more exciting things to talk about. She had gossip.

"Come on, Helen. What has got you so fired up? Tell us please. We're bursting to know."

"Well, Alice, and you, Freya, the matter is a little sensitive to say the least, so what I say must not leave these four walls."

"Oh come on stepmum, you are driving us insane. Just say it."

"Freya, you will remember the night of Alice's birthday when we came into the house on our way to visit her and Freddy and our attention was caught by something that was happening in the study. We had already noticed that a man and woman had passed out drunk in the lounge.

"As we were passing the slightly open door of the study, we noticed a very large pair of women's knickers hanging on the door knob and we heard voices."

"Don't tell me you didn't look to see who it was, Helen?" Alice chipped in.

"Be quiet darling, we are not all perverts and voyeurs."

"Well, Freya and I did just have a peep to make sure that everything was all right, no one being murdered or anything.

"Anyway, everything seemed fine. We didn't stay long, did we Freya? Just long enough to see that Charlie from number nineteen was fully immersed in a private part of the very large Mary from number fifteen.

"As I said before, we didn't stay long, being in a hurry as we were to join you two in the bedroom. But it did seem that they were very pleased to be doing what they were doing, and Mary indicated that she would like to be doing this for ever and ever.

"We were not sure what his reply was, but we suspected his gurgling was in the affirmative."

Everyone screamed with laughter and Freya said how, with great difficulty, she had dragged Helen from the room. Helen pulled a face at her and she and Frederico laughed heartily.

"So! Has this story got a happy ending darling? Have they run off to the Caribbean together or something? Will we be getting new neighbours?"

There followed a general buzz of speculation. I thought that their respective partners should be involved, so that then all would be blameless.

Frederico suggested that partner swapping could become the new norm on the street and began naming neighbours whom he thought he could manage to get off with, to which Helen added her comments: "No, she's a bit of a bitch", or "No, she'd kill you" or, "Yes, Mr So-and-so in number so-and-so is rather interesting."

When they settled down, Freya asked a question.

"So Helen, can we help the lady with the giant knockers, I mean knickers, get more of dear Charlie?"

"A good question, darling. Yes, we can and I have. That is my news. You all need to know so that no one interrupts our lovers. I've given them both a key to the potting shed. As well, I've taken a spare mattress to the shed and some pillows.

Everyone clapped and raised their glasses and cheered, and called out "Well done, Helen."

"But what did they say? Did you seek them out separately? Were they shocked that you knew?"

"Well, I didn't see Charlie. I had seen Harold leaving with a car-load of mates to play golf, so I went in and saw Mary.

"And yes, she was shocked, but not as much as I thought she might be. She had a little cry and professed her undying love for Charlie.

"She was over the moon when I presented her with the keys. Now all she needs to do is simply text him, then nip through the side gate or over the fence and meet him there and give him a key. Bingo, big knickers can hang alongside the onions and the dahlia tubers. What better way to plant the life force?"

"And a happy ending all round, I presume. And we, darling, get our very own garden gnomes with extras."

"Yes, Frederico, and you only get peeping and perving rights, if we do it together."

Lots of hilarity followed and every aspect was discussed, even to concern about their respective spouses finding out.

"I must say that the other two are not especially likeable. He can be particularly rude and she is a snob par excellence. I doubt either has a loving bone in their body," said Helen.

"Now, darling, we mustn't judge them too harshly. Perhaps they just need to get out more."

"Perhaps they could get off together and you could give them keys to your studio?

"Then I could go down with trays of sandwiches and cupcakes and make a few bob. I could offer a shopping service so that they didn't have to stop. And of course, you will have a supply of nudes to paint."

Frederico was loving the story of the neighbours' follies, and milking it for all he could.

"Stop it, Frederico. We've done the neighbours now."

. . .

Through all of this merriment, Freya was watching Frederico. His beautiful olive skin, inherited from his Portuguese great-great-grand-parents, and his handsome face were perfect. His manner was very pleasant. So what was Freya to do?

If she did not yet feel truly excited about making love to Freddy, then her commonsense told her it would be wrong to do so.

Lovely as he was, he was still caught in a crazy world that drags people into it and expunges the passion of their youth. Would Odin have ever been like that, she wondered?

I suddenly asked Helen if they had any photos of Frederico when he was younger, from even before he married Alice's mother.

"I don't remember ever seeing any when I lived at home."

"Funny you should ask, darling. Only last month we were cleaning up in the shed, and there was an old suitcase that Frederico had never unpacked, even when he was with your mum. He thought it was prob-ably empty because it was so light. Turns out there was one large envelope in it containing photos. Give me a minute and I'll get them."

When Helen came back, she tipped the contents of the envelope onto the table in front of me and Freya, then returned to the kitchen to help Freddy.

I got up and knelt on the chair to better spread out the photographs, just as Freya's hand darted out and grabbed a photo.

Freya's face was a study in intensity. It was as though she was devouring the picture. Her hand shook slightly and I noticed a single tear run down her cheek.

"Freya?"

Freya didn't speak or move.

"Freya? What is it, sweetheart?"

Freya looked up, and I saw that her eyes were blurry. I moved across close to her and put my arm around her, and peered at the picture in her hand.

There was the young and smiling long-haired Frederico in his motorcycle leathers, holding a helmet and standing beside a big motorbike .

"Freya? What is happening?" I asked

Freya leant away to the side so that she could reach around me and gather up some more photographs.

Photographs from thirty years ago. Frederico stripping down and cleaning his motorbike; Frederico pulling up beside a petrol bowser on his motorbike; Frederico pushing his motorbike up a ramp onto a ferry; Frederico looking like a bikie, smiling sternly and confidently at the world; Frederico looking as though he knew things; Frederico as his own man.

Freya didn't speak but stood up and headed to the kitchen. Moments later she returned leading Freddy by the hand. They headed out the door and up the stairs.

Helen walked in and watched them go, then looked at Alice.

"Is Freya okay Alice?"

I picked up some of the photos Freya had been looking at and held them out for Helen to see.

"I think, Helen, our love has just turned a corner. Saved by Freddy's bikie past, I hope. I think Freya has a new image to imagine when she makes love."

"Wow! When she came into the kitchen and looked at Frederico, it was as though she was in a trance. She just looked at him and said, 'take me to bed please, Freddy'."

We were silent for a moment, then we went out hand-in-hand to the kitchen to clean up.

When we had finished and hung up the tea towels, we turned and embraced, and planted our lips firmly on each other's. My arms were around Helen's neck.

"I wonder if she will need us now? My guess is that she won't, but we should check on them in a little while."

We both wandered into the lounge and cuddled up together on the sofa.

We tiptoed into the bedroom, listening and looking into the gloom. There was silence. Then Frederico's voice said, "We've been waiting for you two. Get over here pronto."

We stood beside the bed, slowly adjusting our eyes to the low light. Two faces peered up at us, both wearing big smiles. Freya was the first to speak.

"I reckon I could handle a couple of small kisses from girls, but I'm pretty high on a bloke at the moment, so don't expect much."

Everyone laughed and Helen and I headed round to Freya's side of the bed, where we were each allowed one loving wet kiss each.

"What about me? Am I part of the celebration or not?"

But before we could get around to Freddy's side of the bed, Freya swung herself over him and in a very firm voice informed him:

"You're not kissing any other women for at least twenty-four hours. The only lips you will have anywhere near any part of your body will be mine. Is that clear?"

There was much laughter, and for Helen and me a wonderful feeling of relief.

"Congratulations both of you. We'll see you in the morning."

And as we headed for the door, Freya's voice came, unusually loud and clear.

"You might. Goodnight."

8

WET POTS EVERYWHERE

I HAD FORGOTTEN that Bertie had asked me to look after the person coming to measure up and mark the layout for the new ordered wet pots for his vegetable garden. Wet pots were the latest thing in garden drought management, porous slow-release terracotta urns that one buried in the garden and regularly filled with water.

After Bertie had left to catch the bus for his Saturday morning visit to Rosa in hospital, I quietly wandered about the house in my old summer frock, lazily enjoying my solitary time at home, while still revelling in the after effects of my weekly Morning Glory with Bertie.

When there was a knock on the door, I thought twice about answering but then I remembered Bertie's message and went to investigate.

A smiling, good looking young man stood on the door step, wearing a short sleeved jungle green shirt, khaki shorts, a sun hat and boots and carrying a pack on his back.

"Hello, I'm Robert Musgrave. I'm here about your wet pots. I just need to mark out the vegetable garden and count how many pots are required so that they can be put in later in the week.

"You must be Mr Bennett's tenant, Alice?"

"Yes, that is me, and hello Robert. Pleased to meet you."

"You too, Alice. Can you show me Mr Bennett's veggie patch please? It shouldn't take me long. Actually, if you would like to hold the end of the tape measure, it will speed up the whole process. But only if you have time Alice?"

Only this earnest young man with the disarming smile, could have gotten me out of the house at that moment, such was my drowsy happy-go-lucky state of mind. At this point, doing nothing was going to be my project for the day.

"Around this way Robert, and yes, I'll help you with the tape measure."

Robert followed me around to the back of the house. The pavement was hot under foot, but I was used to being shoeless in the garden. It was warm sunny Sydney day but with a soft sea breeze. I thought how this was a nice thing to do, and was pleased that I had answered the door.

"Wow! Mr Bennett does have a fine vegetable plot. Most of the gardens I visit are not a patch on this one."

"So let's start here Alice. If you could hang on to this end, I'll take the tape up this first row beside the path and put in the pegs."

Robert removed the haversack from his shoulder and took out a handful of bamboo sticks. Then he ran the tape out to the other end of the veggie patch and then, crawling on his hands and knees, headed back towards me, placing sticks in the ground at set intervals.

It was nice sitting in the sun and the breeze just watching Robert at work. He had just run the tape out on the fifth and last line, and we were close to finishing.

"Would you like to push a few sticks in Alice? Just pop them in every thirty inches. Simple!"

He'd walked back to where I sat and squatted on his haunch's. I noticed what seemed like some sort of longish lump running along under one leg of his shorts, and surmised that it must be either an essential tool of the professional wet potterer in a hidden long pocket, or maybe, could it be Robert's very own personal tool? I looked back up to Robert's face.

"Yes, Robert. That would be fun. Every thirty inches you said?"

"That's right, if your an inch or two out it won't matter. Off you go."

I set off slowly along the line, on my hands and knees.

Being so close to the warm soft soil felt beautiful. I would stop and sit and reach forward and place a couple of sticks and then swing over onto my knees and move along a bit further.

I hadn't noticed that the breeze had increased until I noticed that my frock had blown up over my back, exposing my rear end. I had also forgotten that I answered the door minus my undies.

Totally unaware, I moved along the row in the strong breeze with my frock blowing haphazardly about. I was also unaware that Robert was following close behind me, rolling up his tape measure.

When I got to the end of the row, I turned and sat down and looked back to admire my workmanship.

I was surprised to see Robert so close behind me, but then I realised that we had finished the last row, and he would now pack up and head off. But there was another much bigger surprise.

Robert's face had turned a darker shade of red, not the sunburnt shade he was when I last looked at him. He was looking at me in a funny way. And then I saw why. That longish lump in his shorts had grown much longer.

There was in fact, something rather interesting peeping out of the leg of Robert's shorts. At first it startled me, then, as I reflected, I remembered the breeze blowing my frock about and saw that my very naked bottom, not to mention all the rest of me, had been subject to Robert's gaze.

I experienced a sudden rush to the head. I had already enjoyed my Saturday morning session with Bertie and I was still a little wet from that. But I realised that, whether it was the laziness of a Saturday morning, or the delicious feeling of my pussy, I still had the capacity for another adventure.

Robert saw me looking at his shorts.

"Do you have time for a cup of tea Robert? We've got some very nice biscuits."

When I led Robert to the sofa and sat him down, he gently reached up and put his arm around my neck and pulled my face to his and we kissed.

I decided things would need to move quickly before Bertie returned home. I reached down and slid my hand up into the leg of Robert's shorts, and wrapped my fingers around his large cock, and not to be outdone, he slid his hand up my leg and gently palmed my pussy.

Our short time together before Bertie arrived home was pleasurable to say the least. Just the thrill of having the surprise of a new cock in my already well loved pussy was exciting and I loved it, and Robert said he did too.

So it wasn't a surprise when Robert asked if he could see me again.

Robert lived at home with his mother Samantha, and younger sister, Megan.

He said he had tried leaving home once but it hadn't worked out, and when I enquired why not, he said that his mother was not happy with his accomodation nor the people he shared with, and made him return home.

It seemed, from what Robert said in conversation, that none of his relationships had lasted. He joked about it and said that perhaps he just hadn't been good enough.

I thought that was interesting. Robert often spoke affectionately of his mother and I couldn't help being reminded of those anecdotal stories about the problems some newly married women or female partners, experienced with their man's mother.

That old saying came to mind. 'A daughter is a daughter for life, but a son is a son until he takes a wife', and could see how easy it might be for there to be friction between the two women, each one vying for his affections. Having a strong dominant mother, it would seem, could be a real problem.

It was only a week after we got together when Robert asked me home to meet his family.

I thought it was all a bit soon really, but in a new relationship one sometimes agrees to things that one might think twice about later on.

Late one afternoon I found myself in the Musgrave's lounge, sitting beside Robert, with Samantha eyeing me from the chair opposite.

"What a beautiful girl you are, Alice. It is so nice that Robert has found you. He doesn't have a good track record of bringing home nice girls."

I wondered what she meant. Did Robert bring a lot of girls home, I wondered?

After we'd had a cup of tea and a biscuit, Samantha suggested that Robert show me the house.

"It's much bigger than we need really, but we do love it so, don't we Robert?"

Robert and I wandered off down a passageway and into an ante room where a wide staircase led up to a suite of rooms. He took my hand and led me up the stairs, and we wandered the full length of a wide passageway with numerous doorways.

"Have the family been here a long time Robert? I asked."

"I was born here, actually. My grand father had it built back in the late thirties, just prior to the second world war. He was in hardware and builders supplies."

Robert led me into different rooms, one was a study with book-shelves lining the walls, others were bedrooms, both large and small.

Robert seemed to suddenly become affectionate and I responded as I thought he would have liked. Wandering and exploring all of these rooms was quite exciting, and I felt like a child looking for secrets places, and having adventures along the way.

We walked into another bedroom. The curtains were partly pulled across and in the dim light, I saw a large bed, in fact it was unusually large compared to those we had seen in the other rooms.

Robert put his arm around me and drew me closer. He ran his hand down over my rear, and down my thigh.

"I love this room. Let's make love here Alice."

He was already reaching around to the front and beginning to lift my dress. I put my hand on his trousers and felt a lump that signalled Robert was quite serious in his intent.

"Yes, Robert, I'd like that."

He led me to the bed and I slipped off my dress and dropped my undies to the floor, and kicked off my heels. Then I turned to Robert and helped him remove his trousers and pants. He sat on the bed and began taking of his shoes while I, having nothing else to do, put his now rigid cock in my mouth.

We were soon on the bed and I reasoned that we should be quick, before his mother started to worry and came looking for us. Robert probably thought the same thing, and he took no time at all to slip his member in.

It was convenient that I was able to get wet so quickly at moments like this.

We were soon happily smiling at one another as Robert shagged me, and I closed my eyes and thought what I nice thing this was to do and how good it was that Robert had suggested it. Then, out of thin air as it were, I heard a woman's voice.

"Move over Bobby darling. Mummy's here to help"

I opened my eyes and looked up. Above Robert's face was the face of Samantha, and as I moved my eyes down, I saw a pair of giant naked breasts, wide hips and, oh my god, a large dildo fixed around a waist.

I felt Robert leave. Then Samantha swung her leg over me and pushed something against my vagina and I felt lubricant being squeezed up into me. Then she pinned my arms to the bed with her strong hands and huge weighty body.

I stared up at this sixty something years women, with her strong heavily made-up face, lit up with lustful excitement. Her newly applied bright red lipstick shone and her tongue slid in and out between her lips.

"Now sweetie, mummy's come to help her little boy do nice things to his girl friend. You just have to lay still, and everything will be all right."

I was in turmoil. What was she going to do? What was this all about? More importantly, how should I be responding at this moment.

Suddenly Samantha launched the dildo into my heavily lubricated vagina, pushing it in hard, and far up into me. I hadn't known that these things could go in that far. It was truly amazing. Then she settled into a regular shagging motion, her brow lined in concentration.

I tried again to assess the situation, calling on my university psychology reading. Would what was happening to me come under the heading of Aberrant Behaviour? Was I part of the fantasy of members of a Dysfunctional Family? Did the mother suffer from a Multiple Personality Disorder?

I came to the decision that, one: I was probably not in immediate danger, and two: that things could have worked out a lot worse, and, however crazy Roberts mother was, she was not to be feared.

Then I heard a whisper in my left ear.

"She loves it if you scream or shout. It makes her feel more potent."

I turned my head. Megan's face was close up to mine and I experienced another 'Oh my God' moment.

The girl was perfectly naked except that she also had a strap-on affixed around her waist.

Megan was very pale and very thin and her breasts seemed under developed. I estimated that the young woman was probably in her late teens or early twenties but given her less than robust appearance she could well have been older. It crossed my mind that perhaps I was looking at the after affects of child abuse.

I now decided that I would be safer if I joined in this fantasy. I would be whatever was required of me. And in response to Megan's advice, I screamed, and yelled.

"Harder Samantha, harder, push it right in. Give it to me, please!"

Samantha's face lit up and her tongue came out and hung over her bottom lip.

"You are a feisty little bitch, Alice. I like that very much. Tell mummy how much you like her fucking your little pussy. Go on!"

Under different circumstances, this could be fun, I thought.

Cathartic maybe. Meanwhile, for safety's sake, I continued with the charade.

Samantha's giant pendulous breasts swung from side to side in front of my face with her nipples sometimes twitching my nose.

"I love mummy fucking my little pussy. Oh yes, please don't stop mummy."

I added a couple of tinny squeals for good measure. Samantha laughed, and told me that she would like her little Bobby to bring me home on a regular basis. I played along with the idea.

"Oh yes mummy, I would love you to do this to me, all the time."

Samantha licked her lips and dribbled on my face. Then she remembered Robert.

"Bobby darling, where are you? You should be in mummies special spot that she keeps just for you. Chop! Chop! In you get. Give it all to mummy like you always do."

I took that opportunity to whisper to Megan.

"Who do you get to shag Megan? Me, I suppose?"

"No, Alice. She only lets me do her. She says I don't deserve any of the girls my brother brings home. I'll get into her in a minute when she tells me to.

I was appalled that a mother could deny her daughter pleasure, even if this whole scenario was extreme and weird and over the top.

I smiled at Megan.

"Megan? It would be an honour to have you as my friend. I'm going to leave my phone number for you. Just tell me where to leave it."

Megan's eyes lit up.

"Oh, Alice, you are so beautiful."

Megan's pretty, but sad face screwed up for a moment, while she thought my proposition through.

"There is an upside down plant pot in the long grass below the letterbox. Leave it there Alice. Oh Alice, you make me feel so good."

"Oh, and Megan? Have you ever been with a man?"

"Yes, but I shot him dead when I was thirteen."

I was speechless. Never in a million years would I have thought this gentle young woman could have been violent. There must have been an extraordinarily good reason for it.

I was being called and I turned back to look at Samantha.

"Alice! Stop mumbling to my stupid daughter."

Samantha had slowed down a little bit. No doubt she was concentrating more on Robert's rear end action. She stopped looking at me, and lifted her head.

"Yes, darling, yes! Give it to mummy. Don't waste it Bobby. Nobody needs it as much as mummy does darling. Give it me! Oh yes Bobby, yes!"

"What happens now," I whispered to Megan.

"When he pops and leaves, I take his place. She loves this dildo and demands I do her with it a least once a day when there is nothing else going on, which is most days. Although, she does go into Roberts room early in the morning to suck him off and make him suck her breasts."

Wow! This must be a case study that I, or any of my fellow student could write up for a university post grad submission.

I felt Samantha starting to withdraw. Just as well, I thought. Despite all the lube, the sides of my fanny were starting to burn.

"Thank you mummy."

"Glad you enjoyed it, darling.

"Megan? Get up here quickly."

Samantha really was a bitch, no matter what disorder she was living with.

I wasn't particularly concerned about Robert. He was capable of making proper decisions if he put his mind to it.

It was little Megan who worried me.

Now that I had an inkling as to why Megan was so thin and looked so anaemic, I knew I had to do something. I made a vow, there and then, that I would help her, somehow and sometime. Just how, I hadn't quite figured.

"Megan! Come along girl. Get it in me. Mummy's desperate."

Robert came around to see me. He kissed me and I looked at him without showing any emotion. I was done with him and his mother. Fun maybe, but no, not a good space to be in.

"All good with you Alice? I heard you enjoying yourself. We must do it again soon. Hope my nutty sister didn't interrupt your pleasure."

Oh, if only you knew Robert, I thought. And I doubt you ever will. Dear Bobby, you or your bizarre mother, will never clap eyes on me again.

9

THE NEIGHBOURS

IT WAS ONLY a few weeks after Helen had played Good Samaritan and handed keys to the potting shed to Mary so that she and Charlie could meet to make love in secret, that Helen, passing the potting shed on her way to her studio, heard a muffled sound coming from within. It didn't sound like a couple making love; rather more like someone sobbing.

Helen stopped and wondered if she should investigate. If there was something going on between lovers, that was their affair, and she should not interfere. But she could hear only one person, and decided to knock and enter.

"Mary? Are you all right, darling?"

She heard Mary blow her nose and then, a few moments later, call out for her to come in.

Mary sat looking gorgeous as only she could, her weight pushing out her stockings, her dress and blouse in Rubenesque splendour, and everything designed to precariously balance on her strappy high heels.

"Darling Mary? What is wrong? Tell me?"

Mary said nothing, but simply passed her phone to Helen. Helen read the message:

So sorry my darling, Hilda has found out and is fearful of a scandal. We are already on a plane heading for an extended holiday on a cruise ship in Europe. She has arranged for number nineteen to be sold immediately we get back. Will be in touch. Much love, Charlie.

"Oh, Mary, you poor darling."

I sat on the bed beside her and wrapped my arms around the large lady. I could feel her shaking with emotion.

We must have sat like that for a good half hour, until Mary could cry no more.

Suddenly she gave a short little laugh.

"Well, Charlie gets a holiday in Europe out of it."

I giggled in response.

"But Mary, that is not what Charlie really wants. He wants to be here in your arms."

That opened the floodgates again.

When Mary had once again become silent, we just sat. Then I adjusted us both to be more comfortable and we lounged back against the pillows stacked against the wall behind us.

"I will especially miss the kissing," Mary squeaked.

After a few minutes of silence, I spoke.

"I think we could possible fix that. Well, sort of."

"What do you mean, Helen?"

I had one arm around her neck and my other arm and hand rested on her large thigh. Then I gently turned the hand over and began to rub her thigh through her skirt.

I drew Mary's head towards mine, and, lifting my hand from her thigh, I turned her face towards me. Mary's still wet eyes focused on my face and I smiled lovingly at her. Then I put my lips on hers, knowing that this could be a terrible mistake.

I left my lips on hers. She didn't immediately respond, but at least she hadn't pulled away.

I was ready to retreat and remove my lips, when suddenly Mary pushed back at me with her mouth, gently. I waited a moment, wanting to give her some space. Then she pushed at me harder.

I put my hand behind her head and pulled it slowly towards me while increasing the pressure on her lips. Then I took a risk and pushed my tongue into her mouth, just a tiny distance, and moved it slowly, side to side.

All of her body shook and as it subsided, I realised that Mary was experiencing a huge emotional release. But there must still have been some tension remaining. I could feel her looking for something, something more, looking for what I might do next.

I decided to take another risk.

I unbuttoned my blouse. I was without a bra and I felt the cool air on my breasts. I picked up Mary's right hand and slowly placed it inside my blouse and waited.

I felt Mary shaking and gasping as she hurriedly moved her hand around, feeling my skin and discovering a nipple. And while she was doing that, she picked up my spare hand and placed it against the exposed skin of her large bosom, and I gratefully slid my hand down inside her top. I too found a nipple and I too, gasped and sighed.

Then Mary began to moan and moved her mouth around on mine, and we both tongued each other.

"I want to help you get through this, Mary my darling. Please let me make love to you?"

I only had to wait a second or two before she answered.

"Oh yes, Helen, please, please make love to me. This all feels so wonderful, so right. Do whatever you want to me, Helen. Anything!"

I held her tight. Then I asked her to follow me to my studio just a few metres away, where we would be much more comfortable.

We stood up and moved to the studio.

We lay down on the big bed and made ourselves comfortable. Mary was desperate to keep kissing me and pawed at me to get to my lips. And when I let her, and our mouths were again fastened together, and we had each resumed our nipple play, I slowly moved my hand down to her crotch and lightly fingered her through her skirt.

"Oh Helen, this is heavenly," Mary whispered.

She reached down and drew up her skirt, then she took my hand and pushed it down into her knickers, placing it atop her huge pouting hairy pussy. We both gave an excited cry.

"Oh yes, Mary! That feels so good. Thank you, my darling."

"Helen, it belongs to you now. Your fingers feel wonderful. Do anything, darling. Whatever you want, and I will love and cherish you for it always."

I lifted my head and gazed down on Mary's enormous stockinged thighs and legs. Her suspenders rolled down and over her fleshy upper thigh, on their way to her stocking tops.

I knew what I wanted next. It was something that my true love, Alice and I shared a lust for: seeing a woman's stockinged legs and shoes waving in the air.

Holding Mary's legs up in the air and looking at them, while I shafted her with the big strap-on, hidden beneath the bed, would be so wonderful and sexy. And I believed Mary would enjoy it too.

As we kissed and I slowly rotated my hand on Mary's pussy, I reached down and brought out the strap-on from beneath the bed. I did not want to frighten her with it, so I knew she had to see it first.

"Mary darling, I've got a special thing that Frederico and I play with sometimes if he's feeling a little flat and I need his attention. Would you like to see it?"

Mary looked at me quizzically.

"What is it, Helen? Can you show me?"

I put the dildo slowly up to my mouth, watching her as I did so. Her eyes were suddenly wide open.

"Oh Helen, it's a giant cock."

I put out my tongue and started licking it, then I put the end into my mouth and as I did so, I lowered myself towards her mouth. I took it from my mouth and placed it next to hers.

"Lick if for me, darling."

Still looking amazed, Mary did not hesitate, quickly pushing out her tongue to touch it. I slowly rotated it and then gently pushed it between her lips. Almost in a trance, Mary opened her mouth and moved it forward, over the end of the dildo. I rocked it slowly backwards and forwards in her mouth, then I put her hand on it and asked her to hold it for me for a moment while I removed her knickers. Mary lifted herself so that I could more easily slide them off.

Then I took the dildo back and she watched, fascinated, as I buckled up the band around my waist.

"Helen? Will this feel like a real cock?"

I squeezed some lubricant into her vagina hidden amidst a jungle of curly hair. Then I placed the dildo against her and moved it slowly in, watching as I did so the magic of her vagina opening up to receive me. It was a beautiful sight.

"Is that okay, Mary? It's not uncomfortable in any way? Say if it is and I will stop immediately."

Mary's eyes were closed and her mouth was wide open. I heard a moaning sound, then suddenly Mary thrust herself up towards me and screamed "Yes, yes, oh Helen, yes!"

Mary had a new special friend, and I had a new lady-love.

I gave Mary a slow but serious shagging with the dildo and we both loved it. I would sometimes stop, but then the lower part of her body would thrust upwards and she would call out "More please Helen, more!"

Now I was ready. I wrapped a hand around each of her ankles, just above her bright blue high heels and lifted up her legs, speaking as I did so.

"Mary?"

"Yes, Helen?"

"Just so that you know. Having your beautiful stockinged legs and your shoes waving in the air in front of me fulfils a fantasy for me that cannot be beaten. If you ever feel that I'm not showing you enough attention, Mary, just say, 'I want my legs in the air please' and I will be your sex slave in seconds."

Mary giggled.

"Oh Helen. Everything about you is so beautiful. You shouldn't have told me that. I'll be texting you every day with that message. I will exhaust you."

We both laughed, then Mary went into a serious panting and groaning mode as I set about finishing off her first strap-on shagging, and with an orgasm that made her cry with happiness.

When we had finished and it was time for Mary to return home, she threw her arms about me and declared her love for me. Then as she was about to leave, she asked:

"Where can I get one of those, Helen? Just in case something was ever to happen to you."

We laughed and I promised to take her on a special shopping spree soon.

"There is another world out there Mary, and it is waiting for you."

Frederico became very excited in bed that night when I told him what had happened between Mary and me in the studio that day.

"Christ! I might get a go at her beautiful backside after all."

"Not so fast, sunshine. I have noticed that my rear has not received any attention from my beloved husband in quite a while. You are therefore banned from any bottoms other than mine, until I give you permission. In any case, I doubt if Mary has ever heard of anal sex."

Frederico chuckled and rolled me over on my tummy and licked my pussy and up between my buttocks.

"How could I have forgotten your beautiful butt, darling? It's your best asset."

I rolled back and whacked him over the head, then we rolled about laughing and I let Frederico have me doggy fashion, his favourite, while I ran images through my mind's eye of my three beautiful lady loves' legs reaching up into the air.

Domestic bliss, with extras.

The day after Mary and I had made love, I received a call from her telling me that Harold had been taken to hospital from the golf club after suffering a severe heart attack. He had died later that night.

Mary didn't sound particularly distraught. I was ready to rush over, then I figured that a lot had happened to her in a very short time, and she needed a quiet spell to digest it all.

"Mary? You must call me or just come over if you need to. Promise you will call?"

"Yes, Helen. Thank you. Love you."

I went and found Freddy and told him the news.

"I always knew that golf was bad for you," he quipped.

"She knows we're here for her, doesn't she darling?"

"Yes, sweetheart. She has promised to phone or come over if she needs us or wants company."

I hugged Frederico. I wonder if he knows how much I love him, I thought.

One afternoon, a couple of days after Mary called to tell me about Harold, she rang and asked if she could visit. I suggested she come for dinner and she said she had a niece visiting from the country and could she bring her along. I told her that would be fine.

Freddy answered the doorbell and I heard him offering Mary his commiserations. Then he ushered Mary and her niece into the dining room, where I was just finishing laying the table.

"Darling, Mary is here with her niece, Sophie. Sophie, this is Helen."

"Pleased to meet you, Helen. Auntie has talked about you a lot," said the young woman, staring intently at me with her very bright eyes.

I almost blushed. What had Mary said? I wondered. Sophie looked like what you might expect a young country girl to look like. Quite tall, fresh-faced and with a slightly naive or innocent expression permanently displayed. She was dressed modestly, with dark trousers and jacket and a simple button-up blouse, and she wore a pair of very sensible shoes.

"Lovely to meet you, Sophie. A sad time no doubt, but I'm sure Mary welcomes an opportunity to see you. You are from way up north, I believe. I hope you will be here for a while, so we get a chance to get to know you."

"Well, Auntie and I are still talking things through. She feels it could be time for me to leave the farm and spend time in the big city, and she's offered me accommodation if I choose to move down here."

"But do you think it's time to leave home Sophie? Don't let Mary talk you into it if it isn't what you want."

"Well, moving out is what I want, so Auntie doesn't really have to do much to persuade me. Being able to live at her house will make everything much easier."

I excused myself to go to the kitchen and check dinner and left Frederico to play host. When I returned, Freddy and Sophie were looking through the DVD's, hoping to find something that Mary would like to relax her after a gruelling week dealing with undertakers and funeral preparations.

I went over to Mary.

"Hello, darling. So good to see you."

"Thank you Helen. I've missed you."

"Sophie seems lovely. How old is she?"

"She turned twenty-two in July just gone. I think her moving to my place would be wonderful, don't you? She doesn't have a boyfriend where she lives, and there are very few young people left on the surrounding farms. I was surprised she was so happy to talk to you. She is usually very shy and rarely talks to people. Maybe having you and Frederico next door will be good for her. You do have a talent for relaxing people, I've noticed."

We both laughed at the innuendo in Mary's statement.

"Dearest Mary, are you OK? It must have been a shock."

"Better than I would have expected, darling. It is strange, and I can only say this to you, but the loss of Harold has been liberating. Already I'm feeling relaxed, knowing that I can do anything I want to, and when I want, and not be answerable to anyone."

I leant forward and kissed her lightly on the lips.

"Well, Mary, it is so good that you see it that way. I wonder what your new liberated life will bring and where it will take you? And of course, they say that good things come in threes. Hmm! Look out, girl! Don't go leaving me for a new hot love just yet. I'm not ready for that."

We both laughed, and I headed off to the kitchen.

"Frederico, will you be able to help me serve dinner, please?"

"Yes, darling, I'll be there in seconds."

On the following Monday, Mary phoned and said things were a bit hectic and she wouldn't be able to meet me the next day as planned.

Then she added that, because she wouldn't be able to make it and she didn't want me to be lonely, she was sending me a present and when I enquired what it was she told me that Sophie said she would happily stand in for her and that she had given her the new key, the one I had just given her for the studio.

I was taken aback a bit, and expressed my surprise and asked Mary what Sophie knew. She said she had told Sophie enough to get her excited. 'The rest is up to you, darling. I honestly want you both to have fun. She needs it, and you, darling Helen, in appreciation of your loving gift of liberation, deserve it."

I laughed and thanked her, reminding her that it was looking even more urgent that we go shopping, and for her to get that special thing, and to keep Friday free to do it if she could.

She laughed and said she would.

I was a little on edge as I walked to my studio. I really hadn't had time to get to know Sophie. I knew she was a very capable farm girl with no boyfriend, and that there were very few young people her age in the region. I also knew that she had a certain look which I liked, and that underneath her trouser pants I suspected she had a nice pair of legs.

I tapped on the studio door to let her know I was there, and went in.

Sophie stood tall on a pair of high heels that she had gone shopping for with Mary the day before. Her stockings were a delightful smoky grey and she wore a shortish but conservative pleated skirt and a blouse buttoned to a frilly lace collar. Her face still wore that naive expression that I noticed when first we met, but there was something else going on suggesting a not-so-innocent state of mind.

"Hello Sophie, and welcome."

Before I could say another word, Sophie crossed the room and threw her arms around me and fastened her mouth on mine. I slipped my arms around her and pushed back on her lips; then her mouth opened and she put out her tongue and explored my now open mouth. We stood like that for a few minutes, then I slid my hand down her back and lightly felt her backside.

We eventually separated our mouths and Sophie smiled.

"Auntie said it would be best if I kissed you straight away, then I wouldn't be so nervous."

I laughed and turned her towards the bed, and we sat down.

"Dearest Mary! Did her advice work, Sophie? You're no longer nervous, I hope?"

"Yes, Helen, I feel relaxed with you now. Do you like my shoes?"

"Good! Yes, I love your shoes. I do have a bit of a shoe and foot fetish. Now Sophie, can I please do something, so that I won't feel nervous?"

Sophie looked at me with eyes shining.

"Anything!" she whispered.

I slowly unbuttoned my blouse right the way down and pulled it open, then I took Sophie's hand and drew it over my bosom and rubbed her fingers lightly on my bare breast.

"Please find a nipple, Sophie, and lick it."

Her face was a picture of surprise, delight and then lust. She put up her other hand and moved her face to my breasts, and within moments was nipping and tugging me with both hands and her teeth.

"Oh, you darling girl. You've made me feel less nervous already," I whispered soothingly.

Sophie moved back and stared into my eyes.

"That's good, Helen. Can I keep playing with you breasts, or would you like me to do something else?"

"In a little while Sophie, you know that I will want to shag you. I'm about to take off your skirt, beautiful girl. I can't wait any longer."

Sophie whimpered and shook as she absorbed what I was saying.

Her long legs swung wide apart and she stretched out, then she pushed her legs out more and pointed and rotated her elegant feet and footwear.

Immediately, I pulled up the hem of her skirt and looked at her.

Sophie's legs were indeed long and beautiful. Her grey elasticised stockings clasped the top of her legs, and above her stockings I saw that she had left her knicker off, probably on Mary's advice, and I stared at the mass of small shiny black curls all around her vagina and up and over her *mons veneris*.

"You are beautiful, Sophie," I murmured, lifting my head and kissing her lips. And when I put my hand out and touched her, lightly running my fingers up her stockings and between her legs, she let out a girly squeal of delight.

"Oh yes, Helen, please touch me! Touch me! Oh yes, Helen! Do anything you like. Anything! Please!"

I reached around and unzipped her skirt, then dragged it roughly down over her legs. Then I dropped onto my knees, put a hand around each ankle and lifted her legs and dragged her closer to the edge of the bed. Then I buried my mouth into that mass of curls in search of her lips and her clitoris, and when I found her surprisingly large soft happy cherry thing, I sucked it and felt her shaking body and her crying, and knew that she was mine.

After a while, I sat up. Sophie stared at me and smiled, then her lips made puckering motions, wanting to be kissed, and her tongue disappeared into my mouth. Sophie would not let my head go, and we kissed and tongued until we both ran out of breath.

"Helen darling?"

"Yes, Sophie?"

'Take off your clothes for me, please Helen. I so want to see you.

"Yes, darling, I will, and I love it that you ask for the things you want."

As Sophie watched, I slipped my frock off over my head, leaving me in my suspenders and stockings, and shoes.

Sophie stared at me, appreciation showing on her face.

"My God, Helen, you are so beautiful."

"Thank you darling. I do love complements," I giggled.

I got up on the bed and straddled Sophie, and backed up to her face. Her hands grabbed me by the hips and in moments she was ravishing my pussy with her mouth. I shuddered and felt my vagina getting extremely wet.

Then I lay down on Sophie so that I could reach her pussy, and we quietly licked and sucked each other for a long time, sometimes having little orgasms along the way, and occasionally Sophie would squeal and shout my name or just a "Yes," or "More please."

Then I turned and went to her, and we put our arms around each other and kissed, and then kissed some more. And then we rested.

I asked Sophie to close her eyes, then I stretched my arm down, felt under the bed and retrieved the strap-on dildo. Then I held it close to her face and told her she could open her eyes and look at the present I had for her. She was at first shocked and then very impressed with it.

"I wish Adele could see this," Sophie laughed.

"Is Adele your girlfriend back home?" I ventured to ask.

"Was, sort of. She lives on a farm about half an hour's drive away. I used to take the ute and go and see her once a month when her folks were away at the big market. Adele never goes to town to the market. She's a big girl, fat I suppose you'd say, and not very good-looking and she can't stand people looking at her. She thinks the whole world is laughing at her."

"That is really sad, Sophie. Surely there is a man for her somewhere?"

"I reckon not. She's never gonna change. It is sad."

"You live a long way from everything too, don't you? You must both get very lonely. Have you ever thought of being lovers?"

Sophie rolled over and looked at me, then leant closer and kissed me.

"Almost, I suppose. I let her lick me a couple of times, a year or so ago, and I gave her pussy an occasional rub and she did the same to me. But we stopped doing it."

I was intrigued. This was an insight into the extremely lonely life of isolated Australian bush communities. These were young women

who lived without access to other people, to anyone with whom they
might find love.

"Oh, Sophie. I can't bear to think of someone like you living
without love. Did the two of you ever talk about what you might do to
change things?"

"Sadly, not. Adele has just given up on life. I guess if she lived in
the city she'd probably be a drug addict. As it is, she's addicted to
Kenny."

"Kenny? I thought you said there were no males around?"

Sophie laughed.

"Sorry Helen, Kenny is Adele's dog. A Golden Retriever. She
spends all her time bathing it combing it and kissing it. She lets ..."

"She lets Kenny what?"

"She gets Kenny to do her."

"I'm sorry, sweetheart, I didn't get what you said?"

"Adele gets Kenny to shag her. She loves it. And Kenny doesn't
seem to mind."

I turned and got up on my elbow.

"Sophie! You are not making sense, darling. People don't fuck their
dogs. You're spinning me a yarn and I'm not happy with this story."

"Gee Helen. I am so sorry. What I'm telling you is true though. I've
seen them do it. Adele invited me out to a little room behind the barn
that she's decorated and it includes a low bed. I thought she was just
going to show me her room, but it was more than that. I saw it all
happen there. Then she wanted to share Kenny with me. That's when
I stopped visiting her."

I was not handling this information very well. Bizarre acts
between people I could sort of handle, but sex with animals? That was
too difficult.

"Sophie! I think this conversation is doing my head in. We better
stop it. Tell me a happy story, please."

There was silence for quite a while. In the end, I thought I'd
spoken a bit harshly to Sophie, so I moved closer to her and held her
hand.

"Sorry, Sophie. I hate to think of you in such unloving circumstances. I just want you to be here with me and Mary, safe, and feeling loved.

"And I want you to tell me you will stay and live here next door to me. And one other thing, wrap that bloody strap-on around your waist and make love to me, please. And kiss me, Sophie. I want your lips right now."

Sophie took a sharp inward breath and moved swiftly, first with a long loving kiss, then she kissed my clit, and then she worked out how to put on the strap-on.

I directed her to the bottle of lubricant and she gingerly wiped some on me. Then she held and inspected her new piece of equipment, laughingly pointing out that she was a "dildo virgin", and hoped I would be gentle with her.

We both laughed and I pulled her head back down and kissed her again.

"I have loved the short time we've had together, Helen. Thought I should say that right now, just in case I get it all wrong and you throw me out in the next few minutes."

"Darling Sophie! All you need do is slide it in. What you do then does not much matter, just so long as you do it with love. Even if you get a little carried away, I will know that you still love me. Pop it in, darling."

Being shagged by my loving new novice was wonderful. I asked her to hold my legs up straight so that I could look at them and include them in my "legs to the sky" fantasy. She did that and said how super cool it was, and that she had never ever been this excited about anything. And then she kissed me behind the knees and touched my feet, and kissed and licked my thighs above my stocking tops.

She was a natural with the dildo, not too hot, not too cold, but just right. And I could see that she loved doing it to me. Sophie's face was alive and happy, reaching around my back to pull my buttocks up towards her. And when I came suddenly, she screamed and came with me, and suddenly Sophie was laughing and crying at the same time.

Then I unbuckled her and attached the magic rubber cock around my waist. Then I turned her over and made her get on her knees, lubricated her and whispered, "This is your reward for giving me such a wonderful shagging."

She screamed in a mixture of anticipation and fear, as I inserted it. I didn't really know what life experience's she'd had and I wondered if the dildo was too big. But it slid in easily and she straight-away settled down to a regular rhythm and was soon calling out words of endearment and encouragement as we went.

I rolled her over so that I could lift her legs up and satisfy my visual lust. She moaned as I lifted them and moaned again when I told her to open her eyes and see how beautiful she looked and how she had the most beautiful legs in the world.

"Oh Helen, I so love what you are doing to me. Please keep going."

I lay between Sophie's legs and shagged the beautiful girl some more, unable to stop myself. But when I slowed, thinking it might be time to stop, she announced in a clear but quiet voice that she would like "some more, please". And when I suddenly began to thrash about and pushing right up into her to test her limits, she screamed out "Yes, Helen, yes, Helen, please Helen, keep doing it to me, Helen!" before she screamed a final "Yes", and exploded in an almighty orgasm which echoed through her body, and mine, for the next five minutes.

We fell into each other's arms and I covered us with the quilt.

"Helen?"

"Yes, my darling?"

"I will definitely stay and live with Auntie. I'm in love with you."

We pulled each other close and kissed; then exhausted, we fell asleep.

10

ROSA'S REQUEST

THE PAST COUPLE of weeks had been very busy for Alice, both at university and in her home life, but she felt surprisingly fit and healthy.

She had done very well at mid-term exams, her love life, not counting the bizarre episode with Robert and his mother, was wonderfully fulfilling and a source of great happiness.

Freya came and stayed on Sunday nights, and of course they saw each other most days when they had lunch together at uni.

Alice's new lady love, her stepmother Helen, came over on Wednesday afternoons and they relaxed and enjoyed each other for hours.

And then there was Freddy, Alice's stepfather, now also a lover. They had only managed to be together on the night of Alice's birthday party, but she was comfortable in the knowledge that Helen would make certain that Alice would enjoy him again.

And there were Alice's visits to Rosa Bennett, Helen's life-long older friend, now in hospital when, more often than not, Alice would subtly encourage Rosa to put her hand up her skirt and touch her. It was only a tiny moment, but they would enjoy kissing and banter, and talk and laugh about what Rosa was going to do to Alice, when she eventually came home from the hospital.

Then there was Bertie, dear gorgeous silver-haired Mr Bennett, giving Alice that wonderful Saturday morning Morning Glory moment. She had never missed having it since they began shortly after Rosa moved into care.

Not only that, Alice was now the keeper of Rosa's secret codes, which harnessed Bertie's amazing sexual potency so that anyone who knew the code could enjoy his loving attention.

Rosa had warned Alice to be careful, that enjoying her husband could become addictive, and if Alice had any concerns it was indeed that deep-down feeling that less and less could she do without Bertie on Saturday mornings and more recently, the newly discovered delights provided via Rosa's Fifi codes.

Only the day before, Alice had discovered that the hot water in her flat was not working, so she hurried over to the house clothed in just a bath towel to use the bathroom in the hallway, just one door down from Bertie and Rosa's bedroom.

Alice had just finished and was leaving, but when she hurriedly burst through the bathroom door, she ran slap bang into Bertie's arms. Her towel dropped to the floor and as Bertie caught her he laughed and stared at her breasts.

"Oh, Alice. You know how much I love your breasts. I know I never see them without commenting. Sorry, sweetheart, I'll try not to in future."

Alice took a deep breath and stared up at him. Her sudden rush to get to university was forgotten.

"Think nothing of it, Mr Bennett. I happen to like you liking and commenting on my breasts. Gives me a sort of buzz."

Whether it was the residual carry-over from a heavy week of love-making, or simply being naked in Bertie's arms, Alice felt a sudden wetness in her vagina.

She didn't want to let go of Bertie and he made no attempt to let her go, preferring to hold her and look down at her bare top.

Alice decided that she wanted Mr Bennett there and then, while she was totally naked and in his arms. Before she could stop herself she was saying the words uppermost in her mind.

"Fifi wants it doggy style, please."

Having mouthed the words out loud, Alice slid dreamily to the floor and knelt down, her knees apart and her completely naked rear in the air. She turned her head to one side and peered up at Bertie.

Bertie was wearing only his pyjamas. He untied the chord and his pants dropped to the floor. Alice watched as his giant cock slowly lifted its head, then Bertie knelt down behind her, spat on his hand and wetted her pussy, then put his cock against the wet vagina. It trembled and, as so often happened recently, her cunt opened and sucked him in. All thoughts of her getting to university vanished as anticipation turned into the reality of Bertie's beautiful cock filling her cunt with happiness.

Bertie went into a serious shagging mode and after only a few minutes, Alice's body convulsed and she screamed.

"Oh yes, Mr B. Thank you Mr Bennett, you darling man."

Then Alice reached back and gently pulled Bertie's big cock out of her and she jumped up.

She bent down and licked her stanchion of pleasure, and then lifted her now radiant face to Bertie's and kissed him.

"Thank you so much, Mr Bennett. Love you lots. Gotta rush."

Alice and Helen didn't see each other on the previous Wednesday. The husband of Helen's neighbour Mary died suddenly of a heart attack and Helen decided that she should stay at home to be there for Mary if she was needed.

When Helen arrived at Alice's house, both women were delighted to see each other. Alice playfully pushed Helen against the kitchen wall, and rubbed herself against her really hard while the two kissed passionately. Then she took her by the hand and led her through the garden to her flat.

We have already noted elsewhere how Helen's and Alice's pleasuring habits were so similar. They could pleasure each other while having conversations about anything, erotic or mundane, and in recent times both seemed capable of having regular orgasms without a lot of effort.

Alice had noticed how quickly she got wet between the legs and on informing Helen of this, Helen laughed and said the same had happened to her to the point that there were days when she was permanently wet.

The two speculated that maybe it was because they were both so emphatically in love, or maybe it was part of the joy of having a choice of desirable and loving lovers.

The two walked hand-in-hand to the bed and lay side by side. Then each lifted the skirt of the other and inspected her delicious partner before they both lay back with skirts pulled up, their stocking covered legs spread open wide, knees slightly bent, and each with one hand on the pussy of the other.

After only a few minutes, even if the conversation had been about the price of copy paper, or an article in the latest *Psychology Today*, one or other would give a little shudder, then the other would do likewise.

This blissful state would only end when the two decided to move on, and prop themselves up and unbuttoned each others shirts. Then they would sit up face-to-face and cup each other's breasts and admire, caress, suck and bite each other.

Today there was much to talk about. Unusual sexual experiences with new people had been had by both women since they were last together, and they were eager to relate their stories.

It was decided that Helen would tell her story first.

Helen began by updating Alice on her encounter with the distraught Mary, whom she had found crying in their potting shed over her loss of Charlie. Helen told about seducing the large woman and how it already seemed to have changed Mary's life.

Alice laughed when Helen talked about her plan to take Mary shopping for a strap-on.

Then Helen talked about the surprise in finding herself with

Mary's country-girl niece Sophie, and how Mary had sent her niece as a present, because she couldn't make it due to Harold's passing.

Helen told how Sophie had rushed to kiss her because she was nervous and how, before they parted, she had declared her love and said she would come and live next door to her forever.

Alice made a face, and asked if these new conquests, so conveniently close to home, would eventually replace her.

"Darling, I will willingly share Mary and Sophie with you. I still don't know Sophie very well, but I feel confident that the two of you would get on famously.

"Incidentally, Mary and Sophie came to dinner a couple of nights after Mary's husband died and I think, from watching Frederico's reaction, he would happily make his contribution between Sophie's legs.

"Now you and Sophie sounds like a sharing plan he'd go for, dearest stepdaughter."

The two laughed.

"I look forward to meeting her."

Finally, Helen told Alice what had happened when she told Frederico about making love to Mary, and how he excitedly said that now he might get a chance to get his hands on her amazing butt, and then she told her how she responded and what had been said.

"He knows I do enjoy it."

Alice looked at Helen and commented that on the subject of butt sex, she was still an anal virgin and that she kept thinking she should do something about it.

"The truth is, I forget about it, and only think of it when it's too late. I'm not sure how to start. I should be able to practise, or something?"

Helen looked at her quizzically, then took Alice's hand in hers.

"Darling, I had no idea that you had this problem. One day, when you feel like it, mention it to me and I'll help you.

"There is a small thinnish pink thingamajig in the box over there, designed just for that purpose. That, and some lube, and we can sort it out in an afternoon."

"Really, Helen? Great! We will do this together then. Love you."

Alice then recounted her story of being taken home by Robert.

Helen couldn't believe what she was hearing and she was angry that this had happened to her true love, Alice. And in her concern and frustration she suddenly showed her anger.

"Why didn't you just get up and leave? Anything could have happened. You might have been murdered and no one would ever have known what happened to you. No, Alice! I'm very disappointed. It's as though you have no regard for me or Freya, or any of the people who love you."

Helen uncharacteristically folded her arms across her chest, hiding her breast, indicating that she was not feeling in any way loving.

Alice was shocked at Helen's response.

"I am so sorry, Helen. I truly am. You are right and it was very wrong of me to stay there. If it's any consolation, it has woken me up to the possibility of unexpected dangers. Robert seemed so harmless. Little did I know that his mother was the one in charge of his life, the one pulling the strings.

"Darling. Please forgive me. I promise I will never get into such a silly situation again. I promise. In fact, anything that seems odd, I will talk to you before going further. I did think it was strange that he wanted me to meet his mother, within days of us starting to go out together, and the fact that he mentioned her so often in conversation was becoming tedious. This was so obviously a sign of something odd."

Helen kept her arms folded and she remained looking angry. Then she spoke.

"I'm going to talk to Frederico and to Freya. And I will say to Freya what I've said to you. You must both be very careful. I can tell you from personal experience that there are some seemingly nice women out there that are mad or depraved but who, when you meet them, seem imbued with sweetness and light. I hadn't thought about how young you both still are."

There was a long silence. Then Alice spoke.

"I am so, so sorry my, darling. I promise you that I have learnt an important lesson. I love you so much, Helen. Please?"

Alice held out both arms, pleading for Helen to hold her. Helen slowly unfolded her arms and looked at Alice.

"Come here and let me hold you. You surely must know by now, how much I love you."

The two made tea. Helen had brought cakes so they buttoned up and sat up at the table for a little time out and nibbles.

Then Helen said that there was something that she wanted to discuss with Alice, something important.

"What is it wicked, stepmother? Tell me."

Helen told Alice how she had visited Rosa recently and they had had an unusual conversation. It was also uncanny, because it was about something that had occupied a little spot in Helen's mind for a very long time.

Helen became silent for a moment.

Helen said how they all knew that Rosa was very perceptive, and as Rosa spoke Helen sensed that she knew that Helen had always had feelings for her husband. Nothing had ever happened, or been said, over all the years, even though the Bennetts had been Helen's parents' best friends and the two families had visited each other often.

"I suppose my admiration for Bertie was noticeable, even if I thought it wasn't. But then suddenly Rosa made everything very clear. She was really talking about her situation, her possible death, and her concern that Bertie might suddenly be all alone in his later years with no one to show him the sort of love he was used to.

"She stated that, while Alice was in the house, Bertie was okay. But Alice wouldn't be there forever. She had her life ahead of her, and that must take her away at some point."

Helen looked at Alice, who was staring at her, fascinated with what Helen was saying.

"Then Rosa said what I least expected. She said she wanted me to try to develop some sort of physical relationship with Bertie. When I was about to say something, Rosa smiled and said there was nothing for me to say. She said she knew I had thoughts about him and now, with her health issues, there was a good and proper reason to put those feelings to good use.

"When she eventually allowed me to speak and I asked if she had any suggestions for how I might go about this if I decided to do it, she said yes. She said I must talk to Alice and enlist her help.

"And then she said, tell her Rosa said she wants her to show me the codes list. When I asked her what that was she simply said, 'Alice will explain'.

"So, Alice. I don't want to burden you with this problem, but you seem to be my only hope if I am to offer my physical affections to Bertie and satisfy Rosa at the same time."

Alice was flabbergasted.

Even though Helen had known about Alice "looking after Bertie", as Rosa put it, details of Alice's amorous adventures with him had remained, as Rosa insisted, a firm secret.

How could she now tell Helen about what she had been doing with her Mr Bennett, especially now Helen had admitted to having feelings for him?

"Helen, darling, you must believe me when I say that this has come as a shock and I don't really know where to begin. It's not that I don't want to tell you. I was sworn to secrecy by Rosa, a secret which I was prepared to take to my grave. Now that has all changed."

The two women entered into a mutual silence. Helen sympathetically studied Alice's face and saw the confusion she was experiencing, and waited.

"Give me a moment darling while I work out where to begin. And Helen? I think this is going to take us a while and it is already five o'clock. It might be an idea if you called Freddy and told him that you could be a bit late getting home. Is that okay? I can't see how we can cover things quickly."

"Good thinking Alice, I'll call him."

"Oh! Before you do, Helen, Freya asked me to ask you if she and I could get some time with Freddy sometime soon? That is if you are okay with that. Please say if you're not."

Helen smiled.

"I thought you two would never ask. Just don't wear him out. He doesn't deserve the attention but yes, that's fine, darling. I'll give him a call."

Helen spoke to Freddy, saying where she was and that she would be an hour or so later than she thought. Then Alice listened as she told Freddie about the girls wanting to see him.

"Oh yes, darling, I almost forgot. Alice and Freya would like to spend some quality time with you soon. If you are up for it, can I suggest Friday night? What will I do? Oh, I thought I might go next door and spend time with Mary. I might even introduce Mary to that little business that attracts you to her large derrière. Who knows? If I'm successful, she might be ringing you up every night and asking you to come over and get a spider out of her bedroom.

"Okay, sweetheart. I'll get something from the fridge when I get home. Love you. Bye!"

Alice and Helen laughed then Alice lent over and kissed her.

"Thanks you so much Helen. I'm sure Freya will thank you properly when she sees you next."

For the next hour or more, Alice walked Helen through Rosa's story, complete with details of her mid-marriage change of heart and then later, seeing her husband differently and loving him as she really wanted to love him.

Helen found herself a bit teary when Alice later spoke of Rosa trying to understand the changes to Bertie's mental state.

When Alice explained the code, and how Rosa came up with it, Helen was amazed, firstly that Rosa had managed to do it; but she was also impressed with the sheer variety of sexual activities that Alice said the Bennetts enjoyed together.

Alice mentioned Maude and her special need following the loss of her husband, in the context of Rosa's ability to train Bertie, in this instance, for something Rosa had no intention of trying herself. And when she said how Bertie had got excited at the sight of Maude's big bottom, Helen interrupted and exclaimed in a loud voice,

"What is it with men and big butts? If they find them so dammed attractive, why haven't we girls all got one?"

The two women laughed and Alice went on with her story. Eventually she paused and told Helen to hang on while she went and fetched Rosa's copy of the code. On her return, Alice handed the six pages to Helen.

"While you have a quick look through it I'll make us a snack, then we can look through it together.

"And Helen, I admit to having used the code a couple of times, and I'm sorry if you find that upsetting. I knew nothing of your feelings for Bertie. I don't want to hide anything from you."

Helen laughed sympathetically at her confession.

"Darling, I can never be anything but grateful for all the happiness you have given me. Sharing you with Bertie, even if I do become involved, will never be a problem."

Alice embraced Helen and kissed her, then went off to the kitchen.

With slices of cheese on wholemeal toast and washed down with glasses of apple juice, Helen and Alice sat side by side, reading the code. Helen's finger moved slowly down the list.

"It is amazing. So comprehensive. What does BF in small letters beside a code mean? And I love these 'side dishes', extras while you are engaged in another activity. My God, Rosa, is extraordinary."

The two agreed that she was indeed amazing.

"Actually, BF beside something means it is a Bertie's Fantasy as against something that Rosa and Bertie fantasised together. And if I tell you I tried that one, the one where your finger is, what will you think of me, my love?"

Helen laughed. "Oh my god! Tell me about it Alice. Wait! I just read the Fifi code you are referring to and I am mighty intrigued, even excited."

"It began with me thinking of trying something and then, feeling a bit guilty I suppose, I thought I should have something marked BF so at least I knew that Bertie would enjoy it. I would simply go along for the ride, if you will excuse the pun."

Alice began to blush.

"Oh my God, Alice. You know I get the hots for you more than ever when you blush. Stop it! Just tell me what happened and, more importantly, did you enjoy it?"

"I absolutely loved it. It didn't sound so special when I read the code, but it was delightfully sexually stimulating, having his cock pushed up in my stocking and him taking my hand and placing it over his member beneath the stocking and asking me to gently rub him.

"And watching him enjoy himself and everything he did was a voyeur's delight. And importantly, Bertie really seemed to enjoy himself."

"Oh, you sexy little whore! Now I must have him. Say you will share him with me my darling, please."

"Helen, if only you knew how often, when I thought about things I could do with Bertie, I thought of you sharing the activity with me.

"Darling, there is much to think about, I know, and I believe you now need to go back to Rosa and ask her any questions you might have after tonight.

"Before I send you home to Freddy though, there is one story I must tell you; it is about something I believe you should use to begin your adventures with Bertie. It is how I got started and I believe it relates to Bertie's mental situation."

"Please Alice, tell me more."

"Well, if I tell you it began when I knocked on Bertie's door a couple of days after Rosa went into hospital, thinking I should check to see if he was okay and would perhaps like me to bring him a cup of tea in bed, or to make breakfast.

"On my way to uni every morning I would meet Rosa in the kitchen putting on the kettle and assumed that she was taking drinks back to bed."

Alice then told Helen the story of 'Morning Glory'. Helen sat and stared at her, with a dumbfounded expression on her face. And she gasped when Alice would come to a part where Bertie would talk about things so innocently and matter-of-factly, like saying he should ask Rosa what she thought, for instance.

Alice finished her story.

"So Helen, I have enjoyed Morning Glory every Saturday morning since Rosa left. I should mention, though, that Bertie and Rosa's special morning start is not confined only to Saturdays."

She stopped speaking and looked lovingly at Helen and smiled.

"An enterprising woman who happened to be in the know might avail herself of Morning Glory at around seven or seven thirty on any of the other six days of the week. And I know that Bertie would appreciate it greatly."

Helen tearfully reached out and Alice slid gently into her arms.

"Oh, darling Alice! How could I not love you?"

After kissing and touching each other's breasts for a little while, Helen announced that she would act decisively.

"I will visit Rosa in the morning."

Helen got up and prepared to leave.

"And Helen?"

"Yes, darling?"

"Assuming you go ahead, can we sometimes do things with Bertie together? When I read the codes, I almost always think of us doing these things with you by my side. Being able to touch or kiss you while Bertie is doing his thing would be wonderful."

"Oh darling, yes, yes, of course we will. We will have Bertie together."

11

HORSES FOR COURSES

WHEN HELEN CALLED Mary and asked if she could visit her and Sophie on Friday night, Mary said that that would be wonderful and they would look forward to seeing her.

"Oh Helen, I've had such a week, you wouldn't believe. Sophie has been on top of me at least once every day with our new strap-on.

"She's a different farm animal each time she mounts me. A couple of hours ago she was a rooster. I hope you will be able to cope with her. She's gone crazy.

"Oh, here is Sophie now. It's Helen, darling. She wants to come over for the evening on Friday."

Helen heard Sophie's screams of delight and laughed.

"What is she saying, Mary? I can't quite hear her."

"She's beside herself with excitement. She says she's going to hide naked behind the front door, just wearing her new strap-on, and she's going to jump straight onto you."

"Gosh, I didn't know she liked me that much. Tell her, if it helps, Helen will take her panties off before she knocks on the door. Oh yes, one more thing, tell her not to forget the lube."

Mary laughed. She had switched on speaker phone so that Sophie could hear everything that Helen had said. Helen heard screams of excitement.

"Sophie says she is so excited and loves you 'muchly'."

It was Friday night, and Alice and Freya had arrived in the late afternoon for their evening with Freddie.

"Freddie will be home shortly. I've left food in the fridge for all of you but if you two wanted to go and get into our bed, I could leave him a note telling him that there are a couple of lemons in his bed waiting to be squeezed."

"What a good idea, Helen. Now that you've got us doubly randy, darling, we will have to run straight upstairs to bed. But I'm sure we'll manage.

"Oh, and Helen. We hope you have a nice night, but we're both a bit concerned about this country girl who's staying with your neighbour and whom we haven't yet met. We're feeling a little insecure, aren't we Freya?"

"Yes, Alice, you are right. Just don't forget who you most enjoy 'titty time' with and who wants to become your favourite 'bottom play' slave, Helen.

There was much laughter and kissing goodbye, as the girls headed for the stairs and Helen looked for a writing pad and pen in a drawer in the kitchen dresser, to write a note for Freddy.

As Helen began to write, she suddenly had a thought that made her get up and call to the girls, asking them to come back down.

"Oh no, you've changed your mind and you're sending us home?" cried Alice.

"No, not at all, I love the idea of you both having time with Freddy. But I have had some thoughts about it. Make yourselves comfortable while I think it through, so that I don't make it sound too complicated."

Alice and Freya smiled and sat down at the table.

"As you know, Freddy works as a flight controller at the airport. It is well documented by psychologists that his occupation is one of the three most stressful jobs in the world. Probably because of this, when Freddy knocks off and comes home, he more often than not needs to come down from wherever he's been in his head all day, and relax. He will usually have at least one glass of red wine while he sits on the sofa, eyes closed and not really wanting to talk.

"I'm telling you this as part of my quick introduction to understanding Freddy, and probably men in general.

"In short, despite what we grow up being told about men, how they are wanting it all the time, or they only want one thing, along with all that macho talk and pictures of 'he' men, the reality is very different.

"If the truth be told, there are times when we women wish that what we were told was true. Surely it would make life more simple. But that is another story for another day.

"Yes, there are men that fit that description, but interestingly enough, they are not the ones we could see ourselves spending the rest of our lives with.

"In short, our ideal man might be both sorts rolled into one, but realistically, thinking of a long-term partner, one to be the father of our children and one we can have good conversations with, we will need to opt for a more sensitive man.

"So! Where am I going with all this? Ah yes, Sex and the Sensitive Man, and subtitled, Getting the Most from Heterosexual Love."

The girls laughed and looked at each other as Helen took a deep breath.

"A woman can get a most rewarding sex life if she learns early in the piece that her sensitive man will need space, room to move, time to observe her and desire her, and then make his moves to win her.

"Sometimes he will want a simple release from a tough working day and this might be as little as a cuddle, and maybe her playing with his cock. Other times, he might allow his fantasies to overrule the left brain machinations of his work day and become a frenzied lustful seeker of orgiastic fantasy. Lovingly, of course.

"In short, a woman needs to be what she is best at, being understanding and, in particular, adaptable.

"Women are multifaceted and can do so much more than men, with their bodies and their emotions. Men's brains run on tracks that keep them focused only on the task at hand. In Freddy's workshop out the back, which is a cross between a farrier's, a cabinet maker's, a sculptor's studio and a laboratory, he could quite easily build a rocket to the moon, if that is what he chose to do. Single-mindedness is their forte.

"Men are different in other ways.

"They unfortunately, depending how you look at it, do not have bodies like a woman, with curves and soft bits, or with nerve endings close to the outside of their bodies or warm wet places that can give them nice sensations all day long.

"Men are stuck with that interesting long thing that we can enjoy – at the right moment, of course – along with a brain that can invent the stainless steel sink or a better mouse trap. As well, many males seem to suffer from a limited emotional capacity, and even that wilts under the impact of a woman's menstrual moods.

"I'll stop talking about all that and finish up with my suggestion for this evening."

"Yes, please! I'm feeling like I've just a spent an hour in a tutorial, Helen," complained Freya.

"Yes, darling Helen, now tell us what we should do," said Alice, taking Freya's hand and squeezing it.

"My suggestion is that you both get into your nighties or pyjamas, pick out a video and just chill out in front of the television with the lights turned low.

"Let Freddy discover you busily watching something and seemingly not even thinking about him in a sexual way. He will then relax and enjoy watching you and slowly he will unwind.

"Even if he does nothing, just stay laid back about things, even to the point of a cup of cocoa together and saying you're tired and being prepared to just get into bed and go to sleep.

"Oh yes, one other thing, don't be obvious in showing Freddy your delicious attributes. But a nightie that works its way up just a little over your bum, or pyjama bottoms that work themselves down, never did the male gaze any harm. Just as long as he doesn't suspect you did it deliberately."

The girls clapped and cheered.

"The trouble now, Helen, is that visualising your last suggestion has made us horny. Come on Freya, let's go and practise and see if we can get to look innocently rude, and we should have a quickie on the stairs to quieten us down.

"Thank you, Helen. You are fantastic."

"Love you both. Have a good night, the both of you. Just don't wear my husband out totally."

True to her word, Helen slipped out of her panties as she knocked on Mary's door, planning to hold them up to the sexually frenetic Sophie as evidence of her willingness to let the country girl have her way. She was surprised when Mary opened the door wearing nothing but a robe.

"Helen? I'm waiting for you," came the voice of Sophie from some-where in the house.

Helen looked at Mary quizzically.

"I should warn you, darling, Sophie seems fixated on farm animals. She's been on and off me all week and role-playing a different animal each time. Yesterday she had me as a billy goat and a rooster. As well as that, she's been back to the sex shop twice and she ordered a special something online as well. I will let you discover what it is.

"Oh, and my friend Janice is calling in shortly for our weekly coffee and cake session. I forgot she was coming and I couldn't get her on the phone to change the arrangement.

"Janice is my oldest friend. We were at school together. She is a singing teacher and helps the choir master at St John's where I sing on Sundays. I'll keep her in the kitchen."

Then a funny look appeared on Mary's face.

"It's odd really when you think about it. Janice has always had a thing for me and will often say that if she had been a man, she would have raced me off years ago.

"Well, Helen, I giggled to myself when I had a sudden thought today. I had the idea that I should hide a dildo under the kitchen table, then, just when Janice says 'If I was a man (etc)' I could pop it on the table in front of her and tell her 'Well here's your big chance Janice. I'm single now and I've got the hots for you too, dearie. How about it?'"

Mary was quiet for a moment.

"The thing about Janice is that, while she acts the innocent, I happen to know, from other sources, that she is far from it. Why she has kept her private life secret from me over all these years, I'll never know. Perhaps she thought I was so proper she couldn't divulge her deeper secrets. Who knows?

"I've always been secretly in love with Janice's skinny body and long legs. Opposites attract apparently, don't they? Now that you have pointed me in this new direction, Helen, I'm keen to get my hands on every skinny bit of her."

The two women laughed out loud. As they were about to walk off, Mary to the kitchen and Helen to the lounge, Helen said, "I think that is a great idea, Mary. But just remember though, they say be sure you really want what you think about, because once you've had the idea, it usually comes true."

Then Mary stopped and stood and looked at Helen and spoke. "Just to keep you up to date, Helen. Sophie applied for a job a couple of days ago and today they called to say she had got the position, meaning she is definitely going to stay here with us. Isn't that great?"

"Yes, that is good news. What sort of job did she get, Mary?"

"She will be a nurse's assistant with a veterinarian working with the racing industry. It turns out that our Sophie had a couple of very good references from her time working on stud farms. She will be able to study and move up to being a nurse if she wants to.

"She's very excited. She is now in a full-on horsy phase. When you find her in a minute or two, don't be too shocked.

"Her latest fantasy is that she is a mare about to be served and she has been restrained so that she won't kick and damage the expensive stud stallion. You will be the Arab stallion, and also the stud mistress who soothes the mare to ensure the mating happens.

"Welcome to Sophie's animal world, Helen. It's been a most entertaining week."

"If I'd known, Mary, I would have worn my jodhpurs and riding jacket, and boots."

"Now you are getting me excited, Helen. I think I could really enjoy a girl dressed like that."

Mary went off to the kitchen to make afternoon tea for her visitor and Helen headed for the lounge.

Helen's first thoughts when she saw Sophie lying naked across two footstools pushed together was how incredibly beautiful she was. Her strong body somehow reflected both her youthful naivety and her farm girl worldliness. In her manner, she seemed so self-sufficient and alive, and without any pretensions.

"At last, Helen darling! We can get started now, I hope," Sophie called.

"You are champion Arab stud stallion Sir Richard Burton, and I am Princess Fatima. He and I are of pure Arab stock and highly excitable, and your job as stud mistress, Miss Hot Pussy, is to get Fatima to take the giant donga of Sir Richard. This could be quite a challenge, Helen.

"And I hope you like the new strap-on. Found it online. It arrived this morning."

Helen saw that Sophie had wide leather imitation cuffs on her wrists and ankles, no doubt supposedly to stop her kicking and injuring the stallion, or moving away. What she also saw was the new strap-on. It was a huge replica of a stallion's penis, bigger than most of the dildos one saw at the sex shop.

Helen looked down at the beautiful Sophie. I think I can do this, she thought, smiling to herself, thinking back to the days at boarding school when the girls would go to the stables after class to groom the horses.

There wasn't a stallion at the school, but often the penises of the geldings would get quite big when they were being groomed, and some of the girls would giggle and make jokes and say things like "I hope I can find a boyfriend with one like that."

Helen could see the appeal and suddenly felt a tiny flutter between her legs. She picked up the heavy horse strap-on and inspected it. Instead of ending in a bulbous point like human dildos, this one was almost flat at the end, like a human one but sliced off. It was nearly twice as long and also thicker.

She removed her dress and attached the horsy thing around her waist and made sure it was firmly in place. Then she found the big bottle of lubricant.

"Ready, darling? I think Miss Hot Pussy is going to enjoy this."

"Ready, Helen!"

Helen added some lube to the end of the rubber donga and moved in to be closer to Princess Fatima. Then she attempted to add lube to the mare, but as she did so Princess Fatima whinnied loudly and moved herself to one side. She was having none of it.

"Easy girl. Take it easy, Princess. Everything is going to be fine. It won't hurt. Just relax."

Little snorts and heavy breathing came from the front of the mare.

Miss Hot Pussy touched Princess Fatima lightly with her fingers, all the while making soothing sounds. The mare responded, opening and shutting her vagina and trembling.

"You clever, beautiful girl. Just relax, Princess. You will like this once we get him inside you, I promise."

But when Sir Richard touched Princess with his penis, she threw her backside up and down and side to side and screamed a horsy scream.

Miss Hot Pussy stopped and reviewed the situation. Then she placed a hand on Princess Fatima's bare back and moved slowly forward along the mare's body, caressing her lightly and whispering nice things to her.

"There, there, Fatima. Relax and let me stroke you. Nothing bad is going to happen."

When the stud mistress got to Fatima's head, she touched her softly around the ears, then she put her mouth to an ear and licked inside it. Fatima gave a little horsy squeal and leant her head towards the stud mistress's face and tongue.

All the while, Miss Hot Pussy's hands were caressing Fatima. Then she ran a hand along the mare's flanks and under the mare, surprised to find, but happy to fondle, a delightful human-like breast. Fatima lifted her body enough so that Miss Hot Pussy could trace a circle around a nipple and stretch it and pull it downwards. Fatima made a not-so-horsy sound, a sort of gasp.

Then Miss Hot Pussy took a risk. She removed the dildo from around her waist and turned it on herself. As she did so she whispered nonsense things to the young mare, in a soothing voice.

The stud mistress was by now very wet, and after a few moments adding lube and spreading her vagina, she managed to insert the huge horse dildo.

Then she moved slowly around to the front of Princess Fatima, and got down on her knees and kissed her pouting lips. Then she licked a tear from Fatima's cheek.

"There, there, good girl. Easy, girl."

When the stud mistress stood up, she presented Fatima with her wet pussy with the giant dildo hanging from it.

"Good girl, Princess, don't be afraid."

Princess Fatima could suddenly smell the stud mistress's wet pussy. She made little whimpering sounds and put out her long horsy tongue and licked Miss Hot Pussy's pussy.

Then Princess Fatima moved her face down and began licking the stallion's penis, as Miss Hot Pussy moved it up and down slowly with her hand. All the while, Fatima gave little snorts and pulled back her lips, and gently nibbled at Sir Richard's penis.

"We like Sir Richard's penis really, don't we, Princess? Good girl," cooed Miss Hot Pussy.

"Now I think Sir Richard would like to offer it to your beautiful rear again. He will do so very slowly, Fatima. Just relax until he gets it inside you, just a little bit to start with. Then you will be in heaven, I promise. Good girl!"

The stud mistress slowly made her way back, kissing and caressing Fatima's body as she went, stopping to touch her beautiful breast again, and at her pussy to lick it and poke her tongue in and roll it around the mare's protruding clitoris.

Princess Fatima sighed and when Sir Richard's penis touched her, she opened up her vagina and sucked him in. Sir Richard kept up the forward movement until it could go no further, then he began a slow rhythmic movement.

When Princess Fatima orgasmed and screamed a horsy scream, Helen came too, much stronger than she had expected.

"Oh my God, Princess, what a darling little filly you are. Sir Richard and Miss Hot Pussy love you very much. Good girl!"

When Princess Fatima had orgasmed and she had hung limply over the cushioned stools for a while, Helen withdrew Sir Richard's penis.

As it left the beautiful Arab mare's pussy, it made a noise like a champagne cork popping, causing Sophie and Helen to burst out laughing.

"Oh Helen, that was amazing, so amazing. You are the most wonderful stud mistress in the whole world. Thank you from the bottom of my heart, oh, and other places too."

The two women laughed and hugged and kissed.

"Would you like to come to bed now, Helen? I would love to snuggle up with you and maybe have a snooze."

"Yes Sophie, I would love that."

Sophie took Helen's hand and joyfully led her along the passageway to her room. They were just passing Mary's bedroom when they heard voices. Sophie looked at Helen in surprise and whispered.

"Auntie has a visitor, I think. Who could it possibly be?"

The two stood outside Mary's door and tried to hear what was being said.

"Mary joked about having a plan to seduce Janice. I thought it was just a joke, but maybe she did. It's interesting, given how totally different their bodies are. But then, as Mary said, they say opposites attract."

Sophie looked at Helen and smiled in disbelief, then whispered again,

"I don't think it would be too hard to get Janice on her back. She is obviously in love with Mary and from what I can tell, having never married or even been in a lasting relationship, and Mary having just lost her husband, now would be the right time."

The two looked at each other and smiled, then Helen quietly turned the door handle and peered around the door.

Sophie squeezed Helen's hand excitedly. There was Janice on her back with her long skinny legs wide apart and high in the air, her feet and black high-heeled shoes and her shiny stocking covered legs twisting wildly in her frenzy. Mary was on top of her, her big bare buttocks rolling methodically as she lifted herself up, then pushed into her old school friend.

"Mary, you shouldn't be doing this. Oh! Oh! Oh! My God! Yes? It's so wrong. What's come over you, Mary, You've always been such a proper person."

"If it's wrong, you silly bitch, how come your pussy is running with wet? Tell me truthfully, Janice, you love it, don't you? Don't you, Janice?"

There was near silence for a few moments, apart from Janice gasping.

"Yes, Mary. I love it," Janice whispered.

"And when I've finished shagging you, Janice, you are going to put this thing on and I will teach you to have me like I'm having you.

"You would like that, wouldn't you Janice?"

"Yes, Mary. Oh yes!"

That thought was probably what caused Janice to suddenly let out an almighty scream and those long skinny legs shook and Janice's body shook and then Mary pushed in harder, right up as far as she could, then her body shook too.

"There Janice, you did enjoy that? Of course you did. I love you, you skinny bitch. We are going to fuck each other every week after coffee and cake, for the rest of our days.

"Now let me touch those beautiful breasts. I've always wanted to suck on them, Janice."

Helen and Sophie heard Janice sobbing and gently closed the door and headed for Sophie's room.

"I'm so wet from watching them. Quick, into bed you slutty country bitch. I want your beautiful legs high in the air. Right now!"

Sophie gave an ironic horse whinny, and pirouetted coquettishly in front of Helen.

"Anything you say, Miss Hot Pussy."

At daybreak, Helen kissed Sophie goodbye and hopped out of bed and headed home through the gate in the fence.

She came into the house expecting the downstairs to be empty, and that she would enjoy a quiet coffee and read the Saturday newspaper she'd collected from the front garden on the way in.

She was surprised to find Freddy dressed in his silk dressing gown and already making coffee.

"There you are darling. I wondered when you'd be home."

Helen noticed how Freddy's smiling face was looking at her more eagerly than she would expect, given the time of day and, she assumed, after a possibly busy night with Alice and Freya.

"Yes, darling. I like to be at home on Saturday mornings, your day off, and looking forward to a weekend together."

Freddy switched off the coffee machine and came over to her. He put his arms around her and gently moved her backwards against the kitchen dresser. He kissed her lovingly and moved his hands up and down her back.

Helen enjoyed this moment, although she was still bringing her brain back from laying in bed with Sophie only minutes before. And her vagina was still wet from when Sophie, seemingly still asleep, rolled over in the early hours of the morning and touched and gently rubbed her pussy.

Helen realised that this was not a simple welcome home from Freddy, and when he turned her around and lifted up her skirt and touched her bottom gently and ran his fingers up and down the crack of her backside, she gasped. And when Freddy leant over to the butter dish and lifted the lid and pushed his finger into the butter, Helen knew where Freddy was heading.

Helen was lovingly enjoying Freddy's sudden obsession with her bottom. It had been ages since he had taken her in that way, and her excitement was palpable.

"Oh Freddy! I so love it when you're naughty in this way. Stay inside my bottom all day if you wish, darling. In fact I want you there all weekend."

"You are so beautiful, Helen. I'm crazy about you."

While this blissful domestic scene was in play, two sleepy girls arrived at the door of the kitchen from upstairs.

Alice and Freya stared at the buggering couple in disbelief. Freya reached out for Alice's hand.

Freddy was rhythmically reaming and disappearing into Helen's bottom while his wife repeatedly gasped, "Yes Freddy, yes Freddy, never stop doing this to me, Freddy, I love you my darling."

Freya took Alice's hand and wetted the index finger in her mouth then lifted her nightie and guided the finger into her bottom hole and wriggled and rolled her tiny bum about. Then she put a hand between Alice's legs and palmed her very wet pussy.

Suddenly Freddie called out to Helen.

"Sweetheart! I want to come."

"Yes, Freddy. Yes! Come in my bottom, you beautiful man."

Then the girls heard that sound again, the beginning of the growling roar they had each heard twice that night, as Freddy had taken each of them in turn.

Helen screamed as Freddy exploded inside. She slumped onto the dresser, sobbing.

"Oh Freddy, I love you so much."

The two girls tippy-toed back upstairs and threw themselves on to the bed.

"That is definitely something that is going on my list of things to do," whispered Alice. "Except Helen hasn't yet given me the anal sex lesson she promised me."

Freya looked at Alice and feigned jealousy.

"It's nice that she has offered to help you. I guess I will just have learn to do it all by myself."

Alice laughed.

"Darling, just ask her. She doesn't realise that folk like you and me don't know how, because she's been a devotee of bottom play for a long time and assumes everybody is the same as her."

"Of course, we'd have to work out how to get Freddy to do it to us first."

"You are right, Freya. And Helen just might not be keen to tell us how. She might want to keep that special thing with Freddy just for herself."

The two girls laughed and rolled about and, in their excitement, took turns lying on each other's backs and pretending they were Freddy, shagging each other's bottoms and yelling out, "Sweetheart! I want to come!"

TURNING THE CORNER

HELEN HAD a funny feeling in her stomach when she headed in to the hospital on Tuesday to visit Rosa, but she didn't know why.

Alice had explained how Rosa and Bertie, the long time close friends of Helen's parents and the young Helen, had gone through a difficult patch in their marriage many years before, and how Rosa eventually changed the situation by taking female lovers and later sharing them with her husband.

Alice also explained the code, the list of verbal instructions Rosa had developed to better cope with Bertie's forgetfulness, and his not-so-obvious mental changes. The code ensured they could continue to enjoy a rich sexual life together.

Now it appeared that Rosa was worried about her imminent demise, putting forward the idea that Helen should replace her as Bertie's sexual partner if and when she died.

So what was causing Helen's concern? Rosa had observed Helen over many years and knew that, even as a very young woman, she had held secret feelings for Bertie.

Suddenly, a thought came to Helen. Why, in all these years, given the closeness of Helen's mum and dad and herself to the Bennetts, Rosa had never expressed any deep affection towards her. Was it really because of Helen's hidden crush on her husband? Why did Helen always feel that Rosa was a little distant, very friendly, but never ever engaging in Helen's personal or private life in the way that close friends usually do?

Rosa greeted Helen with a welcoming smile.

"Well, Helen. Have you survived what Alice told you?"

"It was all a bit of a shock, Rosa, but yes, I'm much closer to understanding yours and Bertie's life together. Thank you so much for sharing that with me."

"So do you have any difficult questions for me to answer, or can I assume that you are able and willing to become my surrogate when I'm gone?"

The two laughed.

"I'm yet to understand why you believe that you are about to leave this world, Rosa, and why the rush to push me into this unusual role. I can't help feeling that there is a piece of the jigsaw missing, at least in my understanding of things."

Rosa looked suddenly taken aback.

"What on earth has caused you to think this way, Helen?"

There was silence. Then Rosa saw that Helen was wiping her eyes. Helen looked up, sniffled and looked at her.

"Rosa? I've always felt that you have kept me at a distance. I accepted that maybe there was something about me that you found unattractive. And I always felt guilty about my feelings for Bertie when I was younger and thought that was probably a reason for you not to want me too close to you.

"So if I am having trouble with your suggestion about me and Bertie, it is because our lack of intimacy seems so at odds with your suggestion of my possible relationship with Bertie.

"Tell me, Rosa. What could possibly make me feel this way? Why have we never held one another, Rosa? I've always wanted to love you and be loved by you. What prevents that, Rosa, what stands between us? It surely can't just be Bertie?"

Helen looked at Rosa and noticed that she seemed to be staring into space. Then Rosa looked at Helen and asked her to go and put the "do not disturb" sign up on the outside of the door, then lock it. And when she came back, she noticed that Rosa was dabbing her eyes with her handkerchief.

"You had better come and sit closer, Helen, please."

Helen moved up the bed.

"What I am about to say will shock you and I'm telling you this secret only because I want you to know how I really feel towards you. Please bear with me, Helen. Things will be painful, for me at least and, most likely, for you too."

Helen felt a moment of turmoil. What could Rosa possibly mean, painful?

"I have always said that Maude was my first female lover. But the truth is your mother, Isabelle, was my first lover.

"Belle and your father Vernon were experiencing a difficult period in their marriage at the same time as I and Bertie were, except they were ten years older than us, which probably made things harder for them. You were living in London.

"Belle had called around to our place one afternoon. Bertie was at work and she had just had an argument with Vern and left the house. It was a period when I was wanting to get away from Bertie, but was either too scared or uncertain about how to do it.

"Belle and I were sitting on the sofa, both crying and blowing our noses, and occasionally saying something or other about our situations. At a moment when we were both overwrought, we put our arms around each other and sobbed.

"We must have both suddenly realised that being close like this was the first instance in a long time that we had experienced affection. Heaven knows how it happened, but moments later we were kissing and sighing and squeezing our hands together.

"Neither of us wanted the moment to end, so beautiful did it seem. We suddenly found that we had put our tongues in each other's mouths and were wildly tonguing each other. The feeling was ecstatic for both of us.

"And it didn't stop there; Belle was the dominant personality, I suppose you would say. Being older probably made the difference and she began to unbutton my top, and moments later, her hand was inside my bra and caressing my breast. I was wild with desire for her, and we quite soon ended up naked on the sofa and very much in love."

Rosa was crying and was forced to stop talking. Helen was also crying. There were so many things she wanted to say or ask, but she could not speak.

After a little while, Helen managed to ask, "So what happened to you both, Rosa? Where did this take you?"

"Your mother led me through, and into, a turbulent time, a time when we both explored other people's love while still maintaining our strong emotional and sexual bond.

"Being younger probably helped me over the ensuing years to re-evaluate how I felt about Bertie and, eventually, to rediscover my love for him.

"For Belle it wasn't that easy. She and your father never really had the close relationship that Bertie and I had enjoyed before things got difficult for us.

"Vernon discovered that Belle was having an affair, I don't know how, and by then it was more than likely the affair was with the one and only man she ever linked up with, and who treated her well.

"Your father suggested that she leave him in the house and go and live with her lover, but Belle knew that she was not in love with that person and would not go.

"It was a most unhappy time for the two of them and something had to give. And it did. Vern suddenly died.

"I'm not sure how old you were then or what you were up to in London, but you will of course remember the event. You returned home for his funeral. I remember seeing you there.

"Belle and I were still the love of each other's lives, and this went on for years. We experimented with other lovers, mostly women, and we often shared them. But then her age began to catch up with her, and Belle slowed down.

"She often would ask why I couldn't just leave Bertie and move in with her. I resisted, telling her that Bertie and I had come to an arrangement and now shared our other loves.

"Belle resisted my sharing her with Bertie, something I would dearly have loved, saying that she was too jealous of him, that she believed he monopolised me and controlled my life. She refused to see the goodness in him and I can only assume that it was something to do with her own marital disappointment."

Rosa leaned back and rested, and Helen blew her nose and stared at her hands.

"We had a terrible row, two weeks before Belle died. I have never forgiven myself for it.

"She asked if I would come home to her house and spend the night with her and for some silly reason which I can't even remember, probably to do with her ongoing rejection of Bertie, I declined.

"Belle cried, and said that if it hadn't been for her I would never have had the opportunity to move forward as I did. She claimed – and I believe she was right – that I was only able to reconnect with Bertie because of her love for me."

Rosa became quiet again. She reached out and took Helen's hand. Then, in almost a whisper, she spoke.

"I believed she died of a broken heart. I killed her."

There was silence. Helen looked at Rosa and sobbed.

"When you came home from London, Helen, it was like seeing Belle again. I cried for a week. Bertie comforted me and told me to go to you. But I couldn't. I thought I had done enough damage and wanted to be sure that you remained safe.

"I eventually saw that I had been irrational, but by then I had kept you at arm's length emotionally for so long, I couldn't change things. I wanted to love you but I was frightened."

Rosa fell silent again.

"But it didn't really work, did it? You knew and I knew that something wasn't right, something was missing.

"I tried to make things right for you except, subconsciously I was making them right for Belle. I could see that you and Freddy might some day need to make some changes, just as Bertie and I had, and Belle had tried to do.

"I took Alice into the house, believing that you and your step-daughter stood a chance of enriching each other's lives, and that perhaps through Alice, and through some miracle, you and I might eventually find each other.

"Finally, I attempted to set you up – or is it Belle I wanted to set up? — with Bertie before I died. I know it could have worked for her eventually if I had just given her more time."

Rosa fell silent except for her occasional sobbing. Helen was deep in thought, fighting her way through an emotional situation that she could never have imagined. She was desperate to find a solution, for Rosa, for her mother, and for herself.

"Rosa?"

"Yes, Helen?"

"It doesn't have to be too late for us. I sincerely want you to do something, at this moment, for you and for me and for Belle."

"What is that something, Helen?"

"If you could pretend that you are sitting here with Belle, and I reach over and kiss you, and maybe we even let our tongues touch, and I put my hand on you, and you put a hand on my leg, I think we could begin to undo all that has happened and turn time back.

"And when you open your eyes, I, Helen, will be your new lady love. I wish for that more than anything, Rosa. It might take time, and it might start awkwardly, but I believe we should give ourselves a chance. We can create a new beginning. And we owe it to Belle, as well as ourselves. Please, Rosa? Will you let me kiss you like that?"

Rosa didn't reply, but looked at Helen. With only a moment of hesitation, she closed her eyes, puckered her lips and moved her head forward towards Helen. Helen met her with her lips and, ever so slowly the two began to hug each other.

"Let us try Helen, let us try."

Helen lay down on the bed beside Rosa, gently pulling her down beside her. Then the two held hands. Then they held each other close. But they were still strangers and confused, and they wept.

Touching each other would be something they would eventually very much enjoy together, but maybe that would have to be on another day.

Helen and Rosa lay still, each happy that they had made this first move, but both wondering what would happen next.

Helen turned her mind to the things that had brought this about, looked at Rosa and spoke.

"I will start with Morning Glory, Rosa. Alice suggested that if I was to go down this path, having Bertie one morning early would be the way to go."

Rosa turned and flashed her beatific smile, and kissed Helen and squeezed her hand. It was though a veil had been lifted and Rosa could suddenly see that there was hope.

"Thank you, Helen. You can't believe how excited I am, both for you and for Bertie and, dare I say, for me too."

The two lay silent. Then Rosa rallied herself and rolled onto her side to face Helen and gave an almost wicked laugh.

"Helen? Your decision to help with Bertie makes it necessary for me to prepare both of us for this event."

"In what way, Rosa?"

"If you are to have my husband, darling, I want to have you first. Bertie and I have both shared partners in the past. Can I please touch you sweet, Helen? Will you allow me have you before my husband puts his beautiful cock in you?"

As the implications of what Rosa had just said became clear in her mind, Helen felt suddenly enlivened. She stared at Rosa, then slowly began to unbutton her blouse, and when she had finished that she unclasped her bra and pulled it off, closing her eyes.

"Oh yes Rosa, you can. Please! Come and get me, you darling woman."

Rosa looked longingly at Helen, then moved her hand across to Helen's breast and found a nipple, already hard and waiting for her mouth.

As she was doing that, Helen lifted herself so that she could divest herself of her panties, then she pulled her skirt right up to just below her breasts, and stretched her legs wide apart.

"Rosa darling, at last! I want to be your lost love returned, Rosa. Whatever you did with my mother, you must now do with me. Please, darling Rosa, I love you."

Then Helen reached over and opened Rosa's top and feasted her eyes on Rosa's beautiful breasts.

"Oh Rosa, you are so beautiful."

"Yes, yes, my darling Helen, we will love each other as we should have been doing for so long. It is now catch up time for both of us, and for Bertie, too."

Rosa moved so that she could run her hand up and down Helen's legs. Helen sighed and moved her legs to better feel the excitement raging in her pussy, and when Rosa's hand reached and touched her clitoris, Helen gave a little scream and thrust herself upwards, just as Rosa drew two fingers across her wet pussy and thrust them into her cunt.

"Oh Helen, you are so beautiful. I love you dearly. Please darling, lick me."

As she spoke Rosa turned herself around and straddled Helen so that her pussy was close to Helen's face. Helen grasped Rosa's hips and pulled her closer and buried her face in her sex.

When Freddy got home that night, Helen greeted him with kisses and told him to hurry and have his shower, and that she had made osso bucco, one of his favourite dishes.

Over dinner, Helen told Freddy her big news of the day about Rosa. He was fascinated to hear that Helen's mother was Rosa's first lover. He was even more excited to learn of their sexual encounter, and particularly what had triggered it.

Helen had kept Freddy informed about Rosa wanting her to spend time with Bertie, and Freddy had agreed with Rosa that, if anything happened to her, Helen was the logical candidate to look after his more private physical needs. Freddy loved Bertie like a father and he did not feel jealous in any way.

After dinner, Helen and Freddy moved onto the sofa in the dimly lit lounge where they always liked to relax, carrying their still half full glasses of red wine.

"Well, darling. I take it you will be heading over to the Bennett house early one morning this week. I know you will be gentle with him. I wouldn't want anything to happen to him. He is my main source of information about the real world.

"This week we will be discussing the role older women once played in educating boys and young men in the art of love.

"Bertie believes that if this idea could be revived and older women, including mothers and aunts, took on this not necessarily onerous task, young men would be far less aggressive, better lovers by far, and women would be better understood, more appreciated, and family violence would be reduced."

Helen looked at her husband in awe. Then in a slightly sarcastic voice she said, "That is great news darling. If there is suddenly a lull in proceedings when I'm with Bertie, and he seems to have lost interest, I'll bring what you've just told me up as a topic of conversation to keep him awake."

Freddy laughed loudly and Helen watched him with the eyes of a lover.

"Oh, by the way darling, I almost forgot. When I was about to leave Rosa today she asked me something, a favour, you might say."

Freddy had put his drink to one side and was removing Helen's glass from her hand. He was moving closer to her and he slipped his arm around her shoulders.

"So what was it darling. Was she after a loan?"

"Well, yes Freddy, you could say that. Rosa asked if I wouldn't mind if, when the moment was right, she could ask Freddy if she could see and feel his cock. She said she hadn't seen one other than Bertie's for so many years she couldn't count."

"My god, Bertie and I are having our dicks traded on the open market by a couple of beautiful, but lewd women. What chance does a man have?"

As he was talking, he was turning Helen around and over so that she was kneeling on the sofa beside him.

"I suppose you said yes, given that she had just given you her husband?"

Helen was wondering what Freddy was up to, but whatever it was she was enjoying his attention.

"Well of course, Freddy darling. How could I deny an elderly and elegant lady like Rosa even my most valued asset?"

Freddy was now on the move, sliding down onto the floor where he sat staring at the backs of Helen's gorgeous stockinged legs. He put out his hand and stroked a leg just above the knee. Then he lifted her skirt and touched her pussy through her knickers. Helen shuddered. Then Freddy slipped a finger in her knickers and drew them down around her ankles and slipped them off over her shoes.

Helen found herself teasing Freddy in a cracked and croaky and quietly excited voice.

"Do you know what you are looking for, my darling? Can I help you find something that has taken your fancy? I'm offering a range of options and I could be easily made happy with any of them, if they received the attention of a man like yourself."

Freddy was now standing up behind the kneeling Helen. He had taken his cock out of his trousers and was holding it firmly. Then he reached under one of the sofa cushions and found the tube of lubricant they kept hidden there.

Freddy bent and licked Helen's buttocks, one side then the other. Then he gently teased her bottom hole with his finger before pressing a dob of lube inside her.

Helen moaned and, as so often happened when Freddy got her excited, she sobbed with the extreme loving pleasure her husband gave her.

Freddy slowly inserted his stiff prick into Helen's bottom and the two of them gasped in unison. Helen never did work out why this was her ultimate pleasure spot. Not that all the other things were not pleasurable, it was just that this one topped the list.

Helen whispered to Freddy.

"Freddy darling, your cock is so beautiful in my bottom that I think that as we go on, I will want to scream and become a madwoman. Am I allowed to become your madwoman, Freddy? Am I allowed to vent my feelings for you and what you are doing to me? I so love you, Freddy. Please say yes."

"Yes, my beautiful madwoman. I will happily bugger you till you scream. And I might call you terrible dirty names at the same time. Is that okay too?"

"Oh yes, Freddy, I would love you to call me names, a whore, a bad little girl. Oh darling, this is bliss. Bugger me silly, Freddy."

And Freddy did.

When Helen arrived at Alice's place on Wednesday, she was a different person. She grabbed and kissed and held Alice so tight that Alice screamed "you're hurting me sweetheart."

Helen took Alice by the hand and led her to Alice's flat.

"Helen darling, what has got into you? You seem different. Are you okay?"

Helen sat Alice on the bed, slipped a hand onto her breast and kissed her passionately.

"I'm wonderful, darling. The world has changed for all of us."

"What on earth do you mean, Helen? What has happened? Tell me, quickly."

"Rosa and I are lovers at last. She told me why she had never let me get close to her."

Alice was wide-eyed.

"Yes. Rosa broke down and confessed that my mother, Belle, was her first lover, not Maude, as she had led us all to believe.

"She told me that Isabelle, after my father's death, was forever trying to get her to leave Bertie and live with her and this, after quite a few years, led to the breakdown of their relationship.

"They had a falling out and my mother died only a week or two later. For a long time Rosa felt that Mum's death was her fault, and that Mum had died of a broken heart.

"Rosa said that when I returned home from living in London a short time later, it was as if Belle had returned, and she was conflicted. She didn't want to hurt me in the way she thought she had so brutally hurt my mother.

"Bertie told her to stop being foolish and welcome me home in the loving way she felt towards my mother, be it erotically or otherwise, but she couldn't and kept me at a distance. As time went on, any thoughts of intimacy between us became impossible."

Helen paused for breath.

"Oh my darling Helen, this is such wonderful news. I don't know how you did it, but congratulations my love. We are now both slaves to Rosa's magic fingers."

Helen squealed with laughter and pushed Alice down onto the bed and rolled on top of her.

"Now I feel okay about being with Bertie, Alice. I told Rosa that, on your advice, I would start with Morning Glory very soon."

Alice rolled Helen onto her back, grabbed her skirt, pulled it up around her neck, and rushed to put her mouth on Helen's panties.

"God, I love you, Alice. Do things to me, Alice. I so want to feel you."

When eventually the two women had put their clothes back in order and were sitting with a cup of tea, Helen retold part of her story about being with Rosa.

"And now, wicked stepmother, tell me the juicy bit. How did you get from a lifetime of separation to having Rosa's lips on your clit?"

Helen giggled.

"Well, we were wanting to break the ice, so to speak, Rosa having confessed and me asking her to kiss me and so on, but we were not going to overcome the long years of denial.

"But then, given what had just happened, I decided that I was now able to go to Bertie's bed, and announced this to Rosa.

"She came instantly to life, informing me that she and Bertie always shared their lovers, and it was always she that went first before introducing him to a new love. Rosa then asked if she could have me right now? I didn't answer, but simply started to unbutton my blouse, then parted my legs and lifted up my skirt. Bingo! Rosa was on me at last, after all those years."

By the time Helen stopped talking, Alice was already running her hands up Helen's legs. Then she lifted them up high and told Helen to point her toes and roll her ankles around.

"Look at you, Helen! We are the luckiest women in the world. Loving you is a new miracle each day. Thank you."

Just before Helen was due to leave, she addressed Alice in a commanding voice.

"Now, while I'm thinking about it, young lady, what on earth did you and Freya do to my husband last Sunday night? He seemed so full of energy when I met him in the kitchen the next morning. Whatever it was, and maybe it was simply a good night's sleep, I hope you two got something out of it?

Alice laughed and recalled the night she a Freya had recently spent at Helen and Freddy's house.

"Well, Helen, we did exactly what you suggested. We were both supper cool, not being suggestive in any way, other than showing a just a little bit of ourselves while lying in front of the TV, my nightie up a little bit, Freya's pyjamas falling down a tad over her bum.

"As you said, Freddy was tired when he got home and seemed happy just to collapse on the sofa with a drink, not saying much other than 'Hello you two' and later 'Goodnight, see you soon'.

"Freya and I went off to bed, happy to be in your bed and not really expecting any interest from Freddy. We were just dozing off when he arrived and stripped off and got into bed.

"I was closest to him and he cuddled up behind me. Imagine

my shock when I discovered that his cock was already huge and quivering against my backside. Then he silently uncovered us both and pulled me up onto my knees and leant across to Freya and woke her up, and said 'Put my cock into Alice's cunt, please Freya'.

"Remembering all your words of advice about men, Freya and I both kept quiet and did whatever he asked.

"Once he got into me he asked Freya to stay where she was and touch his balls and my clit. Then he rapidly fucked me, quite hard, then announced he was coming. I couldn't help but come with him as he let out a roar. He remained in me for a while, his cock twitching and giving me a lot of little orgasms.

"We all settled back down, but after about half and hour or so Freddy got out of bed and went around and got in beside Freya. Moments later, Freya was awake and on her knees. Freddy reached across and found my arm and said, 'Put my cock into Freya's cunt, please Alice'.

"He got into Freya as he had into me, and with me playing with his balls and touching Freya's sex he came with a roar and with Freya screaming, 'Yes Freddy, yes' as she came with him."

"Oh yes, wicked stepmother. There was one other thing of interest that Freya and I really enjoyed."

Alice looked at Helen mischievously.

"Oh? What was that, darling?"

"We woke, but Freddy wasn't in the bed. We decided to go downstairs and make a drink. We sleepily came to the kitchen, a bit bedraggled and holding hands."

Alice stopped talking.

"And?"

"We saw the most exciting thing ever!"

"What, darling? What exciting thing could you possible see in our kitchen? You're being silly, I can tell."

"Standing and watching Freddy buggering my wicked stepmother over the kitchen dresser, that's what. It was so exciting. Freya and I took turns pushing and rubbing each other against the doorway while we watched and listened. You were both beautiful. Thank you from both of us, Helen."

"Oh my God. You saw us. You little devils. We didn't know you were there."

"Of course you didn't, my love. You were far to busy having your beautiful arse ravaged by your excited, sexy husband."

Helen's face was quite red but she could see the humour in all of it.

"So summing up, Alice, I think all three of us girls had Freddy to our complete satisfaction. Would you agree?"

"Oh yes, darling. Both Freya and I thought he was the best."

"So the question of the day must be, whatever we did right by Freddy on Sunday, can we bottle it so that we can do it on a regular basis?"

They both laughed and kissed.

"I only hope Freya and I get invited for a sleepover again soon, my darling. Very soon?"

"Well, to be fair, I guess I'll have to get Freddy's opinion and just hope that he had a good time too. If the sleepover met with his approval, I think we'll all get together very soon.

"I will add one thing, though. Freddy is off limits to any girl who's looking to get buggered. I have exclusive buggering rights until further notice."

Rosa had told Helen that it was best to get into Bertie's bed just after seven o'clock. By then he had gone for a pee, washed his face and brushed his teeth and then climbed back into bed and resumed an almost dreamlike state. Shortly after that, his erection would start to appear, and by seven thirty at the latest Morning Glory would be at the ready and happy to entertain a loving visitor.

Helen was understandably nervous as she found the hidden key under a flowerpot and opened the door of the Bennetts' house. Alice was not in the kitchen, as the two had agreed the day before that she would have her breakfast in her flat, and keep out of Helen's way.

Helen calmed herself and walked down to Bertie's bedroom. She knocked on the door.

"Come in, Alice."

Helen pushed the door open slowly and walked in, closing the door behind her. Bertie was amazed.

"Helen, sweet Helen, what brings you here so early in the morning? Is everything all right? Is Rosa all right?"

"Hello, Bertie. Yes, Rosa is just fine. She sends her love in fact, and, Bertie, she has sent me too."

"Sent you Helen? What do you mean girl?"

"Rosa and I are now lovers, Bertie, and she wants to share me with you, if you know what I mean. And if you are not comfortable with that, Bertie I can leave immediately, or though a cup of tea before I go would be nice."

Helen wasn't trying to be flippant. She was simply trying to avoid any long and overly serious discussion about the morality or appropriateness of what she was suggesting to Bertie.

Bertie stared at her, still in disbelief. Then he motioned to her to come over and sit on the bed beside him.

"Lovely to see you, Helen. I think about you a lot. We don't see enough of each other. I see more of your husband, which is not a bad thing. I love him dearly. He has a good head on his shoulders."

Helen sat on the bed beside Bertie, trying not to let him notice that she was looking for a lump in the bedclothes. Now that she was here she had a moment of self-doubt, of wondering if this had all been a mistake and that she shouldn't have come. Then Bertie made things clearer.

"If I am to share you, Helen, is there something you have in mind that we could do together? If not, I'd like to make a suggestion."

Helen realised that this was about to get serious.

"I would love to hear your suggestion, Bertie. I believe you already know that I have had a bit of a crush on you since I was a teenager.

"Rosa and I made a breakthrough this week, when she told me about her and my mother. During the conversation, she said she had always known how I felt about you and she thought you probably had similar feelings about me."

Bertie sat quietly for a moment. Then he leant forward and took her hand and slipped it under the bead spread and wrapped her fingers around his growing cock.

"Oh Bertie!"

"This would be a place to start, Helen. Rosa, when she is here, has it most mornings. She calls it her Morning Glory. Would you like to try what Rosa likes? We can think of other things we could do, later."

Helen's mind was racing. Yes, it did seem that Bertie's brain was working a little differently from most people's. And yes, Morning Glory was exactly where she wanted to begin.

"Yes, Bertie. I would like to try Morning Glory. Please tell me what to do."

"Before I do, Helen, I would like you to take off all of your clothes. I have wanted to see you naked for many years and it seems that at last, the moment has arrived. Please stand up for a moment and strip for me."

Helen needed no further prompting. In moments, she slipped off her blouse and bra and unzipped and stepped from her skirt. Then she pulled down her panties and dropped them on the floor and slipped off her shoes. She now stood before him in nothing but her grey stockings.

"That will do, Helen. How beautiful you are. Now I know why in times past, I have ached for you. Please come here so that I may kiss you and touch your breasts."

Helen went and knelt on the bed close to Bertie, and while she at first self-consciously tried to hide her body just a little, Bertie drew her close and began to lick her breasts. Then he drew her face close to his and kissed her on the lips.

"Are you ready, Helen?"

"Yes, Bertie."

Just as Alice had explained, Bertie told her to roll back the covers. And when Helen had done that, she reached out and took Bertie's big cock in both hands. Then she put it in her mouth. At last, after all these years she was the beneficiary of a mouthful of what she once craved. And then, when he asked her to swing around so that her rear was exposed to him, she shuddered just a little, knowing what was about to happen, half wishing she did not know what came next so that it could all be a surprise.

But while Helen was enjoying everything that Morning Glory provided, she also was enjoying Bertie for other reasons, one being that she was at last satisfying her desire to be this man's mature sexual partner. In the back of her mind also, were her expectations of adventures with Bertie using Rosa's codes, while sometimes sharing him with her beloved Alice.

When Helen – at what she thought was the end of this delicious adventure – found herself being held by Bertie's hands, tightly clasping her hips, she sensed there was a change of plan.

Bertie rose from the bed and dragged Helen around so that she was kneeling with her rear close to the edge of the bed and close to Bertie's cock.

"Helen. Don't be frightened if I get a little carried away. I don't usually ejaculate, but on this special occasion, I want to celebrate having you, so if you are OK with this, I will give you a very good shagging and come inside you. Can I go ahead, Helen?"

Helen thought quickly, but just as quickly knew she wanted it.

"Yes, Bertie. I'm very happy that you want to do this with me. Please shag me as hard as you want, lovely man."

Like Alice before her, the earth did move for Helen. But not only that. When things subsided and she went and brought the cups of tea and they had finished them, Bertie informed her that he had enjoyed her so much that he was now wanted to shag her again.

Helen lay panting, totally blissed out on Bertie's second magnificent ejaculation, and as sperm dribbled in huge quantities from her stretched and pummelled vagina, Bertie told her that he hoped to see a lot more of her and that he thought Rosa would be very happy to know how well they had got on.

But then it was Helen's turn to have her moment with the man she'd had a crush on all those years.

"Lie back down on the bed, Bertie. I haven't finished with you, my darling."

Helen settled herself on top of Bertie with her back end close to his face. Then she mauled his testicles and his cock, sucking him and licking him and even biting him and rubbing him between her breasts, doing everything she could to make up for those years of wanting him, and in her mind she saw herself with him in her teens, her twenties, her thirties and on and on, until today.

Helen wanted to fulfil and satisfy all those years, and she wanted Bertie to know how she felt. And when Bertie gently licked her, and caressed her buttocks and her shoulders, and lifted both her feet to his mouth and sucked her toes and licked her ankles, she sobbed and she knew that he understood.

"Yes, Bertie. You will see a lot more of me. And yes, I'm sure Rosa will be very happy. Thank you, you lovely man."

Helen couldn't wait until Wednesday to tell Alice how things had gone at the Bennetts' house, so she phoned very early, before Alice started classes.

"Oh Helen, I so wanted to call you, but thought I should wait."

"It all went very, very well, darling. Amazing, in fact. I'll tell you about it when I see you on Wednesday.

"What I want you to do before then, though, is look at Rosa's codes and think about what we could do together with Bertie. When I see you, we should work out a plan. Oh and Alice, that study and sunroom near the kitchen, is that a place we could go? Is there a sofa there? I haven't been in there for years, and can't remember."

"It would be the ideal spot, Helen."

The two chatted on, then expressed their love and said how they looked forward to seeing each other soon.

13

MISCHIEF OR MAGIC?

IT WAS the day after Helen's first erotic encounter with Bertie, and she was feeling very pleased with herself. She had phoned Alice and put her on notice that they should think about what they could or would do on their first 'Fifi' code session with Bertie. Helen had a few ideas which passed dreamily through her head as she settled in her studio.

Helen looked at the painting she was working on. Leaving a work for a couple of days was always a good idea. To look at it with fresh eyes allowed one to see faults and things that could be improved. As she was looking, for some reason she remembered something Mary had said about Janice, something which suddenly fired her thought processes and she remembered something important.

Only a couple of weeks ago, Helen had been at an art gallery opening, and sitting with a group of women, some of whom she had never met. She got on well with a pleasant lady who talked about interesting things, not just the usual boring holiday plans or their forthcoming sea cruise.

Helen could not remember what led to this particular conversation, but this woman's story went something like this.

The woman, Celia Ashbee, had a son teaching at a private school whose friend, teaching at another private school, had a friend who told him a rude story. The friend of the friend of the friend said that one of his senior students and some other lads were in a church choir and that they had a great time each week after choir practice with two women.

Helen suddenly got very interested at this point, but tried to hide her enthusiasm, not wanting the nice lady to think ill of her.

"Did the friend of the friend of the friend say if the student described what happened, Celia?"

Celia poured more tea and selected a savoury *petit four*. Helen estimated that she was perhaps a little older than herself, a well-kept woman in her late fifties or very early sixties.

Celia continued her story, lowering her voice and looking around her as she spoke.

"It seems that the music teacher and the organist would wait until everyone had left at the end of practice, except for a half dozen or more lads who went and hung around in the churchyard.

"Then the two women would go back inside the vestry, change their clothes, putting on stockings and suspenders, high heels and short skirts, along with lots of makeup, then unlock the door and let the boys in."

Helen found the story fascinating, and erotic.

"My goodness, Celia, stories like this could cause a sudden increase in the sizes of congregations across the land. Please tell me more."

Celia laughed, enjoying her new friend's sense of humour and impressed with Helen's seeming lack of shockability.

"Did he say what actually happened after the boys entered the vestry?"

Helen's new friend coloured up and Helen looked at her appreciatively. Celia, on the one hand a very proper upper middle-class woman of impeccable taste, hid a fun-loving naughty side which one would never have observed except via the subject matter of this conversation.

"He did, Helen. He did indeed. He said that in a very small ante-room there was a mattress covered with a bedspread, probably an emergency bed in case someone in the congregation suddenly took poorly.

"He said that the two women knelt on the mattress and called to the boys to come in, in pairs. Then they told the boys to show them what they had in their trousers. Once they were on display, each woman would put a boys penis in her mouth and suck it; then after a while they would look up at the boy's face and say ..."

By this time, Helen was mesmerised by Celia's story and, it should be said, by the delightful Celia. Her looks, her beautiful voice, her smile, even the lines on her face spoke of intelligence and joy. Her fine clothes spoke of finer garments beneath, a satin camisole perhaps, expensive serviceable panties with just a touch of lace? And was she a woman who preferred wearing stockings or did she choose tights? And even though she was slim, would she own a corselet?

"Say it, Celia. Tell me what she said. You are committing story interruptus. Please, don't leave me hanging."

Celia burst out laughing, then put her hand over her mouth and looked around like a naughty girl.

"Suck or fuck?" she whispered.

Helen stared at Celia's sparkling eyes, bright with mirth.

"Gosh Celia, we're getting to the high notes now."

"Then, if the boy replied with the 'f' word, the woman immediately does an about face, showing her rear end and, it is said, not wearing any knickers, at which point the boy has his way.

"If he has any difficulty finding his way, and if the woman beside her is facing the front and has a moment with a free hand, she will lean across and put him in. If not, a hand will come through the legs to grab him and sort him out."

Celia stopped talking and stared at Helen. She looked flushed and excited. She was fascinated with Helen. She loved her relaxed unfazed way of seeing things.

Helen looked back at her, one could even say lovingly.

There was suddenly a hush as people prepared for a final concert piece by three young violinists.

"Celia?"

204 | THE FIFI CODE

"Yes, Helen?"

"Can I write down my telephone number and give it to you? And maybe we could catch up some time soon. I love talking to you, so I hope we can see each other again."

"Please, yes. And I will call you very soon. You are great company and I do get lonely for someone to talk with who is happy to talk about anything."

"Thank you. Oh, I forgot to ask, can you tell me the name of the church or do you need to keep it a secret?"

"Ah, yes. I hadn't really thought about that. Perhaps if I just say it begins with a J, Helen."

"Hello, Helen."

Helen had walked over to the house to get a knife sharpener. She always meant to buy one for the studio but then, when shopping, she forgot.

Helen was startled by the voice. She looked up.

"Sorry Helen, if I surprised you. I came through Mary's gate and saw you leaving and that you had left the door open, so thought you would no doubt return soon."

"Janice! How nice to see you. Are you looking for Mary? I think it's her volunteer day at the Salvos' op shop."

"Sort of. But I really wanted to see you, Helen. Can I come in?"

Helen gestured towards the studio door.

"Be my guest, Janice."

Helen could not move her eyes away from the long, thin extraordinary body of Janice. Her legs and backside were almost a kinky artwork, exaggerated in a way that artists toyed with in their drawings but which quite rightly, no one ever believed depicted a real person.

But what was racing through Helen's mind at this moment was what she had said to Mary, "Be careful what you think about because it usually comes true." She had thought quite a bit about Janice since her conversation with Celia Ashbee about the goings-on at the church, and Helen was convinced that, 'J' must surely have meant St John's, and if it did, then Janice was surely one of the women entertaining the boys after choir practice.

And hadn't Mary said she thought Janice was not as innocent as she looked?

Helen steeled herself. Other than her fascination with Janice's body, she felt no special attraction to the woman. She had no thoughts about loving her and without any emotional ties it would be hard to imagine that anything would ever happen between them.

Helen closed the door and invited Janice to sit on one of the studio's three kitchen chairs.

"Well, Janice. What can I do for you? Is Mary giving you a hard time?"

Janice laughed.

"Not at all, Helen. I'm not sure how to say this, but I was always fascinated with Mary's story of your seduction of her, and how beautiful and loving it was. Over time, I've not exactly been jealous, but Mary took me quite brutally, not showing any love until later. Now whenever I think of love, I can't help thinking of you, Helen. Could we be lovers too, Helen? It would be a wonderful thing, sharing you with Mary."

Helen's mind raced as she watched an increasingly agitated Janice first lift her skirt up just above her knees and then fiddle with the buttons on her blouse, while her mouth began to gape and her tongue wandered over her lips.

Helen could thank her for her compliments and then simply ask Janice to leave. There was no way she wanted to add Janice to her list of girlfriends. And then of course there was the deceit of the woman, if she was one of the women in the story about the lads at St John's. Her story about wanting to be loved did not in any way ring true.

Helen suddenly saw what was going on. Janice was under an influence of sorts. Was it drugs? Helen guessed it was something she had first heard about many years before, when she was working in a clinic in London.

Janice was suffering from what, in the old days, was called

nymphomaniac's disorder, known amongst Helen's co-workers and nurses as nympho block.

The word "nymphomaniac" was no longer in use, having been replaced with the term "hyper-sexuality", but in those days, the term "nympho block", referred to a woman who had engaged in sex continuously over many days, weeks or months, and who was now unable to live without it, suffering a craving like a drug addict looking for the next fix.

Of the various theories that doctors and therapists came up with, the one Helen found most plausible was the idea that these women had experienced a lot of bad sex or, put differently, incomplete sex, sex without orgasms.

Normally, regular sex between partners might be very satisfying, or it might not. The difference was that women who only had sex a couple of times a week, and did not experience regular orgasms, did not suffer this build-up, or if they did it was minor and could be overcome. Sadly, what was more likely to happen was that they just learnt to live with it or should one say, without it.

One solution offered by sex therapists was to teach a patient to orgasm more easily when having sex, and in the couple of cases Helen observed this did, over time, lead to a better outcome for the woman. And of course, the arrival of the electric vibrator changed things for many women.

What Helen was seeing here might well be the result of Janice having a lot of inexperienced young cocks giving her nothing but their quick ejaculations. These lads were not experienced males offering foreplay and long deep thrusting and prolonged enjoyment.

Unable to find a fix, Janice had finally ended up here as a last resort. Subconsciously, she understood the need for real love and, remembering Mary's story of her loving conversion by Helen, this was the only place where she might find answers.

Helen looked at Janice and saw that she now had her hand between her legs, her head had lolled back, and her eyes were closed.

Then she recalled an experience she'd had in London. It was her first real lesbian romance. The older woman was Louise Lazarus, the glamorous bitch secretary of the medical centre's managing director.

Helen was dazzled by Louise's stylish clothes and elegant body, and when she invited Helen to her flat for afternoon tea, one Saturday, Helen jumped at the invitation. After she had arrived and been shown around the luxury apartment, it was only an hour or less before Louise had her tongue inside Helen's mouth and a hand inside her brassiere, and it wasn't long before she was guiding the young woman's hand along Louise's stockinged leg and up to her panties, where she lovingly showed the willing novice how to put her fingers inside her crotch and inside her.

Louise had secrets that she carried from her schooldays, and over time she revealed those secrets to Helen.

Louise had been educated at one of the smaller private girls schools near the Sussex border, in Kent. The school, or rather the staff, were expected to follow the school's long traditions regarding discipline, meaning that girls were regularly thrashed.

Flagellation or "pursuing the path of penance" as it was referred to, was a regular occurrence at the school. So endemic was it that "the art" was practiced, not only by the staff on the senior girls, but the senior girls themselves who would administer it to a select few of the staff, always in secret of course.

Whippings, strappings, spankings, floggings of every description were a major topic of conversation. Everything at school rotated around who had what done to them, or what they had done to someone else.

So popular was this pastime that it would seem to have been the foremost form of entertainment for the hormonally charged scholars, and quite naturally girlfriends looked after one another, tending each other's discomfort with soothing balms and very loving words.

Thus "pursuing the path of penance" facilitated the continuation of the school's healthy lesbian traditions, endowing the nation with the strong women necessary for providing the special sort of workers and wives required to serve alongside the public school men of the aristocracy and the upper classes, and ultimately to ensure the success and safety of the empire.

Stately homes, along with the nice houses of the public servants taking the early morning trains to Westminster or the City in their bowler hats – and with extreme punctuality – were ruled by women of substance, women who knew where their responsibilities lay, along with their understanding of certain things that their husbands didn't know that they knew.

Adaptability was an essential quality for the public school educated woman, especially when she eventually took her marital vows, and shouldered the responsibilities that being a wife demanded, be they judging the flowers at the village fete or organising the house staff on an Indian tea plantation, or overseeing the affairs of the family and the estate, while her officer husband was away on some foreign battlefield.

Within days Louise had made Helen her protege, and shortly after that her sex slave, having Helen whenever, however and wherever she wanted.

From then on, Helen felt a wetness between her legs whenever Louise spoke her name, and she bent her knees just a little the moment her mistress came towards her.

The medical centre where Helen and Louise worked specialised in gynaecological problems. Woman would present with all sorts of situations, and every once in a while, if there was someone with a case of hyper-sexuality who was suffering, the powers that be would give a wink and nod, and indicate to Louise that this might be a case of "nympho block" and that she could perhaps help the sufferer.

Helen remembers returning home to Louise's house one evening after working late. Immediately she shut the front door behind her, she heard screams which she knew could only mean that someone was being flogged.

Knowing better than to disturb her mistress in full flagellator mode, Helen nonetheless, went and listened at the door of the punishment room.

Things had obviously been going on for some time. The person being flogged was well past screaming "No, please, no more" and now sang out in a high pitched wailing scream, "More, yes, yes, oh please, more." This was followed a little later by a deafening scream that seemed to go on for ages, as the woman reached her orgasm.

As Helen turned to leave, the door flew open and Louise walked out and seeing her, and with her eyes shining brightly from the excitement that she had just enjoyed, grabbed her and kissed her passionately on the lips and, pushing her against the wall and with a hand firmly placed between her legs, said "I'm going to give you an orgasm like that, darling, very soon," then headed to the bathroom.

And she did. Only days later, Louise took Helen into the room and closed the door and proceeded to introduce her to the strap. She already new that the pain would turn to pleasure, but when it did became pleasurable, Louise didn't stop. Only when Helen vented the prolonged scream which accompanied a major orgasm did her lady lover stop beating her, and instead, took her in her arms and carried her the few steps to the big bed. But she hadn't finished.

First she lightly rubbed balm on Helen's cut up bottom. Then she put on her favourite strap-on and opened her legs and shagged her, all the time telling her how beautiful she was how sexy she was and how she was going to fuck her forever and a day.

Once a week, after work, Louise would tell Helen to put on her old school skirt and the long school socks she had saved, hidden in a drawer. Then she would make her lie back on the bed while she lifted her legs, staring at her while she ran her hand up her schoolgirl sock to the bare top of her leg, all the while touching herself with her other hand.

Then Louise would give her her evening shag. And when she had given her an orgasm, she would look down at her with her beautiful smile and say "You've been such a good girl all week Helen, Miss

Lazarus is going to let you have her pussy now as a reward. You can shag her just as much as you want, my child."

Then she would lift Helen up and take off her strap-on and fix it to her waist.

As Helen worked the dildo in and out of Louise's splendid pussy, and as Louise lifted up Helen's skirt and touched her legs, she stared up at her young and innocent face and spoke softly to her. "Do you love shagging your teacher, darling? Does being on top of Miss Lazarus excite you my sweet? Yes, I know it does because you are shagging Miss Lazarus so beautifully." And so Helen's introduction to love also included other people's fantasies, and she loved them.

Helen's first lady lover became her yardstick for any future relationships and she chose mostly to be a single person rather than enter into what she always sensed would be a liaison less intense than the experience the dazzling Louise had shown her.

Janice was staring at Helen with pleading eyes.

Helen looked up at objects hanging on the wall. Among the interesting miscellany of items was a well-made leather tickler, a miniature cat-o-nine-tails that Freddy had brought home as a present for her when he had been away at a convention.

She was excited when one day he picked it off the wall and laid into her bottom with it. She screamed in agony, but just as she was beginning to get a wonderful sensation that overrode the pain and would take her "all the way", Freddy stopped, believing he should not hurt his wife in this way. Helen was extremely disappointed. "That is what comes from having such a caring husband, damn it!"

The little tickler had not been taken off the wall since.

Helen was now getting hot thinking about that day with Freddy, and much further back to Louise, and the possibilities in front of her now. She could help Janice and enjoy herself at the same time.

Janice's amazing legs could not be ignored, Helen mused as she stood up and went over to her.

"Janice?"

"Yes Helen?"

"I'm going to do things to you. Okay?

"Oh yes, please Helen. Please give me some relief. If you don't, I think I will surely die. Do whatever you want to me, Helen. It must be better than dying."

"Janice?"

"Yes?"

"I'm going to whip your backside, Janice, until it turns red, and I won't let you leave until I'm finished. Are you ready for this, Janice?"

"Yes, Helen. I need to be punished for I have sinned heavily in the sight of God."

Helen knew enough about addicts. They loved to be theatrical and talk rubbish, though often it did relate to some real event in their lives.

"Would you like me to kiss you first, Janice, before I thrash you?"

"Yes, yes, give me your lips, Helen. I so want to be loved."

At first, she wanted to kiss Janice only to make it easier for her to launch herself on the wretched woman. Now Helen was going to love her properly, regardless. She could whip Janice with love, just as Louise had whipped Helen.

Helen led her to the divan beside the window

She began by kissing Janice, who cried and thrust her tongue into Helen's mouth. Helen accepted it, tentatively at first but then, deciding to let herself go all the way. She put her lips back on Janice's mouth and tongued her enthusiastically, while Janice groaned.

Then she slipped Janice's skirt down over the long legs and made her lie down on her back. Helen lifted her legs high up in the air as she did with all of her lovers, and told her not to move.

Helen grabbed a charcoal pencil and a pad and quickly sketched the magic legs and the unusual bubble backside, incongruous on such a thin body.

Then Helen slowly caressed Janice's legs and kissed the backs of her knees, and all the while Helen couldn't stop touching her own wet pussy and she smiled inwardly, knowing that this was a good sign.

Janice continued sobbing, all the time murmuring, "Yes Helen, yes Helen, please Helen." Then Helen reached for the tickler on the wall.

When Janice screamed the giant scream that accompanied her most extraordinary orgasm ever, Helen orgasmed too, and not just lightly. The excitement she felt while flogging Janice's rear end felt as though Janice was the one who had flogged Helen. It felt truly beautiful.

Suddenly two women, who until now, had been separated by many differences, were sharing feelings that were very rarely available to women other than via a flogging, be it by hand, the rod, or the tickler.

Janice was cured, at least until the next time. Her manner changed and Helen hoped that her habits would change. But that of course, would be up to Janice.

Helen never knew just what happened at the church after that, nor did she bother to ask. Nor did she enquire about what other things her new sexually hyperactive friend got up to.

But she knew that this new secret friend, Janice, would come to her with her long legs and body each time she felt a "nympho block" coming on, and together they would visit that secret heaven.

Helen bathed Janice's backside and delicately applied a healing balm. Janice lay still and quiet as though she was sleeping, but when Helen said in a very quiet and reassuring voice that Janice could come to her whenever she needed special help, she turned her head and with a serene smile murmured "Thank you, Helen."

And when Helen went on to ask Janice if she would keep their special time together a secret, Janice replied, "Only you and me, Helen, I promise." Then she looked up again and added, "and our little leather friend, hanging up there on the wall."

Helen put a hand on Janice's face and kissed her. "Just the three of us, darling, that's right."

Then Helen rolled Janice onto her back and lifted her legs so that they stood high in the air.

"Now Janice, please don't move for a moment. I just want to add the seams of your stockings to my drawing."

14

NEW LOVES

FREDERICO HAD BEEN LOOKING FORWARD to his rostered day off, and as Helen was going to be away for a lot of the day, they decided it would be nice if he visited Rosa.

"Don't forget what I told you, darling. Rosa will be looking out for you, hoping to get that special request," Helen said with a glint in her eye.

"Oh dear. My trouser friend might find a hospital room rather intimidating. I'll have to call on all my resources."

Helen laughed.

"Darling, I wouldn't worry too much. I'm sure Rosa has a way of ferreting around inside a man's trousers that will satisfy her, one way or the other."

Freddy grabbed Helen and kissed her passionately, and pretended to ravish her.

"You had better save your energy, dearest husband. Who knows, when you're with Rosa, her special lady friend, nurse Christine, the freckle-nosed redhead with the green eyes and the large backside, might get her hands on you.

"If she does, just mention that your wife still has the hots for her, would you please, darling? I think she might have noticed me, but putting in a good word for me would be nice."

Freddy yelled and applauded.

"I sometimes think I'm married to the most loveable sex machine in the whole universe. All right, if you insist, I'll try to remember to put a good word in for you darling, just when I've got her skirt up and I'm checking out her butt."

Helen laughed and cracked the tea towel at him like a whip.

"Promises, promises!"

The two kissed and sat down together with their bowls of muesli.

It was mid-morning when Frederico arrived at Rosa's unit. A "do not disturb" sign hung on the door, so Freddy knocked gently.

"Who is it?"

"It's Freddy, Rosa. Can I come in?"

"Yes, Freddy. Please do."

Rosa's room was comfy. A large vase of fresh flowers stood on the little table under the window.

Rosa was lying on top of her bed reading a magazine. She had just emerged from the shower and wore only her dressing gown. Frederico noticed her tiny shapely feet and her painted toenails. And he could not ignore the glimpse he had of the tops of the backs of her legs beneath her cotton gown, as she bent her knees and repositioned herself to make room for him.

"Even older women can never forget the sensual arts," he remembered Rosa's husband Bertie saying, during one of their long conversations on life and love.

There was a gentle and pleasant smell of fresh flowers in the air and Frederico felt comfortable and relaxed.

"Oh Freddy, it is so good to see you, especially now that Helen and I have broken through our silly problems of the past. I so love that girl."

"From what I can see, Rosa, you've made my wife very happy. She's a changed woman."

Rosa patted the bed and beckoned to him to come and sit down with her. They talked about lots of things, about Helen and Alice and Bertie, and the possibility of Rosa coming home soon.

All the while, Rosa's loving smile beamed at Freddy and he knew she had more than conversation in mind. He decided to take the initiative.

"Rosa?"

"Yes, Freddy?"

"I would very much like to kiss you on the lips in the way Helen says you both now kiss. Can I try that, please?"

Rosa's eyes glistened and she couldn't hide her eagerness.

"Please do, Freddy. I would like that very much. But Helen would have told you, I hope, that I was eager to discover your cock? Before you kiss me, Freddy, can I undo your trousers?"

Freddy stood up from the bed, unbuckled his belt and let his trousers fall around his ankles, then he pulled down his underpants to join them, and shook his fallen clothes off all together. He sat back on the bed, up close to Rosa.

"Oh Freddy, that's much better. Yes my lovely man, please kiss me now."

Freddy took Rosa's head between his hands and reached forward to her already pouting lips. He felt her tongue reach in between his lips and slowly roll around his mouth. At the same time, Rosa's hand found Frederico's rising penis and slid lightly down to the end of it; then her fingers moved under his crotch and fingered his testicles.

Frederico moved a hand down and caressed the top of her tiny foot, then slowly moved up her leg under the dressing gown until he touched her already wet sex. Rosa sighed.

"Oh Freddy, that is beautiful. You are the first man other than Bertie that I've touched in twenty years. You feel so good. Don't stop touching me, darling."

The two were still kissing when there was a knock at the door.

"Rosa? It's me, Christine. Can I come in?"

Rosa pushed Frederico away gently and looked lovingly at his face.

"You will like her, darling Freddy. Helen does."

"Come in Christine, if you dare. And lock the door behind you."

The door opened and closed, then Frederico heard Christine's little gasp.

"Rosa? I'm shocked."

"No, you're not really, darling. You remember Freddy, Helen's husband? Come over here, you sexy woman. You might like to share something with me?"

The well-built green-eyed redhead came over and stared at Rosa's hand wrapped around Frederico's cock. Then she looked at Frederico and smiled.

"Hello, Frederico. So nice to see you again. I hope your beautiful wife Helen is well. By the way, does she ever mention me?"

Christine pulled up her tight skirt so that she could more easily kneel down beside the bed, close to Freddy's's bare legs.

Freddy looked down at the tops of Christine's well-filled brown stockinged legs and the tips of her beige suspenders and her brown regulation shoes, trying desperately to think clearly as Rosa lovingly tickled and ran her hand up and down his cock.

"Umm! Yes, she often mentions you. I get quite jealous sometimes. She has a thing for you, Christine, you must have noticed."

Frederico felt happy that he'd fulfilled Helen's request. Then Rosa laughed.

"Well, we had better even things up, hadn't we? What do you think, Christine? Can you do something to Freddy that might make the lovely Helen jealous?"

Christine looked up at Rosa and smiled.

"With your permission Rosa, I'd love to try."

With that, Christina leaned over and took Frederico's cock out of Rosa's hand and slipped it into her mouth while a hand moved under him and touched his testicles. She licked his cock and sucked it, and stared up at Freddy with eager smiling eyes.

"Oh how beautiful," exclaimed Rosa as she watched.

Rosa opened her dressing gown and leant back and began to play with herself. Christine noticed, and slid a spare hand on to Rosa's leg, where it drifted up her inner thigh to caress Rosa's busy hand and tug gently at her pubic hairs.

There came a moment when Freddy knew he had to do something.

"I so want to shag one of you. I will come very soon if we keep doing this."

Christine took his cock out of her mouth long enough to speak.

"I would love you to fuck me, Freddy, but now is not the right time. Can I dare suggest you invite me home to your house so that I could have both you and your lovely wife, Helen? Can I dare you?"

She laughed and popped him back into her mouth, moving her head backwards and forwards with greater vigour.

"You can expect an invitation from Helen very soon, I'm sure," Frederico groaned.

"Now I am about to come, darling woman. Is that okay?"

Rosa screamed in her excitement.

"Oh Christine! Can I have it, darling? Just for medicinal purposes, of course."

Everyone who could, laughed and Christine almost choked.

"Yes, my love, move your head down here and I will share it with you."

Rosa moved forward and leant down, and Christine put Frederico's cock into Rosa's mouth, all the while holding it and leading him up to the moment of ejaculation with her hand movements. Rosa aided her, with her mouth wide open and with a simple gentle tongue movement as she prepared herself for the rush of Frederico's sperm.

Frederico came with his usual roar and deposited it mostly down Rosa's hungry throat before her sexy nurse intervened, swallowing him to get the last of it. Rosa gurgled and shoved her fingers hard into her vagina and orgasmed.

Christine threw herself on the bed beside them and pulled her skirt right up, pushing down her knickers to her knees and exposing her auburn pussy and rubbing herself vigorously, coming only a few moments after Freddy. Rosa saw her and watched and then fell back, pushing her fingers into herself again and orgasming, and shaking all over.

Frederico looked at Christine, now lying still and smiling up at him fully displaying herself to his gaze. He looked at her solid and sensuous legs and body and thought how much he looked forward to possessing every bit of it very soon.

Christine pouted suggestively and moved a hand to play with Frederico's now withered penis.

"You won't forget me, Freddy, will you? And remember, I can offer you more than what you're now looking at, you beautiful man."

Frederico took her words as a hint, and chanced a final move. He wetted a finger in Christine's wet vagina, then slid a hand under her backside and felt for the magic bottom hole between her beautiful buttocks. Christine responded quickly and put her hand around the back to guide his finger to the spot and then she put it inside her. Then she wiggled her bum and smiled, opening and shutting her eyes and sighing to indicate her pleasure as she looked up at him.

"Oh you darling man. You soon worked out what this girl likes."

Frederico smiled down at Christine as she whispered slowly.

"Don't you dare forget me Freddy. I know where you live."

Helen found Celia Ashbee's house. It was very large and set in an acre of trees and shrubs with lawns around the edge of the sweeping driveway. Large iron gates swung closed behind her as she drove in.

She had texted Celia when she was on her way so that the gates would be open when she arrived.

Everything seemed so grandiose, even more so when she was greeted at the door by a pretty maid who showed her through to the parlour.

"Miss Ashbee will be with you shortly, Mrs Alves. Please make yourself comfortable."

Helen thanked the maid, thinking what a beautiful young woman she was.

Once alone, Helen wandered around looking at pictures on the walls and photographs on the cabinet tops.

She was particularly taken by a number of black-and-white photos showing the young Celia in various activities: with other players holding hockey sticks; riding a beautiful horse in what looked like a dressage event; Celia throwing a javelin at an athletic meeting. A picture Helen liked above all others was Celia standing with two girl friends, all three in bathing costumes.

"Sorry to keep you waiting, darling. Phone calls can be such a nuisance. Come and sit down and we'll start with a cup of tea."

Celia went to a corner near the huge fireplace and pulled on a thick silk chord. Almost instantly, the maid appeared.

"Polly, this is my friend Helen Alves. We would like tea for two. Oh yes, and could you bring a couple of meringues too. Thank you, Polly."

The two women had a pleasant conversation about all sorts of things, laughing a lot at shared jokes and stories.

Then Celia invited Helen to follow her to show her a little bit of the house, but in particular her favourite room.

The study was delightful, lots of books and antiques, and quite lavishly furnished with two enormous sofas and two very large armchairs as well as an ottoman and various footstools.

Celia shut the door and the two made themselves comfortable on one of the sofas.

From the very beginning, when first they met, Helen had been fascinated with Celia's wonderful voice and deportment. And the more time she spent with her, the more she admired Celia's trim body; and she adored her face.

The two had just stopped laughing about something, when Celia leant forward towards Helen and smiled.

"I think it's time I kissed you Helen. I hope you will be neither offended or frightened. Come closer, darling."

Helen was mesmerised. She had lived through many seductions and knew what to expect; or not. Celia's offer came not so much as a surprise, but because Helen fully expected that the initiative would most likely have had to come from her.

Helen instantly appreciated the offer.

"At this moment, I can think of nothing I would want more than to be kissed by you Celia. You are an enchantress. I'm feeling a little vulnerable at this moment though, so please be gentle."

Celia smiled appreciatively and Helen moved up closer to her.

"I will tell you what I would like us to do, if that is fine with you Helen?"

"Yes, Celia."

"I have fantasies, Helen. Seductions are a common one, and teasing is another, not that I get to experience them often. Would you accompany me on my fantasy, beautiful woman?"

"Yes, Celia. I have fantasies too, so I can appreciate your need more than you can know. Please Celia, have your way with me in your fantasy, in any way you want me."

"The rules are that you must keep your eyes closed and you must not move. My fantasy is teasing you."

Helen was excited. She felt a tiny moment of excitement in her pussy and a sudden dampness between her legs.

"Please begin, Celia. I am waiting dear, lady, and you are making me wet already."

Celia smiled in appreciation of Helen's comment. Then Celia made sure Helen's hands were properly placed beside her thighs and that her eyes were closed.

Helen surrendered to Celia. All she wanted was to be a part of Celia's fantasy, wherever it took them.

After what seemed a long time, Helen felt the lightest touch on her breasts, but then the touch was gone. Then she felt fingers lightly touching her on her stockinged knee, but then they were gone. A moment later, a gentle rubbing on each ankle made her want to respond and stretch out her legs and feet, but she knew she must not move.

Then, moments later, fingers moved slowly up the backs of her legs along the calves, stopping to pirouette behind her knees before moving further up and under her skirt.

Then Helen felt her skirt being slowly lifted as Celia revealed the tops of her legs. Fingers touched her suspenders, then lightly touched the wet spot on her panties. Helen could not contain a trembling, but managed to stop the tiny orgasm that would normally follow it.

A silent, motionless period followed. Then Helen felt Celia unbuttoning her blouse and when she had undone all of the buttons it fell open, revealing her braless top and her beautiful breasts.

Fingertips touched the tips of Helen's hard stiff nipples.

Helen heard a little gasp from Celia, then realised that she, herself, was breathing heavily.

Then Celia spoke, and when she did, Helen realised that she had heard that voice, long, long ago. Louise Lazarus, her first love, her lesbian mistress and the woman who had converted Helen to a love of discipline. Could Celia Ashbee be another ex-private girls-school student like Louise?

"Now little girl, if you are ready? Open your eyes and unbutton Miss Ashbee's blouse, just as she has unbuttoned yours. That's a good girl. Don't be scared."

Helen was both shocked and delighted. Never ever had she expected to find a soulmate in a fantasy that she held dear to her heart. Helen had no difficulty in reverting back to Miss Lazarus's schoolmistress and schoolgirl fantasy. She had adored Louise playing the schoolmistress.

Helen opened her eyes and smiled at the beautiful Celia. Helen leant forward and began to unbutton Celia's blouse.

"Yes, Miss Ashbee."

Helen noticed a moment of surprise on Celia's face.

"What a good little girl you are, Helen. I might have to think of a special treat for you later."

Helen had undone the buttons and was staring at the lace bra covering Celia's elegant chest.

"Now girl, before we take Miss Ashbee's brassiere off, she would like you to try and put your little hand down inside the garment, and find the nipple on her left breast. Off you go, child. See what you can do."

Oh, what a delight this woman was. Helen figured that she could play this game all day and still some. She was definitely warming to being the little Miss Helen.

Helen's hand touched the top of Miss Ashbee's chest, then she slid it down behind the left bra cup and captured the beautiful nipple, already standing to attention. She fingered it lovingly.

"Oh yes, you beautiful girl, you are making your teacher very happy. Oh yes!"

Then Celia leant forward and, reaching round, unhooked her bra. She slipped off her top and slid the bra shoulder straps off, then she dropped it on the floor.

She lay back for a moment, her shapely breasts staring at Helen, and Helen staring back, running her wet tongue around her lips in anticipation.

"Would you like to kiss Miss Ashbee's breasts, young lady? And would you like to sit on Miss Ashbee's knee little girl, so that you can cuddle up to her bare chest?"

"Oh yes, Miss Ashbee. Please let me. I'm feeling quite queer, but it is a lovely feeling. I think it's because of the things you are doing to me Miss Ashbee. Please don't stop."

"Before we do anything, sweet girl, Miss Ashbee is going to take off her skirt so that she can better enjoy you sitting on her legs. Would you like Miss Ashbee to take some clothes off?"

"Oh yes, I would love that, Miss."

"And I think we should take some of your clothes off too, darling. While I remove my skirt, you take off your top and skirt. Then come and sit on my knee."

"Oh yes, Miss!"

Helen quickly removed her clothes and stood in front of her fantasy school mistress in her panties, stockings and heels.

Celia stared at her, feeding on the beautiful vision. Then she took Helen's hand and sat her on Miss Ashbee's now exposed stockinged thigh.

Celia couldn't stop herself. She groped Helen between her legs and cupped her breasts and eagerly slurped and sucked her very stiff nipples. When she stopped, she leant back and smiled.

"You sweet girl. You are so beautiful, I might never let you go back into class again. I might make you my slave and keep you in my quarters. I would come and make love to you many times every day and teach you how to love and be loved. Would you like that darling little Helen?"

"Oh yes, Miss Ashbee. Please! I would love that. And Miss Ashbee?"

"Yes, darling?"

"Please let me kiss your lips. I love you so much."

"Oh, what a joy you are. Come to me, you sexy little wench. Put your tongue in my mouth while I think about which part of you I want to have next."

With that, Celia rolled back and to the side to lie on the sofa, dragging Helen with her, pulling her face to hers and kissing her passionately while touching and fingering little Helen between her legs. When they eventually stopped, Celia whispered in Helen's ear.

"Darling Helen. Where would you like our fantasy to go? Do you have a thing that you want desperately enough that you would beg Miss Ashbee to do it to you?

It didn't take long for Helen to respond.

"The truth is, Miss Ashbee, I adore discipline. Spanking in particular. But apart from a relationship I was in, in London during my early twenties, I've never found anyone that shared this same urge. I know much about how to "pursue the path of penance", but it is not something others know about or wish to share."

Helen realised that Celia was crying.

"What is wrong, Celia?"

Celia sobbed.

"Nothing, sweet Helen. You have just made me the happiest person in the world. I too had given up on ever experiencing the delight of proper discipline. So often my bottom has longed for a strong loving hand.

Now we can explore each other in that way. I am so happy. Thank you so much."

Helen lay on top of Celia, gently rubbing herself against her. Then she had an idea, and spoke in her pretend schoolgirl voice.

"Miss Ashbee?"

"Yes little Helen?"

"Earlier you said you might find me a special treat."

"Yes child, I did. Did you have something in mind?"

"Yes Miss Ashbee, I do."

"Well, out with it girl. What special thing would you like Miss Ashbee to do to you?"

"It's something that I would like to do to you, Miss Ashbee. I would love it if you let me give you a spanking right now, and later I would like you to spank me, Miss. The older girls talk about it a lot and say they get a lovely feeling between their legs after the first painful moments. And they say you are the best mistress to do it. They all say they love you for it. Please, Miss Ashbee? Let me do it to you. Please?"

Only moments later, Celia answered Helen's call.

"I would love you to spank me, young lady. You can have my bottom and do whatever you want right now and I shall have yours later. How could I not want to feel your hand on me?

"Let us move to that ottoman over there. You will sit and I will bend over your knees and we will spank our way to heaven."

And they did.

Helen and Celia did a lot of kissing after they had enjoyed a marathon of mutual spanking. They laughed and lusted, cried and cringed, screamed and creamed, and all the time made love to each other every which way.

When they had worn themselves out, they still wanted to be together. With their arms around each other's waists the two wandered back into the lounge and Celia called Polly to bring them refreshments.

Polly brought in a tray. She really was a beauty and Helen looked at her with searching eyes, but couldn't help noticing an air of disapproval when they made eye contact.

"Celia? I believe that Polly doesn't approve of me. She gave me a very black look when she came in. I wonder what I've done to upset her?"

Celia smiled.

"I noticed that, darling. I think the young lady is suffering a painful dose of jealousy. I wouldn't mind betting Polly had her ear to the study door earlier, and heard us screaming. I'll sort it out with her later."

"So can I take it that she could be in love with you, Celia?"

Celia blushed slightly, and coughed.

"Let's say she is just discovering life, shall we Helen?" She looked at Helen coyly.

"Ah! So you have practised your seduction techniques dearest Celia?" I responded severely, "And I thought I was the first in recent times."

Celia kept blushing but laughed loudly.

"You might not believe me when I say it was an accident."

Helen laughed, "Pray, please do tell."

"I had initiated the earlier maid, Jacki, into the delights of love over a period of a month, but she was so highly energised by the whole experience that one day she ran out and dragged the young gardener – who worked here two days a week – into the greenhouse and had him on a pile of weed matting, then immediately fell pregnant.

"Fortunately for all concerned, me included I suppose, young Brad was so impressed with Jacki's sexual know-how that he proposed and they are now happily married.

"Jacki made Brad leave my employ, afraid of what might happen if and when the next maid – her replacement – found her handsome man in the garden.

"I should just mention here that, when Brad called in to tell me he was leaving, I thought I couldn't just let him go without giving him something to remember me by.

"I was alone in the house, as I hadn't yet found a maid.

"I got Brad to follow me into the library and sat him on the sofa. I told him how much I had admired him and the work he did, and would he do just one last thing for me?

"Nervous and in a hurry to please me, and I suspect a little besotted with me, he said I could ask him for anything.

"I sat close beside him and took his hand and said that, as I was unlikely to see him ever again, would he do me the honour of pleasuring me with his manhood.

"Then I pulled up my skirt and dragged his hand onto the top of my leg and then I reached across and unzipped him.

"In moments, I had his rapidly expanding cock in my hand, and moments later I dragged off my panties and dress and brassiere while he took off all of his clothes.

"Then he laughed and impaled me on his cock and ran around the room clasping my buttocks in his hands, and lifting me up and down on his cock, while my legs rocked backwards and forwards like I was riding a hack in a cross country event.

"It was a lovely moment, Helen, as I'm sure you can appreciate."

Celia paused and reached across and slid her hand backwards and forwards over Helen's knee.

"Well, you amazing woman. What a wonderful send off-for him, one he will never forget I'm sure."

Helen put her hand on Celia's and guided her to the back of her knee and made her stroke the back of her thigh.

"The truth is, Helen, Brad now pops in every couple of months and I give him what he calls his finishing up present. I do so like a cock occasionally, Helen, it's important for ones health."

Helen laughed as she stretched her leg.

"I suppose I should really call it 'a bit on the side' Helen."

Helen threw her arms around Celia and they kissed passionately. Celia slid her hand further up Helen's skirt and caressed the tops of her legs, snapping her suspenders.

"Oh Helen, you are so wonderful. I'm so wet and it's all your fault."

"I'm falling in love with you more every moment, Celia. And the reason you're so damned wet is the same reason I am, because of your super randy stories, you sexy bitch.

"Now, let's get back to the seduction of Polly, Celia."

"Following the incident with Jacki, I deemed it better to control myself and not allow myself to seduce any staff.

"I do have an older Italian woman come in to prepare authentic pasta meals for the freezer, once a month. Fortunately it's on the last Thursday of the month, which is one of Polly's days off.

"Aurora comes from strong Italian peasant stock and laughingly throws me around the kitchen as if she was a man.

"We have our zucchini time just before she leaves to go home to cook her husband's dinner.

"Aurora's body has some remarkable features that I am sure you would appreciate. Her lower front is covered with a thick mat of curls. It's as though she had a beard, going from her inner thighs up to her navel. Not only that, she has the biggest clitoris I have ever seen, and yes darling, I've seen a few.

"And I believe that, before she comes to work, she fills her knickers with sweet smelling herbs, rosemary and thyme. I can usually get an idea of her moods from her aroma. If she is very quiet and I cannot smell herbs, I say very little. If she smells beautiful and is singing her Italian opera, I know she will be more than happy to play our games.

"On her singing days, I greet Aurora with a big wet kiss. Then she lets me drag down her big knickers and bury my head in her mass of sweet-smelling pubic hair while I search out and mouth her magic clit. It's her very own little penis. And when she comes, I hang on to that superb object with my lips, and my head shakes."

Helen was agog as she slowly unbuttoned Celia's blouse.

"How wonderful, Celia. What happens next?"

"Well, after that, dear woman, I let Aurora have me however and wherever she wants.

"I moved a day bed into a corner of the kitchen, just for us, but Aurora loves to hoist me up on the central kitchen bench and, in her words, eat me out. Then she enjoys doing me with a large zucchini while I lie on top of her on the bed, sucking her giant nipples and almost suffocating in her cleavage.

"Interestingly, Aurora says that after a zucchini day at my place, her husband picks up her hot vibrations the minute he gets home.

"Serge is a concreter, shorter than Aurora and as broad as he is tall. I only met him once when he came to collect her one day. He must be the original ball of muscle.

"The way Aurora tells it is that Serge showers as soon as he gets home. Then he comes and finds her, usually in the kitchen, where he first sniffs her around the neck, then lifts her skirt and inhales between her legs, then he takes her from behind. When he does that, she knows she's in for a busy evening, with him in her for most of the night, every which way, including her backside."

Celia stopped and laughed, and moved her fingers further into Helen's panties.

"Aurora always thanks me, and laughingly says that Serge only started doing this after we started having our zucchini time.

"I would love you to come and enjoy zucchini time with us. Aurora is extremely well built and has such a lovely personality, and she is very appreciative of any lewd attention. She would just love to get into you, I'm sure."

Helen stared at Celia with new eyes. This woman knew what she wanted and how to get it.

"So I guess we should get back to Polly. How did this accidental seduction come about, Celia? Tell me! I so want to know."

"Well, I needed a book from the study and went to get it.

"Unbeknown to me, young Polly had been dusting there and had discovered the cache of adult toys that I keep in a zipped bag inside the ottoman. She didn't hear me come through the door. Polly was sitting back on the sofa with her skirt up and her knickers down around her knees, rubbing herself while enthusiastically sucking on a dildo.

"I watched, enchanted, as you can imagine, but I couldn't contain my excitement and went to her. She was mortified when she saw me and screamed. But I spoke gently, telling her that what she was doing was quite natural, and that all intelligent women and girls did it.

"She was speechless and couldn't stop staring at me. So I slowly lifted my skirt and slid my hand into my panties, and rubbed myself a little. Polly stared with even wider eyes.

"Then I sat down beside her, picking up the rapidly discarded dildo from the floor, then slowly lowered my panties to around my knees to mimic the way she was sitting. I placed the dildo in my mouth as she had. Then I said to her, 'Polly, let me show you how Miss Ashbee uses this thing.'

"Then I slid the dildo into me then, ever so slowly, began to work it. Then I closed my eyes, hoping that Polly would not choose the opportunity to run away. I played with the dildo for a while and when I opened my eyes and looked at her, Polly's eyes were closed and her mouth hung open and she was busy touching herself between her legs.

"She opened her eyes and looked at me and I smiled reassuringly and Polly, looking a little pale and wan, smiled weakly back at me.

"I decided to move on, hoping not to frighten her. I reached across and picked up her spare hand and rested it on my pubic mound, moving her fingers around a little. She jumped a tiny bit but didn't take her hand away, looking at it with bright eyes.

"Then I put my spare hand on Polly's fluffy little mound and moved my hand around a little bit, then put two fingers on her clitoris. Polly gasped. Then I leant over and kissed her on the lips and almost instantly she kissed me back. Emboldened, I offered her my tongue, slipping it slowly between her lips, and moments later she touched my tongue with hers.

"I wasn't sure what I should do next, she was so beautiful and I didn't want to frighten her. But then I reached up and undid the buttons on her top and put my hand in, and slipped two fingers into her little bra and wiggled a very stiff nipple.

"Polly cried out, but stayed where she was. Then I unbuttoned and opened my blouse and reached back and unfastened my bra, and pulled Polly's head down to my breast. Polly gasped again, then pushed her mouth over a nipple and gently licked and sucked me.

"Then I whispered in her ear that I was about to come, and not to be frightened.

"She took her head from my breast and stared down at the moving dildo. Then she gingerly reached out and touched it, then put her fingers around it, clasping it and moving her hand up and down with me as I pushed in harder.

"When I came, I screamed and the darling girl screamed too, staring at my contorted face. Then she grabbed my hair with her free hand and pulled it over, and kissed me passionately. Then she slid her tongue over my bare breasts.

"Then Polly screamed loudly and her body shook as she orgasmed and I grabbed her and held her close to me, and after a little while I whispered, 'Did you like that Polly? Would you like us to do it again one day?'

"Polly put her mouth up to my ear and whispered, 'Oh yes Miss Ashbee, I did love it and yes, I would love to do that again'."

"That was around a month ago, Helen. She and I have come a long way since then. Polly is wonderful and I love her dearly, but I realise now that she has become a tiny bit possessive, so I should do something about that.

"Her petulance might give me a good excuse to introduce her to a little discipline.

"Now you and I have become lovers, I will gently lead her to the idea of us sharing ourselves with you."

Celia and Helen kissed a long beautiful farewell kiss and said their goodbyes, agreeing once again that they had been very lucky to have discovered one another.

Celia's parting words sounded enticing.

"I'm pretty sure that when you visit next time, you will have two people waiting with their lips puckered up looking for your lips

Helen. And who knows, you might find more than just one person willing to show you their derrière.

"Sweet dreams darling."

"How was your day, my love?" said Frederico as he passed Helen a drink and they settled on the sofa.

"Really good. I think I've found you a new girlfriend, Freddy, part of our sharing. Would you like to meet her one day? She's beautiful and very sophisticated and wonderfully randy."

"Sounds good, Helen. I take it she has a loving personality?"

"Of course, darling."

Frederico sipped his drink.

"How was your day? I bet Rosa got what she wanted?"

"Quite good. Yes, she did. Oh and I think I've found you a new girl-friend, Helen, part of our sharing. Would you like to meet her one day? She's got freckles and green eyes, and has red hair and a slightly pronounced backside; oh yes, and she is desperate to get her hands on you.

"Oh, and something she said, but which I didn't understand, was that she looked forward to being the meat in the sandwich. Now what is that all about?"

Helen laughed loudly, poking her husband in the ribs.

"Sounds good, Freddy. Seems like the gal knows what she likes. I definitely would like to meet her. Oh, can I take it she has a loving personality?"

Frederico paused before answering.

"She's so hot for you, I don't think you'd give a damn about her personality, my love."

Helen threw herself on Freddy, nearly spilling his drink.

"I must be the luckiest woman in the world, having you for a husband, Freddy. God, I love you."

"The feeling is mutual, sweetheart. We are very lucky, Helen my love."

15

SUNROOM DELIGHT

WEDNESDAY WITH ALICE was going to be exciting this week, thought Helen, as she drove into the Bennetts' driveway, thinking about their forthcoming adventure with Bertie and the codes.

Alice smiled lovingly and kissed her at the door. She was feeling exhausted from her hectic exam week at university and explained this to Helen saying that she was not feeling very loveable.

Helen laughed out loud.

"What could your lover possibly do right at this minute that would help you take your mind off this? I'll do anything."

Alice kept her unhappy look on, then, taking advantage of Helen's sympathy, and like a spoilt child, demanded to know when she was going to get her anal sex lesson.

Helen laughed, thinking this was incredible. Then, in the most matter-of-fact voice she could muster, she replied.

"Right now, actually. Will I remove your knickers, or will you do it yourself?"

It was Alice's turn to look stupefied.

"You aren't serious, are you?"

Helen got up and walked over to the sex toy box.

"Never more serious, my darling. I am going to enjoy myself

having your beautiful backside for my very own today. If you lighten up, I might even make it work so that you can enjoy it, too."

Alice's face was changing. She was suddenly eager and willing to enter into the spirit of the game.

"All right, wicked stepmother. I will allow you access to my posterior on one condition."

"And what will that condition be, my darling?"

"You have to immediately come to me and take off my bra and kiss my breasts, spread my legs wide apart and lick my pussy, then roll me over and have your way with me with that pink thingy you're holding in your hand."

The next few minutes saw the two screaming at each other while grappling with their clothing and body parts.

Alice tore Helen's top off and bit her nipple so hard she shrieked in pain. Helen lay on top of Alice and pretended to shag her very hard. And finally, they threw their arms around each other and hugged and kissed and rolled around the bed, passionately devouring whatever body part they could get their mouths on.

Finally, Helen rolled Alice over on her tummy.

"Pink thingy time, darling. Hope you like it."

"Oh no!"

Alice lay quite still as Helen squeezed some lubricant into her bottom. Then she closed her eyes and screwed up her face as she felt Helen's index finger in her; then the pink thingy slid effortlessly into her smooth bottom passageway.

"There, darling! So far so good, would you say?"

"Yes Helen. Now what?"

"Now, sweet girl, we play mummies and daddies, or if you prefer, just girlfriends. But I'm the daddy one. So look out mummy."

Helen began a slow in and out with the pink thingy and Alice lay still, reflecting on what was going on.

Then Helen increased the speed a little and Alice began to get a feeling she hadn't known before. It was all so slippery and soft, but also so very nice. Helen thrust the pink thingy in and out, and as she did so, she put the fingers from her other hand on Alice's pussy and gently played with her clitoris.

Alice relaxed her backside, and began to move it around in time with Helen's bottom play. Then, as she felt her clitoris yearning for more of Helen's attention and as she visualised images of Freya and Helen's beautiful legs in the air, Alice orgasmed, and as she did so she felt an exquisite echo of it in her backside.

"Oh yes, Helen. That was beautiful. A two-in-one happy ending. I love you, Helen, and I'm going to love anal sex. Thank you, you wicked stepmother."

"You can seduce me with your bottom anytime, darling. I'm on call twenty four hours a day."

Alice rolled over and grabbed her and showed her appreciation with her lips.

As Alice made tea and toast for the two of them, Helen reviewed the code list and called out to Alice and asked if she had made her list.

Today was the day they were going to decide which codes they would use when they shared Bertie later in the week.

Bertie was out on a coach trip learning about drought management techniques on farms. Saving water was one of Bertie's big interests.

As they finished their late-morning tea and toast, Alice suddenly suggested that, with Bertie away, they could nip down and see the picture of Fifi fixed to the inside of his wardrobe door. Given that Fifi was the motivating key word in all of Rosa's codes, this seemed quite a good idea. They too would then have an image of her when they went to Bertie and requested his services.

Alice and Helen felt like naughty children as they stole into Bertie's bedroom. They had, of course, both been in there before, but for just one purpose: Morning Glory.

Alice opened the wardrobe and the two crowded in to meet Fifi.

There she was, the classic, alluring, sexy French maid, guaranteed to excite the carnal lusts of any man, and many women too.

The Fifi postcard was not alone. A postcard depicting a large pair of smiling, bright red lipsticked lips was stuck to the door, along with another card showing just a pair of feet wearing high-heeled fashion sandals.

Helen laughed.

"We'd better pile on the lipstick darling, and make sure we've got the right shoes. We want Bertie to have his fantasies satisfied too."

Turning to leave, the two faced the bed. Both stopped, unable to leave the bedroom without remembering what they usually came in there for. Then Alice looked at Helen. In a flash, the two were rolling on the bed, each holding a handful of wet pussy and yelling: "Morning Glory! Morning Glory! Thank you, Bertie."

Alice and Helen sat on the sofa in Alice's flat, drawing up their Bertie Menu, as they called it.

Alice was back on form, energised no doubt from Helen's attention, both to her front and to her backside.

"We mustn't be too greedy or demanding, I suppose? Do you think we can have more than three things? Can we have seconds? Are side dishes counted as one? If there are two of us, does that mean three codes would equal six as we are sharing? We mustn't exhaust him!"

"If it's between Bertie and us, from what I've seen of him I'd bet that we'd be exhausted before Bertie was."

"Oh, darling Helen, I so look forward to that exhaustion, specially as we will be doing it together."

The two laughed and compared notes, and eventually agreed on their list and also which Fifi code they would ask for first.

Then they did a last-minute check of the sunroom and set a day and time for their Bertie adventure.

Helen made a note to buy another lipstick and Alice thought it was a good time to shop for new shoes. They were both extremely excited and when they kissed each other goodbye they agreed that the planned adventure was going to be exactly that, a real adventure.

Alice and Helen had picked a day when Bertie played bowls in the morning, then came home and showered, and spent the rest of the day in his greenhouse or garden shed. Alice had a pretty good idea of the time they should approach him, but they decided, just to be sure, they would make certain to be in the kitchen a half hour beforehand.

The two dressed themselves in Alice's flat. During a phone call a couple of days earlier, Helen had said that she was thinking of wearing a black corselet she had bought earlier in the year, but had never worn. Alice liked the idea so much that when she was out shoe shopping she lashed out and bought a black corselet too.

The two women had a lot of fun dressing for their Bertie adventure, all the time deliberately avoiding the temptation to touch each other in their lascivious enthusiasm.

"We must save ourselves for Bertie, Helen."

"Can't I unbutton your corselet just the once Alice? Please?"

Applying their makeup felt like dressing for a pantomime. Face powder, mascara, eyeshadow and lipstick.

"Perhaps Bertie would like us as geishas?" Alice suggested.

"He might. He served in the Far East and might have been in Japan on leave. Must ask him one day."

Alice pranced around the bedroom wearing her new shoes, getting used to them and worrying that she might not be able to walk far. Helen looked at her and burst out laughing.

"Darling! You only have to waddle from the kitchen to the sunroom. After that you'll be either on your bum, your knees or your back," to which Alice replied,

"I just don't want you beating me to it, wicked stepmother."

The two went over to the house and mucked about in the kitchen enjoying a constant banter, things like who looked the most like a tart, or how they would be received if they went to the mall dressed like this.

Suddenly, they heard Bertie coming along the passageway. Both women experienced a short pang of excitement and a sort of panic, but when he saw them, kissed each one on the cheek and commented on their beauty, they knew that it was game on.

"Seeing you two together dressed up like this is really exciting. Where are you both off to? The races perhaps?"

"No, Mr Bennett. We thought we'd play dress-ups and then hopefully, hang out with you for a while as we see so little of you. Helen agreed to come over to help me enjoy the end-of-term holiday. We were just thinking of moving into the sunroom and would love you to join us."

Bertie looked at the two women, inspecting them from head to toe.

"I would be mad to refuse such an offer. Lead the way, Alice."

Helen and Alice each put an arm through one of Bertie's and led him through to the sunroom.

"Is there a game or activity that either of you had in mind?"

Helen and Alice looked at each other. This was the moment when Alice would ask the question.

"Well yes, Mr Bennett, there is. Mr Bennett, Fifi and her friend would like to suck your cock."

There, it was done. What would happen now? The two women looked at Bertie's face. Were they conscious that they were wearing an exaggerated adoring eyes look?

Bertie looked at each of them in turn then clasping each of the women's elbows in his large hands, he led them to the sofa and turned and looked at them.

"Now, Helen, and you too, Alice, it will be truly delicious for me and I will enjoy our time much more if you were both to take off your dresses so that I can see more of you. I would like to see your breasts. Please do that now."

The two women looked at each other, then reached down and raised their dresses above their heads and took them off. Bertie stared at the two beauties in their corselets and stockings and shoes.

"You are both very beautiful."

Then Bertie leant forward, first to Helen, loosening her corselet so that the part covering her breasts fell forward and exposed her nipples. Then he did the same to Alice.

Then he undid his belt and dropped his trousers and underpants around his ankles and, as the two women stared, lifted his heavy penis out from between his legs, holding it up as he sat down on the sofa.

"Now, kneel down on the carpet, the two of you."

The two women went down on their knees in front of him.

"Sweet Helen. Would you like to start?"

Alice watched, fascinated, as Helen moved her head forward, taking Bertie's huge cock in her hand. Then Bertie reached a hand forward, grasping Helen gently by the hair and dragging her head and those bright red lips to his cock. Helen opened her mouth wide and engulfed Bertie's manhood and began to slowly move her head up and down.

"Alice dear, you could touch my testicles and help Helen when she needs it. I'll leave it all up to you. Thank you. Oh, and I must tell you that you both have beautiful breasts."

Alice ran her fingers around Bertie's testicles while she looked at Helen and at her stiff nipples.

After a little while, Helen turned her head towards Alice and removed the cock from her mouth and offered it to her. Alice took it and straightaway began to suck it. Helen's hands were suddenly free and she reached over and fondled Alice's nipples.

Alice flashed her smiling eyes away from Bertie long enough to acknowledge her appreciation of what Helen was doing.

"You are both amazingly beautiful women. I love you both dearly and I love what you are doing."

After what seemed a considerable amount of time, Helen signalled Alice that she was happy to move on.

"Bertie, Fifi and her friend would like you to have them over the back of the sofa please," Alice said softly.

Bertie smiled and stood up, lifting the two women by their arms as he did so. Then he led them around to the back and one at a time bent them over at the waist and placed them over the back of the sofa and pulled down their panties. Then he spent a little time, inspecting and touching them and making sure his entry to their vaginas was not impeded by their corselets or suspenders.

Alice and Helen, hanging over the sofa back, were free to exchange adoring and delighted looks, and exchange kisses, and touch each other breasts.

"You first this time Alice."

Bertie took hold of his member and rubbed it up and down against Alice's vagina to wet it before inserting it. Alice gasped and closed her eyes while Helen held her hand tight against her bosom.

Then Bertie started to shag Alice, gently at first but then harder, until he reached his preferred rhythm.

Alice looked at Helen and smiled, then whispered.

"Darling, I think I'm going to orgasm shortly. Just letting you know."

Helen squeezed her hand, acknowledging her message, then purposefully took one of Alice's nipples and clutched it tightly, so that she could better feel Alice's explosion.

After Alice screamed and convulsed her body and yelled 'yes Bertie', he stopped his thrusting, but remained in her for some minutes, allowing her to have a second and third tremor.

Helen had also experienced a small orgasm as she held Alice's breast.

Then Bertie slid his cock out of Alice and straight into Helen. He moved it slowly around and around, as if he was searching for something, or maybe wanting to stretch her vagina, but the effect on her was significant. Helen fully appreciated his "looking around inside me" action before beginning to shag her.

When the girls resumed their mutual touching and kissing while Bertie did his job on Helen, Helen whispered that she would come quite soon too, and Alice moved a hand to hold one of Helen's nipples, as Helen had done with her.

Helen didn't scream but she did a lot of noisy groaning, climaxing with three very loud explosive grunts, while Alice experienced ongoing trembling, resulting partly from her earlier orgasm but triggered by Helen's deep release.

Again, Bertie chose to stay put inside Helen until he was sure she had been properly fulfilled. Then he withdrew.

"Thank you, Bertie. That was truly beautiful."

"For me too. Thanks. I do love both of you."

After a few moments, and furtive looks and smiles at Helen, Alice plucked up the courage to make one more request.

"Mr Bennett?"

"Yes, Alice?"

"Fifi and her friend would like to have you on your back."

Bertie laughed.

"I could probably do with a bit of a lie down."

Then he walked around to the front of the sofa and lay down, his massive cock waving happily at the ceiling.

"Who's first?"

Alice and Helen stood up straight and stretched, and looked at each other and laughed. Everything was certainly going to plan.

Having Bertie on his back would give them an opportunity to ride him and be totally in control. They had earlier speculated whether they would be able to experience yet another significant orgasm. Also, having Bertie this way would be a lot like having Morning Glory, and they wanted to know whether it would feel the same.

Alice went first, clasping his cock, then climbing on him and sliding him in to her very wet vagina.

She was now in charge of their movement and the speed and impact of him against her body. What was different from Morning Glory was having her lover Helen with her, touching and kissing her.

Moving up and down on Bertie was a wonderful sensation and she could have happily done it for a lot longer, but there was a mission, and Alice dedicated herself to seeing if she could orgasm a second time.

Helen touched her with light finger caresses as she moved. Sometimes she would touch Alice's nipples as they bounced around in front of her, and with her other hand she palmed her own pussy. The two were indeed sharing every moment.

Alice came, again with a scream; not only that, but she remained sitting quietly on Bertie's cock, then felt the urge to repeat what she had done and very soon screamed and came again. Then she did it a third time.

Helen stared at Alice in amazement.

"I doubt I'll be able to do that, darling. You are amazing."

When Helen climbed onto Bertie and began her ride, she wasn't sure how things would work out. She'd had the super orgasm earlier. Did she deserve another? Even with her darling Alice's caresses, was it even possible?

Another lot of noisy groaning and climaxing with loud explosive grunts heralded the success of her efforts. She slipped off Bertie's cock and lay on top of him. He put his arms around her and kissed her, and Alice bent her head down and kissed each in turn.

Just when Alice and Helen thought that they had all finished, Bertie spoke.

"I would very much like to shag your beautiful mouths, dear ladies. If you would both sit up on the sofa, side by side, I will have you; very gently, I promise."

Helen and Alice looked at each other with raised eyebrows, then smiled.

"Are we side dishes or dessert, I wonder?" murmured Helen.

Bertie thought what a picture they made, sitting on the sofa, looking quite dishevelled but happy, legs slightly apart and their breasts sticking out above their half-opened corselets, and showing off their beautiful stockinged legs and suspenders, and their delightful feet and high heels. And he loved the way his two favourite women kept a hand between each other's legs. And here he was, with two bright red open mouths waiting to be fed with his big cock. It couldn't get better than this.

Bertie's cock moved in and out of Helen's heavily lipsticked lips and mouth, then he transferred it to slide in and out of Alice's mouth and then back to Helen again and then back to Alice.

The girls managed to get a quick smile at each other, and even a whispered message, in between their mouths hosting Bertie's member.

"I am so loving this," said Helen.

"Me too! I'm going to stock up on lipsticks."

"We should buy in bulk. I think we're going to use a lot."

"At this moment, I just want to be a Lippy Whore."

"Me too!"

"Helen! Do you know if there is going to be another book, a follow-up to this one?"

"There will almost certainly be one, Alice. Sorry, I forgot to tell you when I arrived. We just received word that Rosa is coming home from hospital next week, which means that things will change around here. There will be plenty to write about, Rosa will make sure of that."

Alice and Helen noticed that Bertie had stopped his gentle thrusting and looked up at him.

They all agreed to stop. Alice and Helen thanked him for a most enjoyable afternoon and Bertie thanked them both for their delightful company. Then he excused himself and headed off to tend to what he described as a "pressing orchid pollinating event" in his green-house.

"I think pollinating could be Bertie's middle name."

Alice laughed, enjoying the irony of Helen's remark.

"Oh yes! There is another thing I haven't told you, Alice. Number nineteen next door to us has been sold, and you will never guess who's bought it!"

"Who has bought it, Helen?"

"I mentioned it to Rosa in conversation when the billboard went up. And guess what? She made a phone call to a friend who bought it two days later. Want to have a guess who the friend was, or will I tell you?"

"How could I possibly guess? Tell me, Helen. Who is your new neighbour?"

"Maude!"

"Oh my God! I knew she was tired of all the travelling and wanted to move in from the country, but this is certainly a bit of a shock. Look out Helen and look out Freddy too. And wait till I tell Freya. We are already worried about all your hot action with your other neighbours."

"And that is not the only change happening in the street, Alice.

"Right next door to Maude in number 19, number 21 has a new owner. They've apparently inherited the property.

"Word has it that the new owners are a successful author currently living in London and his step-sister. Both will be moving back to Australia shortly. I don't know their names. I have been given to understand that they are both single.

"It is a huge old two-story house with a separate unit at the back, much like the one Bertie and Rosa have here. It is a beautiful property set in an established garden and on a double block. It will be interesting to see what they do with it. Exciting times Alice, don't you think?"

"Indeed, Helen. Eros Crescent might never be the same again."

FIND US

Publisher or review enquiries should include your full name and details in all correspondence.

Email address:
admin@richardlee.biz

RICHARD LEE PUBLISHING

Erotic Fiction

The Eros Crescent trilogy in separate volumes:

The Fifi Code

Eros Crescent

Eros Park

Eros Crescent Trilogy (Due mid 2020)

———

Literary Fiction

Australian Short Stories (2020)

Restless: A novel about two young men growing up
in Australia between 1900 and 1936 (Due early 2021)

———

Out of Print Titles

Mathematics for Young Children by Helen Western

ISBN - 978-0-909431-01-3

Currajong: For Those Whom Schools Have Failed

by Bruce Wicking

ISBN - 978-0-909431-03-7

The Puppetry Handbook by Anita Sinclair

ISBN - 978-0-909431-04-4

Wordswork by Chris Davidson & Bruce Wicking

ISBN - 978-0-909431-06-8

Sheep Production by Murray Elliott

ISBN - 978-0-909431-07-5

Ducks for Starters: A Practical Guide to

Backyard Duck Keeping by Bruce Wicking

ISBN - 978-1-875207-00-8

Sweethearts by Colin Talbot

ISBN - 978-1-875207-02-2

www.ingramcontent.com/pod-product-compliance
Lightning Source LLC
Chambersburg PA
CBHW031312170626
46807CB00001B/380